Certain Dark Things

by
Erica Abbott

Bella
BOOKS

2012

Bella Books, Inc.
P.O. Box 10543
Tallahassee, FL 32302

Printed in the United States of America on acid-free paper
First published 2012

Editor: Katherine V. Forrest
Cover Designer: Judith Fellows

ISBN 13: 978-1-59493-295-3

PUBLISHER'S NOTE

Other Bella Books by Erica Abbott

Fragmentary Blue

Dedication

To love, always and forever.

Acknowledgment

My deepest thanks to my brother, sister-in-law, niece, and nephew for their continued love and support.

A special word of thanks to my certified massage therapist. Several plot problems were worked out on the therapy table.

I am grateful to my readers and their kind words. Authors write for readers, and to be appreciated is humbling and gratifying.

To everyone at Bella Books, you have made the publishing process a real joy. My thanks especially to Karin Kallmaker for her friendship and her advice.

To the amazing Katherine V. Forrest, who edited the manuscript, my thanks for both her words of encouragement and her willingness to drop the hammer on me as needed. As always, any book is much better for having passed through her hands.

Finally, to Kathryn, who gave immeasurable help to both the manuscript and the author, I am forever grateful.

About the Author

Erica Abbott was born and raised in the Midwest, and is a graduate of the University of Denver. She has been a government lawyer and prosecutor, a college professor, sung mezzo-soprano onstage, and played first base on the diamond. She likes dogs, cats, music of all kinds, and playing bridge. She also has a love/hate relationship with golf. She lives near Denver, Colorado.

CHAPTER ONE: MONDAY

Lieutenant CJ St. Clair pulled her car to the curb at the entrance to the park. She could count five Colfax Police Department patrol cars, including a supervisor, two ambulances, a crime scene truck and two other unmarked police cars.

She took a breath of cold morning air and pulled her leather jacket closer. The sun wasn't completely present yet. Fall would be giving way to Colorado winter before long.

CJ was not a morning person, and she wished fervently that she'd had time to get coffee before she'd had to drag herself away from the warm body in her bed to get to the scene of a police-involved shooting. When she'd taken the job as the Inspector of Internal Affairs for the Colfax PD, she had been sorry to leave her friends in Investigations at the Roosevelt County Sheriff's Office, but she hadn't missed the early morning calls. IA was almost a nine-to-five job. Almost.

The harsh red and blue lights on the patrol units looked garish against the soft color of gold leaves still clinging to the trees. CJ draped the lanyard with her badge over her neck, and found the patrol supervisor on the scene.

"Sergeant Gonzalez," she greeted him. She knew him as a solid patrol supervisor, an officer who could follow instructions, but not a cop who took a lot of initiative.

He turned to her. They were almost exactly the same height, and she saw his eyes widening a little, with just a touch of apprehension. She was used to that, after more than a year on Internal Affairs. Cops were never glad to see her.

"Um, Inspector. Thanks for coming," he managed.

"Of course. You all did a good job remembering the Internal Affairs protocol on an officer-involved shooting. It's so much easier when you call us right away. I appreciate it." Her soft Southern drawl evoked magnolias and steamy nights instead of a cold autumn morning.

"Sure," he said, still uncertain in the face of her friendly greeting.

"Did you call the Officer Support Team?" The team consisted of volunteer police officers who acted as moral support for cops who were involved in traumatic incidents. CJ herself had served with them until she was assigned to IA—two shootings in her career had made her deeply empathetic.

"Uh, no. I suggested it, but the officer declined," he said stiffly. CJ thought he spoke as though he were writing his report in his head. "You're gonna talk to the officer now?"

"Why don't you tell me what happened first?"

"Okay. Off-duty officer on a morning run, sees a guy assaulting a woman jogger. She yells at the guy, he takes off, she takes off after him, runs him down. He pulls a knife and she draws her weapon, tells him to drop it."

"Wait," CJ interrupted, confused by the pronouns. "Female officer?"

"Yeah."

"I see," she said. There weren't that many women in Colfax PD, and CJ wondered if she knew her. Of course, there were at least a dozen women in uniform she'd never met. "Go on."

"He keeps coming, and she shoots him."

"Fatal?"

"Oh, yeah. They didn't even bother to transport him. Body's still there. The guy was DRT."

Dead right there, CJ translated in her head. She blew out a long breath. "Okay. How's the victim?"

He looked puzzled for a minute. CJ realized why and clarified, "The assault victim, I mean. Not the shooting victim."

"Oh," he said. "Problem there."

"She's hurt?"

"No. She's gone."

CJ was shocked. She combed a manicured hand through her red hair, which fell perfectly back into place, the benefit of a very expensive haircut.

"She's dead, too?"

"No, Lieut…I mean, Inspector. She took off, left the scene. We don't know where she is."

Damn it. CJ allowed herself another few curses. "Is our officer hurt?" she asked.

"No, she's fine," he answered, seemingly happy to be able to give her one piece of good news.

"All right," CJ said briskly. "Then priority one is finding the assault victim. I assume you're canvassing for her."

"Well, no," he admitted, his tone a little defensive. "We were securing the scene."

CJ tried not to frown at him. "I see. I'm not in charge of you, Sergeant, but I'd strongly recommend starting a search for her before Captain Robards gets here. The assault victim might be hurt. And the officer definitely needs for us to find the only other witness."

His surprise was obvious. "You're worried about the witness coming up with a different story?"

CJ sighed. "No, I want to find her to confirm the officer's story. Believe it or not, Sergeant, I'm one of the good guys. I love protecting good cops. I like it a lot better than finding bad ones. So how about you get some people on the canvass? Have you called Captain Robards yet?"

"Uh, no," he asked, puzzled again. "Why?"

"Don't you think you should inform the patrol captain that one of his officers was involved in a shooting?"

His face cleared. "Oh, no. Inspector, she's not Patrol. She's in Investigations. She got promoted to detective a couple months ago."

Hell's bells. CJ knew who the detective had to be. She turned and saw the woman standing a few yards away. She had her arms wrapped around her own athletic-looking body for warmth. She was wearing track pants, running shoes and T-shirt. Standing alone, the blonde looked younger than she had the only time CJ had met her, shortly after her promotion.

To Gonzalez, CJ said mildly, "I see. Go ahead and get started on finding the witness. I'll call the investigations captain myself."

He looked relieved. He knew the captain in charge of Investigations was tough, and he didn't want to make a call at six thirty in the morning to provide the unhappy news that an off-duty detective had put several holes in some guy in a park. "Thanks, Inspector," he said gratefully to CJ.

She nodded at him, and walked away, pulling out her cell phone. Sighing, she punched in her own home phone number. When she got only voice mail, she disconnected and hit the speed dial for a cell number.

"Ryan." The contralto voice was still husky—she hadn't been awake long.

"Hey. It's me." CJ kept her voice low. "What are you wearing?" she asked playfully.

"Is this an obscene phone call?" Alex's voice was dry.

"Yes," CJ said, wanting to have fun for a few seconds before she had to break the news.

"Sweatshirt and running tights. Black sports bra. Very sexy. Under the tights, I'm wearing French-cut bikini briefs. Also black."

CJ shut her eyes, just for a moment, against the picture that formed in her mind. "Stop it."

"Hey, you started it."

"Did I interrupt your run?"

"Still doing the pre-run stretch. I tried to go back to sleep after you left, but for some reason it's hard to do after you've left the bed."

"Miss me?" CJ asked softly, so no one could overhear.

"Just to say 'Yes' is an understatement, but it'll work. What's up? I thought you had an officer-involved." That was her Alex, always focused, always getting back to business.

"I do. I'm sorry, Alex. One of your detectives shot a possible would-be rapist in the park while on a morning run. I thought you should be here."

CJ could hear Alex jogging back upstairs to their condo, caught the sound of jangling keys.

"God damn it to hell! Is the guy dead?"

"He's dead. And I'm sorry, darlin'. It gets worse."

"My detective's hurt?"

"The officer is fine, as far as I can see. The problem is that the assault victim has disappeared."

"Damn it! We're looking, I assume." CJ could hear Alex grunting as she pulled off her running shoes, preparing to change and come to the scene.

"We are now. Apparently it took an Internal Affairs Inspector to figure out that clever strategy."

"Oh, for God's sake," she said, exasperated, and CJ knew what she was thinking. Alex really hated sloppy police work. Sometimes when you screwed up at the scene, you could never get the case back on track. "Look, I'll be there in twenty or so. Which of my guys is it?"

CJ suppressed a sigh and just told her. "Not a guy. It's Chris Andersen."

There was silence. In her mind, CJ could see Alex sitting down heavily on their bed. "I'm sorry, Alex. I know you were a little worried about her..."

"Tell me this is a good shooting," Alex pleaded.

"I hope so. I can't tell. I haven't talked to her yet."

"Yeah. Okay." The potential disaster of the case hung suspended, unspoken between them. "I'll be there as soon as I can."

CJ ended the call and let a long sigh loose. Her life had changed forever when she took the job as the Internal Affairs officer in Colfax, a suburb just south of Denver. She loved her job, but more importantly, she'd fallen in love with the captain in charge of the Detective Bureau. She reported directly to the police chief, so Alex wasn't in her chain of command.

They'd had a rocky start. CJ had been on an open investigation of Alex's involvement in a murder soon after they met, and she'd been afraid that they would lose each other before they'd barely begun. But they were together, and CJ had never been happier.

Alex stayed meticulously out of her way, since IA cases were all confidential. But they still had the comfort of being able to talk about their work in generalities with someone who really understood. CJ could trust Alex, who could offer insight, information and sympathy. Alex could grouse about her detectives, or brag on them, with someone who really cared.

So most days the choices were easy. But not today.

CJ walked over to Chris Andersen, thinking about what Alex had told her. The woman was young for the promotion to detective, not quite thirty yet. Alex had been worried about her from the day she showed up. CJ remembered asking, "You don't think she's ready?"

"Yes and no. She's very smart, has good instincts and works like a sled dog team."

"Sounds like someone else I know." CJ had grinned at her.

"You're referring to yourself?" Alex asked, dryly.

"No, smart mouth, that would be you."

Alex shook her head. "I just don't think she's mature enough. She drove her patrol unit through a plate glass window once going after a suspect."

"You think she's a cowboy."

"I'm afraid she might be. Now that Stan is retired, I'm partnering her with Frank, hoping that will help."

"That makes sense. He's the most experienced guy you've got, and you know you can trust him. Frank will help settle her down."

"I hope so," Alex had said.

Apparently Frank hadn't had enough time to be a good influence, CJ thought wryly as she walked toward Detective Andersen.

She offered her hand to Chris. "I'm Inspector St. Clair," she said. "We met once, just after you were promoted."

Chris shook the hand warily. "I remember."

"How are you all doing?" CJ asked, the Southern drawl in her voice strong.

The question surprised her, CJ could see. Everybody expects me to be the Wicked Witch of the West, she thought in exasperation.

"I'm okay," Chris replied tautly.

"You look cold."

"A little. I expected to be running, not standing around."

CJ signaled one of the uniformed officers and asked him to get a blanket from one of the patrol units. Chris took the blanket, but said tersely to CJ, "You don't have to play good cop with me."

CJ said easily, "I'll keep that in mind."

Chris was trying not to snap her head off, CJ could see that. The tension was rolling off her in waves. Her mouth was held in a firm, straight line.

Clearing her throat, CJ said, "If it helps, I do understand a little. You had a lot of adrenaline going, and it takes a long time to come down from something that intense."

Chris snorted. "Nice speech. Did you learn that in IA school?"

"No," CJ responded, her voice still mild. "Experience."

Chris said, surprise in her voice, "You've been in a shooting?"

CJ nodded. Maybe this would get the woman to relax a little, if she thought she wasn't the only cop in the world who'd had to shoot somebody. "Twice, actually," CJ admitted.

"Fire your weapon?"

"Yes."

A little disdainfully, Chris said, "Hit anything?"

CJ tried not to lose patience with her. "I did, actually." CJ wasn't proud of it, exactly, but she was far from ashamed. "He didn't make it."

Chris turned to her, frankly surprised.

"You killed a suspect?"

"Yes."

Chris seemed to digest this a moment.

Suddenly, without planning it, CJ unbuttoned the top two buttons of her blouse. Chris could see the faded ribbon of raised skin, the top of a scar on her chest.

"Jesus," Chris breathed in. "He shot you?"

"Not that time. The second time I didn't have time to return fire. He was coming after my partner." She knew Chris would assume that she meant a partner on the job.

"No vest?"

"I was off-duty. Part of the bullet lodged near my heart."

"You should be dead," Chris said flatly.

"I imagine so," CJ answered cheerfully. It was getting shot, and almost dying, that had finally resolved the case and brought Alex permanently into her life. Far from hating the faint scar, CJ felt grateful for it. It had been worth it.

"Partner make it?" Chris asked.

"Oh, yes." CJ smiled. "She's still on the force."

Chris froze. CJ realized her tone had hinted at more. "She?" Chris asked.

"Yes, I'm pretty sure you've met her," CJ said brightly, trying to lighten Chris's mood with the joke. "That would be your boss, Captain Ryan."

***

Fuck me. This woman used to be the captain's partner?

Chris looked CJ over. She was, in her wide and varied experience of women, gorgeous. Not her type, exactly, but one gorgeous redhead.

The problem was the mild manner and Southern accent were undoubtedly just clever disguises for a barracuda. Every cop knew how vicious Internal Affairs inspectors were.

CJ re-buttoned her blouse, and Chris took one last glance at the full breasts in the ivory satin bra beneath. Very nice, she thought. She wondered, as she did with almost every woman she met, if CJ might just be gay.

Not my type, Chris mused again, but I certainly wouldn't kick her out of bed.

Chris glanced down and saw a gold wedding band on CJ's left ring finger, under a pretty impressive diamond solitaire engagement ring. Her partner, Frank Morelli, had told her that CJ had money, and from the car she'd driven up in, and the jewelry, Chris could believe it. She was probably married to some vacuous rich guy, commuted in from Cherry Hills, and had two point three kids. Too bad.

CJ asked, "You gave a description of the victim, the woman, to the uniforms?"

"Yeah. I can't believe she just took off."

"People do that sometimes. They're afraid, not thinking clearly. She'll be back, or we'll find her," CJ said reassuringly. "Don't worry."

Chris felt a crushing in her chest. She'd managed, for just a few minutes, not to think about what had happened, that she'd...she'd killed someone. She thrust her hand through her short, white-blond hair. "I didn't want to shoot him. He just kept coming..."

"I know. Sometimes it's the bad guys or us. We have to pick us. Do you usually go jogging with your gun?"

"I...what?"

"Just wondering," CJ said, her tone casual.

Chris glared at her. "Yes. I take it to the grocery store, and to restaurants, and to bars. Last time I checked, we're always on duty."

"That's true," CJ agreed cheerfully. "I just have enough trouble running a couple of miles as it is, without a pound or two of semiautomatic weapon weighing me down."

Chris looked at the woman beside her more carefully. She was tall, even taller than herself, and a real redhead, with creamy, perfect skin. Chris tried to guess her age. She looked really young for a lieutenant, maybe mid-thirties at most. She had generous curves, not slender, but well put together. Nice cleavage, long legs. Definitely would not kick her out of bed.

"What do you carry?" Chris asked her suddenly, trying to think of a safe subject to talk about. One that would not let her think about the man she'd shot dead.

CJ unholstered her gun and showed it to her. "Sig Sauer P229. This one is a .357. A Secret Service agent I met a few years ago recommended it, it's what they use, only they might use the nine millimeter. I don't remember."

Chris looked at the weapon. She didn't really care, and said only, "Very nice."

CJ didn't ask any more questions, and they stood quietly together, an island in the river of people in uniforms flowing around them.

***

A sleek black SUV pulled up as close to the scene as possible, and CJ knew Alex had arrived. The vehicle had been Alex's present from CJ for her fortieth birthday. CJ had endured several minutes of protest over the extravagant gift.

"For God's sake, CJ, I can't drive something this expensive," Alex had complained. "It must cost as much as I make in a year. Everyone will think I'm on the take."

CJ had playfully tugged at her blouse. "Then, as the officially appointed Inspector for Internal Affairs, I'll just have to investigate you. Let's start with a strip search."

"Stop it. I'm serious. It's beautiful, but...I am a public servant, you know."

"Come on, Alex. I drive a new sports car every other year, and nobody says boo to me."

"Yeah, well, you're rich."

"And you married money. Just say 'thank you' and enjoy it, will you?"

Alex had finally accepted the SUV with ill-grace, but CJ knew how much Alex loved the gift.

CJ watched as Alex got out and started to wind her way through the emergency vehicles, stopping to talk briefly with several of the officers on the way.

CJ watched her partner approach. It wasn't that Alex was so striking in appearance. She was average height, trim, with a face that was interesting more than classically beautiful. She was wearing black denim jeans, a white shirt and a black leather jacket, cut like a blazer. The only color from her was a flash of silver earrings and her blue-gray eyes.

CJ loved watching Alex walk. It was the way she moved. Not a swagger, but confident, poised, ready for anything. Anyone could see that Alex was secure, comfortable with herself, a woman who knew who she was, what she could do. Alex's calm self-confidence, CJ thought, was one of the sexiest things about her.

And Alex was so...intense. She cared deeply about only a few things, but what she loved, she loved with her whole being. Alex loved her family, and she loved her work.

She watched as Alex talked to Gonzalez, nodded to a crime scene tech, and then lift her head and search for CJ. When Alex spotted her, she smiled, just a little.

And me, thought CJ, happiness flooding her body. She loves me.

When Alex reached them, the smile was gone, her face set into her Captain of Investigations mode. "Inspector St. Clair," she greeted CJ.

"Captain," CJ responded, keeping her amusement at this formal exchange of titles well-hidden. Alex was all business when they were working. It was with an effort that CJ pushed another picture away from her mind: Alex lying beside her last night, dark hair tangled, the lids over the blue smoke eyes heavy with satisfaction.

"Captain, I…" Chris began, but Alex lifted a hand, still looking only at CJ.

"Have you given Detective Andersen a Garrity advisement?" Alex asked.

CJ shook her head. "We haven't really talked yet about what happened. We were just chatting."

Alex gave her a sharp look, and CJ tried to look innocent. She knew very well that Alex was aware that she typically got more information while chatting than most investigators got during a comprehensive interrogation, but Alex let it slide. CJ continued, "I'll just leave you two to talk. Detective, I'll see you later, at headquarters."

Chris muttered, "Yeah, I'm sure you will."

Alex turned away from Chris and walked with CJ a few steps toward their cars. She said in a low voice, "I drove through on the way and got you a latte. It's in my car. I didn't know how long we'd be here. I left my doors unlocked for you."

"Thank God," CJ said fervently. "And thank you. I'm crazy about you, Captain Ryan, you know that?"

Alex flushed, but her expression didn't change. "You can thank me later, Inspector. Did we call Officer Support?"

"Chris turned it down. She's wound pretty tight, Alex. Don't be too tough on her."

Alex said grimly, "We'll see."

CJ brushed her fingers very lightly against Alex's arm and moved toward her latte.

***

Standing alone, Chris pushed both hands through her hair in frustration. She had just been doing her job, for God's sake, and instead her days to come would be eaten up with interviews and more interviews.

She was not looking forward to the formal meeting with Internal Affairs, but it was nothing compared to her apprehension about the conversation she was about to have. Captain Ryan did not suffer fools at all, and after a couple of months of working in Investigations, Chris was still waiting to hear her laugh, or make a joke, or even crack a serious smile.

And it's too bad she's my boss, Chris thought. Because the dark, serious, brooding ones really are my type.

Alex approached her and said, "How are you doing?"

"I'm fine," Chris said, trying to sound casual. "He's the one going home in a body bag."

Alex gave her a sharp look and said, "In that case, let's walk through exactly what happened." She meant it literally.

They went over to the jogging trail, strewn with golden leaves, and began to walk.

"What time did you leave your home?" Alex began.

Chris answered, "I got back to my apartment about five forty a.m. I figured there was no point in going to bed, so I changed into my running clothes, and drove over. I got here a little before six."

"Got back," Alex repeated. "You were out all night?"

"Yes."

"Alone?"

Chris almost laughed. "No, Captain. Do you need the details?"

"It's probably not relevant, but you never know. I think you should tell me, yes."

"All right," Chris answered. She realized that part of her wanted to tell Captain Ryan about herself. Her sexual orientation hadn't really come up in conversation with her boss, and she wanted to see Alex's reaction.

"About nine last night, I went to a bar in LoDo called Regina," Chris continued. "I was there until around one o'clock, and left with someone. I was at her place until a little after five this morning." She carefully emphasized "her" in the sentence.

She watched Alex carefully, but the captain's face didn't change. Alex said only, "How much did you have to drink? Tell me the truth."

Chris knew what Alex was probing for, and she didn't like it. "I wasn't going to tell you anything except the truth," she bristled. "I had three beers in four hours. I'd eaten something before I went to the bar, and I was not impaired when I left. I was also not hung over when I left her apartment."

"And you left at five in the morning. I assume you weren't playing backgammon all night."

Chris laughed. Apparently Captain Ryan liked precision. "No," Chris told her. "I picked her up, I'd never met her before last night. Her name was Sherry. I don't recall that I ever heard her last name, but I can give you her address. She has an apartment, a place up in Northminster." She stopped and added, with emphasis, "Just to be clear. We were having sex. I trust that's not an issue for you."

"That you slept with a woman, or that you had a one-night stand?" Alex asked evenly.

"Either one," Chris said flippantly, wondering how judgmental Alex was going to be about the situation.

"Your off-duty activities are none of my business, Detective, assuming they're legal. Tell me what happened after you got to the park."

Chris pushed her mind away from her speculation about Alex's reaction and brought her mind back to the morning. "I stretched, then started out, going this direction. I wasn't going very fast, still warming up, when I came around here."

They went to a curve in the path, where it wound through trees.

"I saw two people," Chris continued, "about here. Her back was to me, he was facing me. He was yelling, and so was she. I thought it was just an argument, so I was going to go back the other way, but then she screamed at him, and he punched her. She stumbled, and he hit her again. She fell down, and he drew back a leg to kick her, so I yelled at him."

"Did you identify yourself as police?"

"Yes. I called out that I was a police officer and ordered him to stop. I'm not sure he even heard me. But he saw me coming toward them, so he took off. And I yelled at him to stop, said again that I was a police officer."

"What was she yelling at him?"

Chris stopped for a moment, trying to remember. "Just 'you stupid bastard,' I think. And she called him something else, a selfish son-of-a-bitch or something like that."

"She knew him," Alex concluded.

"Yeah, I thought so," Chris said. "But he'd already hit her twice, and it looked like it was going to get worse, so I didn't have a choice."

"I agree," Alex replied. "Did you see a weapon?"

"No. I didn't pull mine, either."

"Okay. He sees you, takes off. Then what?"

"I ran by her, glanced at her. Her shirt was torn open a little, but she seemed pretty much okay, so I chased him. He ran down the path for a while, but he wasn't in good shape, and he couldn't keep up the pace. I ran fast enough to keep him in sight, and when he started to slow down, I closed on him. He didn't like that, so he started off the path, down among the trees, trying to lose me, I guess."

"Did you follow him?"

"Yeah. I called out again that I was police officer, just as he started off the path. He fell, over a branch or something on the ground, and when he got up, he turned around to face me. That's when I saw he had a knife in his right hand. I don't know where he had it, in his jacket or pants pocket."

"He wasn't carrying it as he ran? You didn't see him threaten the woman with it?"

Chris shut her eyes briefly, running the events over in her head again. When she opened her eyes again, she saw Alex looking at her very intensely. "No," Chris said, after a moment. "I didn't see any weapon until that moment."

"How far away from him were you when you saw the knife?"

Chris considered. She was trying to detach herself from the way she'd felt when he'd turned on her. Her heart had already been pounding from the run, and when she'd seen the flash of the blade, it felt as though time had slowed to a crawl. "Thirty feet, maybe."

"What did you do?"

"I pulled out my weapon, and identified myself one more time as a police officer. I told him to drop the knife."

"What did he say?"

"He said something like, 'Get away from me, bitch.' He waved the knife at me, as if he wanted to scare me away."

"And what did you do?"

Precise and methodical, Chris thought. Aloud she answered, "I pointed my gun at him and ordered him again to drop the knife. That's when he started to move toward me."

"Did you back up?"

Chris knew this was an important point, and she'd had a few minutes to think about how to explain what she'd done. "No," she responded. "The ground was uneven, there were a lot of leaves. I was afraid I might slip, and I didn't want to take the chance. I stood my ground and instructed him, again, to put down the knife."

"What else did you say?"

Chris gave her a sideways glance. How did she know there was something else? "I told him," she said, "that I would shoot him if he took another step."

Alex nodded, as if she'd expected the answer. "What exactly did you say?" she pressed.

Chris took a deep breath of cold air and answered.

"I said, 'Put the damn knife down right now or I'll blow your fucking head off.'"

Alex nodded again, as if she were satisfied with the answer, and asked, "And then?"

"He..." Chris faltered a little for the first time, and then continued, angrily, "He sort of lunged at me, with the knife. So I pulled the trigger."

"How many times?"

Chris could still feel the gun bucking in her hand. "Twice. He staggered, then he just fell down."

For just an instant, Chris saw Alex's face change, as if she remembered the sound of gunfire in her ears, not at the range where they wore protection, but the way it sounded when it was real, when the bullets had been aimed at her. And her partner. Chris caught the look and said abruptly, "Inspector St. Clair told me."

"Told you what?" Alex was startled. Chris guessed Alex might be wondering what Inspector St. Clair might have disclosed.

"I think she was trying to make me feel better," Chris said wryly. "Anyway, she told me about the time she got shot. She said she was shot by a suspect who was coming at you."

"Did she?" Alex said, her voice neutral. Chris couldn't read either her face or her tone of voice. After a moment, Alex said coolly, "I want you to come down and look at the body. Can you do that?"

Chris squared her shoulders and tried to look calm and collected. She didn't want the captain to remember how young she was. "Of course, Captain."

They went down the hill, sliding a little on the leaves. There were still two technicians there, one finishing taking pictures, the other taking a measurement. Alex said to the second tech, "Can you tell where she was standing?"

He showed her the cartridge cases from Chris's 9mm, measuring out the usual arc from where they were ejected as she fired. Alex stood in the spot, and looked down to where the body lay in the leaves. Over him a green tarp had been erected to protect the body. Ten feet away, maybe, when she'd shot him.

Alex said, "I admire your self-control. If it had been me, I doubt I would have given him a third opportunity to surrender. He could always have thrown that knife at you."

Her mind still on what St. Clair had told her, Chris asked abruptly, "What happened to the perp? The one who shot St. Clair, I mean, the one who was coming after you?"

"I shot him," Alex replied evenly. "He died at the hospital." Abruptly turning away from Chris, she asked the crime scene technician, "Have you bagged the knife?"

He showed it to her, displayed in the evidence bag. More than just a switchblade, it was a wicked looking Special Forces type of knife, with finger holes in a molded plastic handle, and a six-inch blade.

Chris stared at it a moment, then turned away. Alex led her to the body and they stood together under the tarp.

"Look closely," Alex instructed her. "Know him? Be sure."

Chris stared long and hard. An hour ago he was alive, and now he was dead. Because she killed him. He was just an ordinary looking man, early twenties, maybe, a couple days' growth of beard. One of his eyes wasn't quite closed all the way, and that bothered her.

Chris tried to figure out, just for a second, what she was feeling. She felt odd, not bad exactly, not good, just weird, uncomfortable. It was like a graduation ceremony, where she thought she should feel different afterward, but didn't.

She shut down the emotion. "I've never seen him before this morning," she said, her voice firm.

Alex said, "All right. Let me tell you what happens now. You go home, clean up and come in to work. When you get in, report to Inspector St. Clair. She'll interview you, get you to sign a statement. We'll farm out the criminal investigation to another agency, since you're one of our officers."

"Criminal investigation?" Chris tried not to sound alarmed. Stay cool, goddamn it. She's your boss, you don't want her to think you're going to fall apart, do you?

"Yes. I don't anticipate a problem, but it's important that another agency review the incident. IA will review what happened for excessive use of force. While all this is happening, you're on paid administrative leave."

"I'm suspended." For some reason, Chris hadn't thought of that.

"Yes, until this is resolved. It will be several weeks, probably. You come up and see me when Inspector St. Clair is finished, and leave me your badge. We've already got your service weapon. Someone will contact you in a few days or so to make an appointment with the department consultant to talk to you."

"A shrink?" Chris asked disdainfully. The last thing she wanted was some head doctor rummaging around in the dirty, cluttered maze that was her brain.

"Even if the criminal investigation is resolved without charges and IA clears you, you can't come back to work without a fitness-for-duty report after a shooting incident of any kind," Alex said, in a firm voice that left no room for argument. "I know you turned down the Officer Support Team, which is your choice, but this is not optional. Do you understand?"

"You're very clear, Captain," Chris said tersely. Great, just great. I get to sit around for a few weeks and think about this.

"Glad to hear it."

Alex walked Chris back to her car, a shiny red Mustang, and watched her drive away.

***

Alex got into her SUV. CJ was still in her passenger seat, drinking coffee. She had run the engine for a bit, so the leather interior was comfortably warm.

Alex allowed herself the pleasure of gazing for a few moments at CJ. Alex loved the leather jacket, especially the way it was just short enough to give her an unobstructed view of CJ's curves and long legs. It had been nearly a year since they had moved in together, become partners, and she still liked looking at CJ's shape. It was almost unfair, she thought, that someone so beautiful should also possess a mind sharp as a new razor—and the biggest, most loving and open heart Alex had ever known. Alex felt fortunate beyond her imagination.

"How'd it go, darlin'?" CJ asked.

Instead of answering, Alex took the paper cup from CJ and drank the last of the latte.

"You could get my germs doing that," CJ observed, smiling.

"Really? More than, say, when I was french-kissing you on the sofa last night?"

"That was a whole lot more fun than watching you drink my coffee."

Alex put the empty cup in the holder and said, "She did okay, I think. You'll have a shot at her later. If there's more to it, I know you'll have it out of her by lunchtime." She glanced at CJ and then asked, "Did you know she's gay?"

CJ lifted an eyebrow in surprise and said emphatically, "I most certainly did not. She told you that?"

"She told me she picked up a woman last night and, to use her words, they spent most of the night 'having sex.' One-night stand, she didn't know her last name. Picked her up at some bar named Regina."

"Ah. One of Vivian's favorite new hangouts." Vivian Wong was CJ's friend, a mortgage banker and relentless serial dater of women. "And you're pronouncing it incorrectly. It rhymes, perhaps not surprisingly, with 'vagina'."

"Why am I not surprised? So you didn't know Andersen was a lesbian?"

"What, you think I'm still using my gaydar?"

"Gaydar? What the hell is that?"

"All this time, and you're still such an uninformed excuse for a lesbian."

Alex said primly, "I'm not really a lesbian."

"You're not?" CJ said, in amusement. They'd had this discussion before. "What are you then, other than in denial?"

"I never look at other women," Alex said solemnly. "I would think that would be the prerequisite for being a lesbian. Now, what the hell is gaydar?"

"Well, fortunately for you, I am a lesbian." CJ grinned at her. "Gaydar is what those of us who admit to being gay use to determine whether someone is similarly inclined, since it's not always possible to take the easy route and just ask. It's somewhat true, and somewhat a myth. Contrary to popular belief, you can't usually tell just by glancing at someone whether they're straight, gay or bi. But some people are very good at picking up signals. Vivian can spend two minutes watching a woman across a crowded room and tell, with about ninety percent accuracy. Although I'd like to point out that Viv had no idea of your woman-loving-woman potential."

"It's surprising you're so witty this early in the morning."

"Ha, ha. Wish I'd known about Andersen's sexual orientation before I showed her my scar in an attempt to bond with her," CJ added, a little ruefully.

"Yes, she mentioned... Wait, you showed her?"

"Two buttons only," she said modestly.

"Damn it, CJ, I didn't realize I had to institute a rule about you not taking off your clothes in front of my detectives. Especially my female detectives. Particularly and especially my one gay female detective. Don't do that."

"Love it when you are a little jealous, Irish."

Alex growled, "I'm not kidding. Keep your clothes on, especially in front of Andersen, okay? She sounds like a player, and I don't want her getting even the remotest idea you're available."

"Yes, Captain, ma'am," CJ said solemnly. Alex wasn't really worried—she knew how important fidelity was to CJ.

Alex stared out the windshield, then said, "I told her to report to you when she gets in."

"Okay."

"I'm sorry for her. I'm sorry the guy is dead. I'm sorry the woman was attacked, though I wish like hell she hadn't run away. Mostly, though, I think I'm feeling sorry for us. The timing on this could not be worse."

"Yes," CJ agreed. "Police brutality and the election for DA."

Alex sighed. "Tony will probably be calling me later today, demanding to know why I did this to him."

"Two years of marriage to the man ten years ago, and he still thinks he has the right to call and yell at you," CJ complained.

Alex gave her a sideways look, not quite hiding her smile at CJ's protective tone. "Just don't care for him much, do you?"

"He makes you unhappy. He's a pain in the neck. I mean, he actually accused you of trying to ruin his chance at getting elected DA by choosing to be with me."

Alex had to smile. " 'Alex, people will think being married to me was so terrible it turned you into a homosexual!' Really, can you believe him?" She shot a sly grin at CJ and added, "Everybody knows you're the one who persuaded me to bat for the other team."

"You are so funny. But you're probably right about what Tony thinks. That's why he hates me."

"He doesn't hate you."

CJ disagreed, but wasn't going to argue about it. Instead she observed, "Well, he's going to hate this a lot more."

Tony Bradford had waited years for John Blumenthal to retire so he could have a shot at running for DA. To his dismay, criminal defense attorney Robert Carlson had decided to run against him, and Carlson was racking up headlines by accusing the Colfax Police Department of excessive use of force.

"Just lousy timing," Alex conceded. "Carlson jumped all over the traffic stop shooting last summer, and now this. It looks clean, but…"

CJ promised, "I'll try to wrap it up as quickly as I can. I don't like Tony, but at least he's been in the DA's office for years. He'd be a much better prosecutor than some defense attorney. Who are you going to get to do the criminal investigation?"

"I was thinking Rod Chavez might agree to do it," Alex said, naming CJ's former colleague in the Roosevelt County Sheriff's Office. "What do you think?"

"Great idea, if he can," CJ said enthusiastically. "Unless you're concerned our friendship would taint things, somehow."

"I'll think about it. See you later?"

"Yes. I'm going to check and see how the canvass is going. We really need to find our assault victim."

"Good luck with that."

***

As she returned to the scene, CJ carefully skirted the news camera and reporter getting ready to do a standup report. The cameraman was on the sidewalk, and the reporter was standing with a nice view of the park in the background, microphone in hand. CJ watched the reporter look at her, speculating whether she was someone important enough to try to interview. CJ walked briskly by, and the reporter dismissed her, turning back to the camera to begin with, "We're here at the scene of this morning's fatal police shooting at Ross Park in Colfax..."

CJ smiled to herself. She looked nothing like a cop, and that often worked to her advantage. The smile faded as she thought about the news reporter. The local station had gotten there quickly, and she wondered if they had been listening on a police scanner or gotten a tip. Either way, the political response to the news reports wouldn't be long in coming.

Sergeant Gonzalez called out to her.

"What have we got, Sergeant?" she asked.

"We ran the plates of the cars parked in the lot," he said. "We got a hit."

"Stolen?" CJ asked.

"No, but one of the owners has a record. Looks like our guy. The dead guy, I mean."

"How nice of him to drive his car here," CJ remarked cheerfully. "I think it's time for me to get a warrant and let's just see what we can find."

By the time the warrant arrived and the locks on the car were opened, the morning had begun to warm a little, the fall sun bright and shiny autumn brass. The sunlight warmed her shoulders through her jacket as CJ stood thoughtfully gazing into the trunk of the old Subaru sedan while a couple of uniformed officers searched the interior.

"No registration in here, Inspector," one of them called to her.

"I'm not surprised," CJ remarked. "Come on back here, will you?"

Both uniformed officers joined her at the back bumper. "Well, shit," the first man said.

The trunk was filled with an assortment of devices: several cell phones, laptops and computer tablets, several with cords still attached like long, black tails.

"Maybe he was a used electronics salesman," the second patrol officer joked.

"You think?" The first man laughed.

"Or," CJ joined in the conversation, "he just might be a thief."

"Hell, you could be onto something there, Inspector." They were all laughing now.

"I'm starting to get an inkling about why the wife or girlfriend took off," CJ mused.

"Maybe she was more of an accomplice," the first officer suggested.

"I think you're right," CJ said. "Time for me to do some police work, I think."

CHAPTER TWO: MONDAY

Chris listened unhappily to CJ's patient explanation.

"It's called a Garrity advisement," CJ said. "You need to read it, and sign it, before we continue."

Chris read it, and then stared down at the document. They were in a small interview room near Internal Affairs, just gray chairs and a gray table between them. There were no windows, and the artificial lights made the red sweater Chris was wearing seem garish and harsh. CJ's pale cream blouse fared better. Chris thought it looked like silk.

"This says I can claim my Fifth Amendment right against self-incrimination. But if I do, you can fire me?" Chris asked.

CJ said, "Yes. This isn't the criminal investigation. That will be handled separately. You can answer all my questions fully, or you can decline to answer based on your right not to incriminate yourself, but if you do decline, you can be disciplined for refusing to answer. The discipline can be anything the chief thinks is appropriate, up to and including dismissal. Still, we can't use anything you tell me in the criminal investigation. Do you understand?"

Chris glared at her. She had known the woman was going to turn out to be a shark.

"Yeah, I get it. I'm between a rock and a hard place. Don't worry, Inspector, I'm not planning on refusing to answer you. I didn't do anything you wouldn't have done. Or actually have done."

CJ sat back in the padded chair and Chris figured she was assessing what approach to take. Chris herself had done it plenty of times with witnesses—and suspects—but being on the receiving end felt really uncomfortable. She tried not to fidget.

"I'm going to record the interview," CJ said. "I just want you to start from the beginning, and tell me what happened."

"You want me start at the park this morning, or before that?" Chris realized she already sounded defensive.

"You told Captain Ryan you were out all night, right?" CJ apparently was not going to play games.

"Yeah. And what I was doing. And with whom. Is there a problem with that?"

CJ sighed. "Look, Detective, could we move a little farther away from 'you versus the world'? I'm not judging you, believe me."

"Forgive me, Inspector, but for all I know, you've got a major problem with me because I'm gay. I just wanna make sure I'm getting a fair shake here, because I didn't do anything wrong."

CJ folded her hands, and Chris could almost hear her thinking. At length she said quietly, "Chris, I'm a lesbian, all right? Now can we move on?"

Chris gaped at her. "You're kidding," she said flatly.

"No, I'm pretty sure," CJ said, trying to lighten things up. "Doesn't sleep with men, check. Only sleeps with women, check. Yes, I'm a lesbian, all right."

Chris looked down to CJ's left hand. "You're wearing a wedding ring," she said.

CJ said, smiling, "Very observant, Detective. I'm a married lesbian, at least as married as I can be in this state. And to eliminate any further discussion, I'm committed to another woman. Are we all clear on that?"

Chris was still trying to wrap her mind around the concept. "Jesus, Inspector," she finally managed, "what's the point?"

"Excuse me?"

"I mean, really, why? I'm not making a pass, but with your looks you could score every hour God sends if you wanted to."

"Very flattering," CJ said calmly, "but I'm not interested in scoring. I can recommend marriage to you very highly, but I think that's a discussion we'll need to have off-duty and after this investigation is over. Believe me, a good relationship beats a one-night stand all to pieces. Now that you're reassured about my credentials, could we actually do the interview?"

CJ started recording. Chris, focusing on being serious and factual, went through the morning one minute at a time. Then CJ started in the middle, took things out of order, and went through it all again until she was satisfied.

"Okay," she said at last, and Chris was surprised to see that she'd been there almost two hours. "If there's anything else, we'll be in touch. Captain Ryan told you about the procedure from here?"

"Yeah, she was very thorough. And why do you keep calling her 'Captain Ryan'?" Chris felt back on solid ground since the interview was over, and tried to regain her usual air of casual indifference. "You were partners, after all. I certainly call my partner by his first name."

"I can call her Alex," CJ said, smiling, "but you can't, so I didn't want to lead you into temptation."

Chris didn't want to like the woman, but she had to admit she had a sense of humor. And she was clearly wicked smart. Chris knew she wouldn't want to try to hide anything from her.

***

When Chris went upstairs to the Investigations bullpen, she started toward Alex's office. From his desk nearby, Frank Morelli moved to intercept her.

"Hey, Hans," he greeted her. "How are you doing?"

Chris made a face at the nickname. "I'm just great, considering I missed my morning run and had to shoot some guy before breakfast," she answered tersely.

A lock of dark brown hair fell over Morelli's wrinkled forehead, and his brown eyes looked concerned. "The Cap told me. She said you were okay. Are you?"

Chris sighed. Morelli was really a good guy, kind of conservative and a straight arrow, but okay for a married, father-of-two, Italian-Catholic man. They were about as opposite as they could be, and she figured that was why she'd been assigned to work with him.

"I'm okay, Frank. It was solid self-defense. I just wish his damned victim hadn't fled the scene."

"Don't worry," he said, and sounded supportive. "I know Lieutenant St. Clair really well. You'll get a fair deal from her."

Chris, watching him carefully, said, "You've known her a long time, right? She just told me she was gay—she was trying to reassure me she'd treat me fairly."

"Lesbian solidarity, and all that?" he joked.

Chris had told him she was gay their first day working together. When he didn't react negatively, she'd wondered why. Now she wondered if his friendship with CJ St. Clair had something to do with it. "Something like that. You knew about her, I guess."

He smiled. "I told you, I've known her a while. Jennifer and I were at the big bash they threw after they had a commitment ceremony. It was the best damn party I've ever been to."

Chris was really interested. "Really?" she began. "So you've met her..."

"Andersen," Alex's voice interrupted her from across the room.

Chris winced, and said to Morelli, "Gotta go get my knuckles rapped. They said I'd be off for a while—sorry to leave you in the lurch."

"We'll figure it out." He gave her arm a reassuring squeeze. "You'll be back before you know it."

Chris walked into Alex's office, frowning. Alex said, "Sit down. You look unhappy. Did Inspector St. Clair give you a hard time? Or did Morelli call you 'Hans' again?"

Chris looked up in surprise. "He told you about that?"

"He may have mentioned it," Alex said, gently amused. "With a name like Christian Andersen, I imagine it's not the first time you've been called that, in school, or..."

Chris said abruptly, "I was never in one school long enough for anybody to bother with a nickname."

Alex sat back in her chair. "Your parents move around a lot?" she asked casually.

Chris gave her a sharp look. "Is this part of the investigation, too?"

"Detective, relax. I'm not out to get you. I'm on your side," Alex said in a reassuring tone.

"Everybody keeps telling me that," Chris muttered.

Alex continued, "I don't know you all that well, and I like to know everybody I work with."

Chris took a deep breath, and released it slowly. She didn't do small talk, and she didn't let people in, but she did really like her job, and being snarky with her boss wasn't going to help her career. "I never met my father, at least that I know of," she admitted. "He took off before I could talk. My mother was an…alcoholic is the nice word. She went from boyfriend to boyfriend, so I was all over the place. When I was nine, Social Services took me away and put me in foster care. I was always getting moved around there, too."

Alex didn't react to the story, except by pushing a pencil around a piece of paper on her desktop. "Sounds lonely," she said, her tone even.

Fuck, Chris thought, I don't want her to feel sorry for me. "It made me self-reliant," Chris said calmly. "Put myself through the criminal justice program at Douglas Community College. I've been on my own since I was seventeen."

In a sudden change of topic, Alex asked, "What will you do while you're off?"

She made it sound like a vacation. Chris answered honestly, "I don't know. I haven't thought about it."

Alex explained, "I'm trying to understand if you have a support system of any kind. Family, friends, somebody you can talk to who isn't in the department."

"I don't actually like talking to anybody," Chris said suddenly. "This is the most personal conversation I've had since I was fifteen and seduced my first girl under the stands after a football game."

Chris kept waiting for Alex to react, but she was impervious. Must have been all those years as St. Clair's partner. Wonder if St. Clair ever made a pass at her. I sure as hell would have.

Alex said calmly, "Everybody needs somebody to talk to, sometimes." She took one of her cards, scribbled a number on the back, and handed it to Chris. "This is my cell phone," she said. "Call me, if you want to talk. I hope the investigation won't take too long."

Chris stared at the number a moment. Something stirred inside of her, but she shut it off and put the card in her pocket.

"Thanks, Captain," she said coolly. "I think you wanted my badge." She took out the leather case and handed it to Alex.

Alex said, "One more thing. You need to go down to the evidence room and identify your weapon. Some chain of evidence mix-up. They need it before they can do the ballistics test."

"Yeah, okay." Chris felt drained for some reason she couldn't name.

Alex stood up and they shook hands.

Chris met Alex's eyes, and wondered for the first time exactly what color they were—somewhere between blue and gray, it was hard to tell.

"I'll see you back soon," Alex said.

***

Alex escorted Chris out of the squad room to the stairway door, then walked back to Frank Morelli.

"How's she really doing, Cap?" he asked.

Alex had a lot on her desk, but for some reason she had felt a sudden impulse to connect with Chris Andersen. Alex felt protective of all her cops, and Andersen had killed someone a few hours ago. Chris's isolation made her infinitely sad. Alex remembered clearly what it was like to live alone, to let work consume your life. It was only CJ that had saved her from some version of Chris Andersen's life.

Thinking of CJ, just for a moment, still gave her a nice, warm flutter in her stomach, even after all this time. Alex said to Frank, "It's hard to tell. Is she always so closed off?"

"Yeah. She had a rough time as a kid, I think. She can be a good cop, though. I think she just needs to grow up a little."

"I hope she gets time to do that," Alex said, frowning. "Come on into the office. We need to figure out how to get you some help. I might actually pick up a couple of your cases myself."

He grinned up at her from his desk chair. "Wow, are you actually allowed to be out on the street again?"

Alex shot him a look. "I was already a sergeant when you got here, Detective. You want to compare clearance rates from my tenure with your current caseload?"

He laughed. "No, I don't," he admitted. "Most of that time you were single and worked, like, sixty-hour weeks or something. I was busy getting married, divorced and married again, not to mention the two kids. I know you can work the cases. I just didn't know you were allowed to actually go into the field again."

"Why the hell not?" Alex was frowning again.

"Because I didn't think the Inspector for Internal Affairs would let you," he smirked.

"She is not the boss of me," Alex growled in mock fierceness.

"The hell you say. I say you're whipped, but good."

Alex gave him a glare, only half real. "How about I suspend you for having a smart mouth," she said jauntily, "and handle your entire caseload by myself, just to prove how independent I am?"

"Be my guest," he joked with her. "You could do everybody's cases, and I'd still say she's got you wrapped around her little finger."

"She does not," Alex snapped, still pretending to be indignant.

But she remembered Frank had seen them together plenty of times away from work. She watched as he gathered case files, got up, and she turned to walk back toward her office.

"You are so whipped," she heard him mutter at her back, and she could hear the grin in his voice.

***

There was a clerk Chris had never seen before in the evidence room. Her name tag said Rivera.

Chris said to her, "I'm Detective Andersen. My captain sent me down to identify my service weapon."

"Oh, yes, Detective," she said in a quiet voice. "It's right here."

She turned to a wire basket and lifted the Glock nine millimeter out carefully and handed it to Chris. Chris automatically checked to make sure it wasn't loaded.

The clerk said, softly, "I'm very sorry about what happened."

Startled, Chris looked at her for the first time. She was a petite woman, with shoulder-length dark hair and olive skin. She was young, maybe only twenty-one or two.

"Uh, thanks, um…"

"Elizabeth," she shyly offered a hand. "I've only been here a few weeks."

"Elizabeth," Chris repeated. The woman's hand was warm, and Chris said again, "Thanks. Yeah, it was not my favorite way to start the day."

"The crime technician told me a little about what happened. I think you were very brave," Elizabeth said suddenly. "I can't imagine how frightened you must have been."

Chris realized she herself couldn't imagine how frightened she must have been, either. She'd turned the feeling off, like she shut down everything she didn't want to feel.

Elizabeth was looking at her with warm brown eyes, and Chris thought she should say something else.

"It's my job, you know, what we go through all that training for," she answered. "Hours and hours, and then you only have a few seconds. I'm just glad, if somebody was gonna die, that it was him and not me."

Elizabeth just continued to look at her, and Chris returned her attention to her gun. "Yes, this is mine," she said. "Do I need to sign something?"

Elizabeth had her sign a receipt and also an identifying tag. She took the gun away carefully and said, "Don't worry. I'll take good care of it."

"Yeah," Chris said, suddenly a little choked up without knowing why. "You do that. I'll see you."

"Yes, I hope so," Elizabeth Rivera said sincerely.

***

When Alex got home to their condo, CJ was there already, in the kitchen. Alex could smell baking bread and something cooking, meat and spices. She hung up her jacket, stepped around CJ's shoes left carelessly in the entry hall, and walked into the kitchen.

"Smells good," she said. "What're we having?"

"Beef stew. Okay? It was cold today, and I just thought it sounded good."

"Sounds great. You know I'll eat anything you make, anytime, anywhere. Should I open some wine?"

CJ gestured to a half-full glass beside her. "Already done. There's a bottle of burgundy breathing on the table, and another half of one in the stew."

"Where's the rest?" Alex asked. She leaned in for a kiss and caught the flavor of red wine on CJ's lips.

"In the cook," CJ admitted.

She said it lightly, but Alex felt a tinge of concern. CJ wasn't much of a drinker, and if she'd already had a couple of glasses of wine, something was up.

It usually worked better if she let CJ tell her rather than asking, so Alex said only, "What else? Green salad?"

"Yes, that sounds good."

Alex assembled salad, mixed oil and vinegar, and they sat down to dinner. CJ already had jazz on the CD player, and Alex poured herself her first glass of red wine as CJ worked on her third.

After dinner, Alex rinsed and stacked the plates in the dishwasher, and wandered into the living room to find CJ already stretched out on the couch with a book of poetry.

"You want coffee?" Alex asked. CJ typically read until midnight most evenings, with Alex fading as soon as the ten o'clock local news was over.

"No, darlin'. It was an early morning, and I'm not sure how much longer I'm going to be awake. I don't want anything to interfere with my impending slumber."

"I could make decaf."

CJ looked up and said, "Okay. Drop of whiskey?"

Alex said mildly, "You drank most of a bottle of wine by yourself. You want to tell me what's going on?"

CJ said shortly, "No, I don't. Don't worry about the coffee."

Alex was a little shocked. CJ always wanted to talk. It was Alex who usually shut things down. She responded, "No, it's fine. I'll make it."

Alex went back into the kitchen and exercised technical skills on the incredibly shiny and complex coffeemaker CJ had insisted on buying. Alex coaxed two cups of decaffeinated coffee out of it, and added a finger of whiskey to both mugs. She put a healthy dollop of cream into CJ's cup and stirred it until the coffee was the color of caramel. When she came around the breakfast bar into the living room again, CJ had changed books, and was reading a new Lincoln biography.

Alex handed her the cup and said, "I still can't figure out how you do that."

"Do what?"

"Switch between books like that."

CJ shrugged and drank coffee. "Keeps me from getting bored. The coffee is perfect, thanks. Are you going to read?"

Alex sat on the couch and touched CJ's bare feet. "No," she answered. "Tell me what's bothering you."

CJ sighed. "I can't, darlin'," she said quietly.

Alex slowly began to massage CJ's feet, pressing her thumbs gently into her insteps. CJ groaned happily, set her coffee on the table, and let the book slide, open, onto her chest. "Not fair," she complained.

Alex said nothing, but continued the massage, working her way up to the Achilles tendons.

"Ow!" CJ complained. "Take it easy."

"You have got to quit wearing those high heels. They're killing your feet," Alex said mildly.

"Yes, but they look so good. A little higher."

"Geez, Red, you're already five ten. Why do you need to be taller?"

"It's not about height. A woman's legs look better in heels." She had a blissful smile on her face.

"Your legs would look good if you were standing ankle-deep in the mud. Please tell me what's bothering you. It's Andersen's case, right?"

CJ sighed. "Right. And we can't talk about it."

Alex stopped the massage, picked up her coffee mug and said, "The hell with it. Yes, we can."

CJ looked at her, her expression wide with alarm. "Alex, I can't contaminate an investigation about one of your detectives."

"We're not going to contaminate it. Whatever the hell is

going on is bothering you, and you're a lot more important to me than department protocol, or any investigation."

"Am I?" CJ gave her a little smile.

"Don't change the subject. Talk to me, Red."

CJ still looked worried, but relieved at the same time. She sat up a little and said, "Are you sure?"

Alex leaned over and kissed her on the mouth, lightly. Alex savored the luxurious flavor of CJ infused with the taste of coffee and whiskey.

"Very sure," Alex answered quietly.

CJ picked up her own coffee, fiddled with her cup a moment, and then said, "I pulled the victim's record. Chris Andersen knew him."

Alex started. "What? She told me she'd never seen him before."

"In fairness to her, she probably just didn't remember him. It was a minor arrest, when she was in Patrol. Criminal mischief. He'd just turned eighteen, so it was an adult charge, but they did a deferred sentence, so she probably never saw him again after booking him. It was over three years ago."

"Damn it!" Alex said forcefully. "I really hate coincidences. Anything else on his sheet?"

"Yes. A domestic violence conviction, a couple of burglary offenses, knocked down to criminal mischief. No weapons charges, though."

Alex sat still, frowning. CJ, who knew her thinking face, said, "Tomorrow's priority for me is finding the witness. Chris told me she was sure the witness knew the victim, so I'm pretty sure I know who our missing woman is."

"Let me guess. The victim in the DV case."

"You really are a good detective," CJ said. "Sometimes I wish we could work cases together."

Alex smiled a little and said, "Just as well we don't. You're really distracting."

"What a nice thing to say. Anyway, darlin', I went to her last known address, but she and the victim had been evicted the day before. I've got a lead on her sister, but she wasn't home when I went by this afternoon, so I'm going by again tomorrow. I will find her."

The phone rang. Alex went over to pick it up, looked at the caller ID, and made a face. "Wonderful," she said bitterly.

"Let me guess. Candidate for district attorney Tony Bradford?"

"Got it in one."

Alex punched the phone on and said, "Hello, Tony."

"What the hell is going on?" he demanded, without preamble.

"I'm fine," Alex responded evenly, returning to sit on the couch. "How have you been?"

"Shitty. I just got a phone call from some reporter who wants to know about a police shooting this morning. What the hell happened?"

"And CJ is fine, too, thanks for asking."

At the other end of the couch, CJ laughed a little, as if certain that Tony Bradford had not asked about her health.

"I don't give a shit about your fucking dyke girlfriend..."

Alex punched the phone off angrily without another word. "He'll call back," Alex said shortly. "But we're not talking until he apologizes. And he knows it."

CJ leveled her green eyes across the sofa. "Hmm. Let me guess. Something less than complimentary about me? What was it last time? 'Red-headed bitch,' I believe?"

"That's the general vicinity," Alex hedged. She wasn't going to repeat Tony's words to CJ this time.

"And you wonder why I don't like the man. He keeps this up and I'm voting for his opponent."

Alex chuckled, but CJ grew serious. "Alex, I'm sorry."

"Sorry for what? It's not like you did anything to cause him to act like this."

"I'm just sorry that Tony continues to give you all this crap about me."

"You do know that I don't give a damn what he thinks, don't you?" Alex said firmly. "He can feel whatever he wants, but he cannot talk about you that way to me. So he can choose—stop talking to me altogether, or stop being an asshole."

The phone rang again. She picked it up. "Round two," she said, glancing at the caller ID.

"Look, Alex…" Tony began.

"We're not talking," Alex said, her voice brittle. "Goodbye."

"Wait a sec, goddammit. I'm the Chief Deputy DA. You have to talk to me."

"I don't, actually. You're rude, insulting and unprofessional. You can apologize for being a jerk, or we're done."

"Look, it's not personal, you know that. It's this damn campaign…"

Alex flared. "That's bullshit, Tony." She flashed a quick look at CJ, who was trying not to watch her, apparently concentrating on the rim of her coffee cup. "You don't say things like that because you're worried about the campaign. You say shit like that because you can't cope with the fact that I love her. And that I didn't love you. I'm really sorry you're still hurting after all this time, but that is no excuse for acting like a petulant child."

CJ looked up, mouthed "petulant", and murmured, "Nice use of our vocabulary word for the day."

Alex threw a sofa pillow at her and CJ, holding her coffee cup safely away, laughed.

Tony began again, "Alex, listen to me."

"Nope. Haven't heard an apology yet. Bye."

"Wait! Damn you, Alex, you are the most stubborn woman. I'm sorry. I just don't like CJ."

"Bullshit," Alex said again. "You gave me all kinds of crap about selling the house so I could move in with her. You liked her just fine until you found out I'd fallen in love with her."

CJ smiled to herself, gazing into her coffee. Alex caught the look, and it gave her a moment of calm.

"I…" Alex heard Tony breathing heavily for a moment, then continue. "Fuck it, Alex. Could we just talk about the shooting?"

"Not really," she conceded. "It's under investigation, you know that."

"Criminal or IA?"

"Both, which is standard operating procedure. On the preliminary look…" She glanced at CJ and got a nod. "It seems like a good shooting."

"Are you going to be able to comment on that for the morning paper?"

Alex grimaced and answered, "You know better than that."

"Yeah," he muttered. "Look, I'm going to call the chief. We may need a press conference on this."

"We?" Alex queried.

"Alex, for God's sake. We both know that asshole Carlson is going to be accusing the DA's office—me—of covering up police brutality. Some nice clean-cut citizen gets shot down last summer by a cop, and now this."

"I don't want to remind you, again, that Mister Clean-Cut Citizen was drunk and tried to wrestle a gun away from a police officer. The guy in the park this morning assaulted a woman and pulled a knife on my detective. Relax, will you?"

"I'll relax," he snarled, "in November. I'm calling Chief Wylie."

"I can't stop you. Good luck. And I'll give CJ your best."

"Fuck you, Alex!" he barked, loud enough for CJ to hear.

***

CJ leaned over, took the phone away from Alex, and said into it, "Great idea, Tony. Someone should do that. I'll just take care of that myself, shall I?"

She punched the phone off and dropped it onto the cushions in disgust.

She had had enough. It was one thing for Tony to call her names, but she drew the line at his abuse of Alex. Alex should be relaxing, not working on deepening the twin furrows that were just beginning to appear between her eyebrows.

"He makes me mad," CJ grumbled. "He calls me names, he treats you like you're some kind of personal whipping girl. I'm sick of him."

"Really?" Alex said, smiling. "I couldn't tell."

"And we've got five weeks left before the election. I don't know if I'm going to make it, darlin'."

She moved across the couch. Alex shifted a little to get into position, and CJ settled happily into her embrace. Alex stroked her down her arms, calming her with a touch.

After a while CJ said, "I'm really beat. You want to come to bed, or are you staying up for the news?"

"I am definitely not interested in the news. I'd much rather watch you brush your teeth."

"Cheap thrills." CJ laughed a little.

When CJ crawled into bed, she wrapped herself easily around Alex, arms around her waist, long legs curving along Alex's legs.

"You're cold," Alex murmured.

CJ moved even closer and nuzzled into her neck. "I wouldn't be if you would let me wear any clothes to bed."

"I like to feel skin."

"That would explain why you don't wear anything either."

"Guess so." Alex smiled.

CJ snuggled happily for a minute until Alex said, "It's really amazing how well we fit, isn't it?"

CJ dropped a kiss on her shoulder and said, "True in so many ways."

Alex said softly, "Don't worry. I'll figure out a way to get Tony out of our hair."

"Don't spend any time worrying about it," CJ answered, her voice already thick with impending sleep. "He doesn't really matter. I love you, Irish."

"Love you, too."

***

The young woman with long, dark hair unlocked her door, and reached for the light switch.

Chris put her hand on the woman's fingers and said, "Don't."

Chris pushed inside behind her and shut the door. A little breathlessly, the woman said, "It's early yet. Don't you want to…"

Chris snapped at her, "I had a really bad day. Let's not talk, okay?"

She put her hand on Chris, under her jacket, and said, in her best sultry voice, "If you don't want to talk, baby, what would you like to do?"

Chris pushed her up against the wall, and kissed her, hard. There was no hint of tenderness or softness, just a demand for heat. Chris pulled her own jacket off, then stripped the other woman of her coat and sweater, still pressing her with bruising lips.

"God…" she heard the woman gasp.

Chris all but dragged her to the bedroom, shoved her

onto the bed. The woman looked up into Chris's flushed face, and struggled to get her boots off.

"Leave them," Chris ordered, pulling off the woman's skirt, unhooking her bra and throwing it on the floor. She jerked down the thong the woman wore, somehow sliding it down to catch on one ankle. Chris could finally get her legs apart.

Then Chris was on top, her hands on the woman's breasts, one leg pressed hard between her thighs. She closed her fingers on hard nipples, squeezing almost to the point of pain.

"Oh, honey!" the woman said, twisting unsuccessfully under Chris's weight.

She tried to bring her hands up, to pull at Chris's shirt, but Chris elbowed her away and resumed hard thrusts with her leg against the woman's crotch. Under her the woman was moaning, grinding her hips against Chris, trying to get enough contact to satisfy her need.

She groped again at Chris, trying to get her hands on skin, somewhere, but Chris moved her own hands to the woman's wrists and held her down as she sank her teeth lightly into the woman's shoulder. The woman groaned again, in pain and desire. Chris thought she tasted like beer and cigarette smoke.

Chris moved her head down to the woman's breasts, seizing one nipple in her mouth and sucking hard. The woman bucked under her, twisting again as if to push her whole body into Chris's mouth. Chris moved to the other nipple, biting lightly.

"Oh, baby, please, baby!" the woman was almost screaming.

Hope the walls aren't too thin, Chris thought briefly, but she didn't really care. All she wanted was this: hard, mindless fucking, hot enough to burn away the memory of a dead man's face.

Angry with herself at remembering what she was trying to forget, Chris brought one hand down and shoved her fingers inside the woman. The woman groaned loudly, raising her hips to meet the welcome intrusion.

Chris began thrusting, sliding up a little and using her thigh to press her hand hard and deep. The woman wrapped her legs around Chris. Still with her knee-high boots on, she urged her on by pushing against Chris in rhythm.

Chris shut her eyes, put her head on the woman's shoulder and simply shoved her hand in and out, fast, then slow, then fast again. The woman was clawing at her back. Chris could feel her nails through the fabric of her shirt. She was pummeling Chris with the heels of the boots, and Chris thought she'd be bruised tomorrow.

"Oh, fuck!" the woman gasped, and Chris felt the body under her jerk, the muscles contracting around her hand as the woman came, hips grinding wildly. Then she dropped as her body's energy drained away. Chris withdrew her hand.

Chris, sweating a little, pushed herself up on her knees, straddling the woman's limp body. Her stomach was still tight, her need burning inside of her. She unzipped her jeans and worked them down enough to get her hand between her own legs.

The other woman stirred, opened her eyes. "Hey, baby, let me..." she said thickly.

She reached for Chris, but Chris pushed her hands away, the woman's arms flopping down on the bed. Chris worked herself down to her swollen center, her fingers still moist and slick from the other woman.

She watched the woman watch her as she rubbed, fingers sliding easily over herself until she felt the orgasm hit her as if she had been standing in surf when a wave seized her. Chris felt the wave take her far away from this dark room, the stranger underneath her, the dead man in the park, everything and everyone.

It wasn't really good. It never was. But it was, for the moment, enough.

CHAPTER THREE: TUESDAY

After her morning run, Alex sprinted up the stairs to the condo. She was still getting her wind back as she let herself inside. She dropped her keys on the table in the foyer and inhaled appreciatively. The smell of coffee, freshly brewed, met her as she went into the kitchen.

CJ was leaning against the counter, looking a little sleepy, wearing her green silk robe and drinking coffee. When she saw Alex, she wordlessly poured a second mug and handed it to her.

"Thanks," Alex said. "And good morning."

She leaned across the breakfast bar for a kiss. CJ lifted a hand to Alex's face and said, "Ah, my favorite. Breathing hard and a little sweaty."

Alex pushed a damp strand of dark hair back, smiled, and drank coffee. "What's your day look like?"

CJ rubbed her forehead with long fingers under a lock of red hair that had fallen over her forehead. "Black suit day," she answered, thinking. "This morning I have a hearing panel."

"I love the black suit. Makes you look like a lawyer."

"That's hardly a compliment," CJ objected.

"I'll tell my sister the lawyer you said so. Will it take all day? You said you were going to try to hunt down the witness for Chris Andersen."

"We'll be done with the hearing in a couple of hours. It's as close to a slam-dunk IA as I've ever had. The idiot, who will go unnamed to you, actually drove his car to work after he lost his license and then lied to me about it. He deserves to get fired. When we're done, I'm going out to find Eddie Nero's girlfriend."

"That's the name of yesterday's victim?"

"Yes. Sounds like we need to take both cars, since I'll be in and out all afternoon. What's your schedule?"

Alex thought. "I've got to finish helping Frank figure out his caseload now that Chris is out for a while. I'm gonna call Rod and see if he can do the investigation from the criminal side."

"Tell him hi for me. I think we owe them dinner."

"I'll mention it. Roger and Kelly need some guidance on a case, there's the usual glut of paperwork, and I'm assuming there will be a conversation with the chief in there somewhere."

CJ finished her coffee and said, "If there's a press conference, call me, will you?"

"I'm sure you'll hear about it from him before I do," Alex pointed out. "You want to shower first?"

CJ said, "No."

Alex put her mug down and said, "Okay. I'll go."

"No," CJ said again, grinning.

Alex tried glaring at her. "I don't think we have time for that."

"Don't be silly, darlin'. Showering together saves water and time."

"No, it doesn't. It takes three times as long, and you know why."

"Just showering this time, I promise." Her expression actually managed to hold a look of sincerity, but Alex knew better.

"Please. When have you ever been able to do that? We both know there will be very little showering and a lot of fooling around."

"Absolutely," CJ said, the grin getting broader.

Alex checked the clock on the microwave over CJ's right shoulder, and did a swift calculation.

"Is your hearing at eight?" she asked CJ.

CJ was smiling so much Alex thought she could count every white, perfect tooth.

"Not until nine," CJ answered encouragingly.

And Alex had a sudden image of hot water running down CJ's shoulders, darkening the bright red hair to rust.

"Oh, all right," Alex agreed, trying for an air of martyrdom. "But you have to wash my back."

"Of course," CJ said, gracious in victory. "May I wash your front, too?"

***

CJ went to her office after the morning's disciplinary panel hearing. She had a small private office, sandwiched between a tiny space for her sergeant and an interview room on the first floor of the Colfax Police Station. She did have a single window that looked out over the parking lot, but across the way there was a small park that gave her a view of some trees and grass.

As always, the office was a complete mess, folders strewn across her desk, piled on top of filing cabinets, even tucked under her one visitor's chair. She hung her jacket on the back of the door and carefully picked her way through the file folders stacked haphazardly in random piles on the floor. Just as she sat down, her colleague poked his head in the door.

"How'd it go?" Sergeant Chad McCarthy asked.

CJ grinned at him. "They're deliberating now, but when the defense is made up pretty much of 'I'm really, really sorry I got caught,' I think we've got a winner. What's going on here?"

"Nothing new since yesterday. I was just going out to interview the complainant on the Deavers case. Do you need anything on Andersen?"

CJ shook her head. "No, I'll handle it myself. Political hot potato, so I don't want you getting yelled at by the brass. That would be my job."

McCarthy grinned, leaning against the doorjamb. "Are you saying it's your job to get yelled at, or that it's your job to yell at me?" he asked, smiling.

"Both," she answered his question. "I'm the only one who gets to yell at you, and they pay me extra to take heat from up above."

CJ liked McCarthy. He had already been in Internal Affairs for several years when she'd taken the position as Inspector, but he hadn't disappointed her with any bad habits. He was a little older, somewhere in his middle forties, but didn't seem to resent her rank. Early on, he'd gently explored her social availability, so she'd told him truthfully of her lack of interest in men. He reacted with some mild surprise at her sexual orientation, but had accepted the later news of her relationship with Alex calmly.

"Always wondered about her," he'd said.

CJ hadn't had the nerve to tell Alex the story, but it amused her every time she thought about it. Alex "I'm not really a lesbian" Ryan. So much for stereotypes.

"I don't mind you getting screamed at, Lieutenant," he said earnestly. "Just so long as it's not the Investigations Captain doing the yelling," he added.

"Believe me," CJ chuckled, "Captain Ryan knows better than to yell at me if she expects to get any…"

She left the sentence hanging, to enjoy the slightly shocked expression on his face before she finished.

"…expects to get any dinner."

He snorted in laughter. "Jesus, Lieutenant, you're a riot. It's not nice to put mental pictures like that in the head of a poor, single, straight guy."

"Hey, what you do in your own head is none of my business. Now, where did I put Nero's sheet?"

He found it for her in the mess, and said, "Call later if you need something."

"I will."

She read Nero's arrest record again, then stared out her window a few minutes, thinking about her approach to the interview with Nero's girlfriend. CJ double-checked her sister's address, and decided to stop on the way and get something to eat. It was not that far from noon, and she tried never to miss a meal.

***

The apartment house was close to the park where Eddie Nero had died. The complex had the unoriginal name "Mountain View," and the sign outside the leasing office proclaimed that the rents were the cheapest in Colfax.

From the outside appearance, CJ could easily believe it. As she climbed the battered concrete stairs to the second floor, she wondered if the residents would have been willing to part with a few extra dollars a month for a new paint job on the building.

Probably not, she decided as she knocked firmly on the apartment door. If she'd ever seen a place more likely to house a meth lab, she couldn't remember where.

A little to her surprise, the door was jerked open a few seconds later. The woman who opened it looked angry, an impression reinforced by the ugly bruise marring her left cheekbone.

"What the hell do you want?" she demanded.

She looked enough like the driver's license picture CJ had seen that she asked, "Marina Sanchez?"

"Yeah. Who're you?"

CJ produced her shield. "I'm with the Colfax Police Department, Internal Affairs. May I come in?"

She looked ready to refuse, but CJ had her best friendly smile and her thickest drawl already on display. Marina stepped away from the door.

"Is your sister at home?" CJ asked. It was important during any interview on-site to know who else was around.

"She's at work," Marina said brusquely. "I guess my bastard ex-landlord gave you this address."

CJ didn't respond. She needed to get Marina into a better mood if she had any hope of this interview going well. "Thanks for seeing me," she said. "This won't take too long, I hope."

The arms of the couch were shredded and the edges of the cushions worn to threads, so CJ chose the chair. It was upright and hard, but since it wasn't upholstered, she figured it might be marginally cleaner. Marina sat in the middle of the faded flowers fabric upholstering the couch and picked up a bag of frozen peas to apply it to her cheek.

"You're here about Eddie," she grunted.

"Yes. I'm sorry for your loss."

Marina made a noise that was almost a laugh. "Are you really? I doubt it."

"I am, actually. I'm sorry he's dead, I'm sorry you were hurt, and I'm sorry one of our police officers had to shoot him."

"Had to? That's a joke."

CJ controlled the twinge of dismay she felt, and calmly took out a small digital recorder and put it on the white plastic Parsons table that served as a coffee table. "I want to hear everything that happened yesterday."

Marina shifted the peas against her face and said bitterly, "What difference does it make? Eddie'll still be dead, and you'll just cover up anything you don't want to hear."

"You're right, it won't bring Eddie back," CJ said, "but if we did something wrong, we need to know about it. That's my job. There will be another investigation, too, a criminal investigation, to see if any charges should be brought."

"Against Eddie?"

The question surprised CJ. "No."

"Against me, then."

CJ cocked her head a little and said mildly, "Why would you think you would be charged with a crime?"

She wondered if Marina would admit to her involvement with the stolen goods in the trunk of Nero's car. Marina seemed to be giving the matter careful thought, and CJ reminded herself not to underestimate her—just because Marina was poor didn't mean she was stupid.

Marina came up with, "Because I left the scene without talking to the cops."

Nothing like getting to the heart of the matter. CJ said, "I'm not interested in charging you with anything, but I would very much like to know why you left."

"Why do you think?"

Not stupid at all, answering a question with a question. CJ said, "I'm not here to try to trick you, Ms. Sanchez, but I'm not going to play games, either. I want to hear about what happened yesterday, that's all."

"Nero," she said shortly.

"I'm sorry?"

"It's Marina Nero. We were common-law married," she said defensively.

"Of course. Ms. Nero. Why don't we start at the beginning?"

CJ switched on the recorder and the contradictions from the version she'd gotten from Chris Andersen began immediately. Marina insisted that Chris hadn't identified herself as a police officer, and when she'd run after Nero, Marina had gone after them.

"What happened when you reached them?" CJ asked.

Marina plucked at her old sweatpants with her free hand. "What do you think? I had to watch her shoot Eddie down."

"Did you see the knife?" CJ asked, concealing her growing distress.

"I never saw a knife," Marina insisted.

"Did Eddie usually carry a knife? For protection, perhaps?"

She shook her head vehemently. "No, never. Absolutely not. I never saw him with anything like that. He wouldn't, he wasn't the violent type."

Except for beating up on you. CJ bit her tongue. There was too much denial about the knife to be true, she thought. People telling the truth usually said "yes" or "no." The more they added, the more suspicious she got.

Switching topics abruptly CJ asked, "You said you were fighting with Eddie when Detective Andersen saw you. What were you fighting about?"

Marina threw the peas down on the table and muttered, "He couldn't even pay the rent on the crummy dump we were living in. How the hell was he going to support…"

She broke off abruptly and unconsciously dropped a hand below her waist. CJ asked gently, "Did he know you were pregnant?"

She looked ready to deny it, then CJ saw her shoulders sag. "I told him that morning. We got back to our place late, but we were locked out with this stupid legal notice on the door, so we went to the park and I told him. And he was an asshole about it, but it was nobody's business but ours. Your little bitch cop had no reason to…to…"

Marina began to cry, and CJ dug in her purse to come up with tissues. When most of the mascara had been wiped away, CJ asked again, "Why did you run away?"

"For all I knew she was going to shoot me, too. I didn't know who she was or anything."

"She says she identified herself as a police officer several times."

"Well, she's lying. And I never saw Eddie with a knife. So go away and leave me alone."

CJ decided she wasn't going to get what she needed today. She stood, and laid one of her cards on the table next to the bag of peas. "We'll need to talk again, Ms. Nero. We still have some areas to cover, and I think you should think carefully about what you're going to tell me next time."

"What the hell does that mean?" she demanded, crumpling the stained tissues.

"Among other things," CJ said quietly, "you could tell me where the two of you were most of the night. We opened the trunk of Eddie's car, you know."

She stopped, using one of her best interrogation techniques: silence. Marina was shredding the tissues. "I had nothing to do with that," she said.

"But you apparently know what we found," CJ pinned

her down. "If you were involved in theft and I can prove it, we'll need to change our mind about those criminal charges. You don't need that, especially not now. With the baby coming, and all."

"You're threatening me, so I'll say what you want," Marina sneered.

"Not at all. I repeat what I said before: I want you tell me what really happened. All of it, not just the parts you choose. Please think about that. I'll be calling you soon."

CJ wondered as she left which of them was more unhappy with the interview.

***

The wind picked up late in the day. Gray-white clouds scudded in over the Rocky Mountains to the west of the city. Yellow leaves that had abandoned their trees flung themselves at the windshield of her car as CJ drove back toward the station.

When her cell phone rang, she pushed the hands-free button and said, "St. Clair."

"It's me," Alex said. "Where are you?"

"I'm on County Line Road. Why?" CJ could tell that something was wrong.

Alex said, "David called. His mom fell at home."

"Oh, no," CJ exclaimed, trying to remember where the mother-in-law of Alex's sister lived. "She's in Trinidad, right?" The town was almost to the New Mexico border, south of Denver on Interstate 25. "How is she?"

"Hospital. They don't know a lot yet. David needs to drive down right away. He's not sure how long he'll be there. And Nic's still in Houston for that trial."

CJ made a U-turn at University Boulevard, beginning to head back toward the highway. "You need me to go get Charlie," she guessed.

Alex sighed into the phone. "Could you? That would be great. We'll figure out what to do with him tonight later. I'd go, but I'm supposed to meet the chief at four thirty."

"About Chris Andersen?"

"Yeah. I assume he already told you about the press conference in the morning."

"Yes," CJ answered, unwilling to discuss it. Talking about her cases in confidence with Alex was one thing; talking about an IA investigation on one of Alex's detectives made her uncomfortable. "Don't worry about my favorite nephew, we'll be fine."

"Are you sure this is okay?"

"Alex, of course. Is David calling the preschool to get me permission to pick him up?"

"He said they told him to fax an authorization, so I'm sure it will be there when you get to the school. I really appreciate this, Red."

"Alex," she said quietly. "This is what families do. Stop thanking me."

She could hear Alex's unspoken thought: Not what your family would do.

CJ had worked hard to forge a good relationship with Alex's younger sister, Nicole, her husband David, and son Charlie. CJ tried to treat Alex's family as her own, and Alex had told her more than once how much she loved CJ for it.

"How did the rest of your day go?" Alex asked. They hadn't talked since leaving the condo that morning, and CJ felt her need to reconnect.

CJ pulled onto the Valley Highway, heading toward Lone Pine, the southern suburb where the Castillos lived.

"Good, bad and ugly," CJ admitted. "The good part was the cop from this morning's hearing is so fired. Fastest disciplinary panel deliberation in history. Lieutenant Baker kept looking at him and saying, 'You actually told St. Clair you hadn't driven to work, then went out to the parking lot and drove away?' If it weren't so sad, it would be hilarious. I mean, we actually gave this moron a gun."

Alex snorted into the phone. "Good help is hard to find," she said dryly. "What about the bad and ugly parts?"

CJ narrowly avoided rear-ending a slow-moving truck in the far left lane. She was still reluctant to discuss her case, but she answered, "I found our missing victim in the Nero case."

Alex was quiet for a minute, and then said, "I would say, 'Great job and you're a hell of a good investigator,' but I sense we're not happy about it somehow."

CJ swerved around an SUV and pulled back into the fast lane. "We're not happy," she confirmed.

"Hell," Alex said gloomily. "You want to tell me?"

"No and yes. No, because it's not your case. Yes, because you have to go talk to the chief and he already knows, so you might as well hear it from me as from him."

"How does he know already?" Alex demanded.

CJ sighed into the connection. "I called him an hour ago," she admitted. "He needed to know before the press conference tomorrow."

Alex was quieter for a longer period this time, then she said, "Yeah, I get it. He's your boss, not me."

"I didn't mean it that way, darlin'," CJ said gently.

"Just tell me."

CJ said, "I found her at her sister's apartment. She claims to be his common-law wife. Her name is Marina Nero, and she's the one who'd filed a domestic violence charge against Eddie a year ago."

Alex said heavily. "And let me guess—she says there was no assault."

CJ hesitated once again, and then said, "No, she admits they were having a fight. It would be hard for her to deny, she's got a pretty bruised face. It's worse than that."

"How much worse could it get?"

CJ summarized the interview.

"Jesus, CJ," Alex breathed into the phone. "What in the hell is going on?"

"I don't know," CJ admitted. "Maybe she just didn't see or hear what really happened. Maybe she thinks she's got a big, fat lawsuit. Maybe she's just covering up her involvement in Nero's stealing. I'm pretty sure she was lying about a number of things."

"I know she's a liar," Alex said harshly. "We found the damn knife."

"I told the chief we'd better get the first press conference tomorrow, because we're in up to our necks if she gets her story out first."

"She's not the one I'm worried about. It's Carlson."

"Yes, darlin'. When Tony's opponent gets this, the fat is really in the fire. Look, I just thought you should know before you go in to talk to Wylie."

"God damn it all. What the hell is going on?" Alex repeated forcefully.

"Don't kill the messenger," CJ said, a little defensively. "The guy had a weapon, he threatened a police officer. It'll be a good shooting."

"Christ, I hope so," Alex answered. "I called Rod this afternoon, and he thought he could start on it tomorrow."

"That's good news." She deliberately changed the subject once again. "Look, I'll call you when I've got Charlie in the car, all right?"

"Yeah. You've got the car seat in the trunk still, right?"

"I never leave home without it."

"And drive carefully for a change, will you?"

"You're just worried about your nephew."

"I'm worried about you."

CJ heard what she wanted to hear behind the words and said, "I'll be careful. Good luck with the chief."

"Thanks. I'm gonna need it."

***

CJ sighed. "I'm sorry your fax isn't working, but I can promise you Dr. Castillo authorized me to pick Charlie up. I do appreciate that you're being careful."

The school director looked thoughtful, clearly assessing CJ. She was tall and thin, with black-framed glasses, and her bulky cardigan hung off her shoulders.

"And you claim you're a relative?" the thin woman demanded again. "Because you don't look as if you can be related to Dr. Castillo, and Mrs. Castillo has just the one sister, and you're not her."

CJ said carefully, "Do you have Alex Ryan's number in the file?"

She glanced down and said, "Yes."

CJ rattled off the number to confirm that she knew it, and said, "You can call her, but she's in a meeting with the Chief of Police right now, which is why she sent me. I'm willing to wait until you can contact her if necessary, but I'd really like to get Charlie home."

The director narrowed her gaze and persisted with, "So what relative are you?"

Admittedly, CJ had been trying to refrain from giving her the explanation, but saw no way to avoid it. "I'm his aunt. By marriage."

"By marriage? You're married to Dr. Castillo's brother?"

"No."

"I don't understand."

"I'm married to Alex."

"But Alex is…"

The director got it and her mouth tightened. "I see," she said tautly.

CJ knew she was not going to convert the woman into broadening her viewpoint, so she continued in her best mollifying tone. "I appreciate that you're protecting him, I really do. Maybe it would make you feel better if I tell you I'm a police officer."

She produced her badge and the woman eyed the ID card with CJ's photo carefully. Finally she said, "Does Charlie know you?"

For the love of..."Of course," CJ said, trying to stay calm. "Why don't you ask him?"

An aide brought him out at last. With his dark hair and eyes, he was like his father, but he had his mother's smile, the same face-transforming smile CJ loved so much in Alex. When he saw CJ at the counter he let go of the aide's hand and ran to her.

"Hey!" he squealed happily.

CJ bent down and swept him into her arms. She kissed him on both cheeks and he started to squirm. "Oh, no, you don't!" she exclaimed, and began to tickle him.

He giggled, still squirming. Behind them the director said, "Yes, I'd say he does know you. Charlie, who is this?"

He stopped laughing and looked at her, puzzled. "My Aunt CJ. We have the same letters in our names."

"Your aunt?" the woman probed.

"Yep," he answered. "She's married to my Aunt Alex. They're both girls. Is she here?" he asked CJ.

"No," CJ responded. "She's still working, so I came to get you."

Charlie looked over at the director and said, "My Aunt Alex is a policeman. So is my Aunt CJ. Where's Daddy?"

CJ answered, "He had to go out of town for a little bit, but he'll be back really soon. Would you like to have dinner with Alex and me tonight? We want you to."

"Yes! What are we having?"

"We can talk about that on the way home. Okay?"

"Okay!"

CJ glanced back at the director, who finally said, "Okay. Bye, Charlie. See you tomorrow."

***

When Alex got home, it was already fully dark. As she pulled into the parking lot, she glanced up automatically at the top floor to see the lights on in the condo. Usually just the thought that CJ was home, waiting for her, was enough to ease the kink between her shoulders from a tough day.

It was going to take more than that tonight.

In the foyer she had to step over CJ's discarded shoes. When she got to the living room, she saw CJ and Charlie down on the rug, playing with the LEGOs they kept in the house for Charlie.

"Hey," Alex said, trying to sound normal. "What are we building?"

Charlie looked up and said, "Aunt Alex!" and ran over to her.

Alex got down on one knee and hugged him. "Hi, you," she said, kissing him. "I'm glad to see you."

"Me, too," Charlie said. "Aunt CJ came and got me 'cause Daddy's gone and Mommy's gone, too."

"Yes," Alex said. "We're happy you're here."

"Aunt CJ says we are getting spaghetti for dinner."

"Cool," Alex said. "I love spaghetti."

"Me, too!"

Alex looked over at CJ, who had unraveled her long legs and was standing, barefoot, wearing jeans and a green V-neck cotton sweater, the sweater cut low enough for Alex to glimpse a hint of cleavage. The color made CJ's eyes look lovely, but Alex could see that CJ was battered from the day. There were fine lines visible around her eyes.

CJ said, "Tell you what, Charlie. I'll put on the dinosaur DVD and you can watch it while Alex helps me fix dinner."

"Okay. Can I still play with my LEGOs?"

She touched his dark hair fondly. "Of course."

After he was happy, the two women went into the kitchen. CJ got out a large pot, filled it with water, and set it on the gas burner to heat.

As they waited for the water to boil, CJ said quietly, "You look worse than I feel, and that's saying a lot. How did it go?"

Alex answered unhappily, "It went like hell. Tony apparently spent an hour last night yelling at the chief, so he managed to dump some of that on me."

CJ looked at her, her mouth tightening with distress. "Alex, what on earth were you supposed to do about it? It's not like you're responsible for what Chris Andersen did."

Softly, so that her nephew couldn't hear, Alex responded, "Chief Wylie disagrees with you. And apparently they're gonna try to make the dead guy look like he should have been on the Ten Most Wanted List to somehow justify the shooting. It won't matter anyway, and there's a rumor that Carlson will also hold a press conference tomorrow. If he does, you can guess what it will be about."

The water began to boil, and CJ dumped pasta into the pot. "God, Alex, I am so sorry."

"Yeah, me too. Mostly I feel for Chris. She's really going to go through hell."

She fell silent. CJ stirred the pasta, the spaghetti swirling like loose-limbed dancers in the boiling water.

After a minute CJ glanced at her partner. Alex was staring at Charlie, who was enthusiastically swooping a LEGO airplane off the coffee table.

"Alex? Where did you go?" CJ asked.

Alex said suddenly, "Do you want a child, CJ?"

CJ dropped the spoon into the boiling pasta. "Where on earth did that come from?" she asked, in shock, groping for the tongs to fish the spoon out of the pot.

"You and I…We've never really discussed it, not seriously," Alex said slowly. "But we don't have much longer if one of us wants to do it the usual way and get pregnant."

CJ blinked, still a little shocked. "Darlin', why are we having this discussion now? Is there something you want to tell me?"

She was obviously kidding, but Alex caught the note of apprehension she always got from CJ when anything seemed even vaguely threatening to their relationship. The damage of long-ago betrayal still echoed in CJ, and she'd never fully regained her confidence in her ability to hold onto love.

Alex tried to reassure her, and said lightly, "Of course not. The only way I could be pregnant is if you somehow figured out how to accomplish it. We can talk about it later, it's just that…"

The timer went off, and CJ dumped the water out, the spaghetti landing in a wet heap in the colander.

"We'll talk later," she agreed softly.

***

The dinner table discussion centered around Charlie's day. He launched into an elaborate tale about the playground that afternoon, involving a fort and some sort of boys versus girls encounter. Alex listened and nodded and said, "Uh-huh" in the right places, but CJ actually seemed to follow the story and asked questions.

She is so good with him, Alex thought again.

"I think you need to go home and sleep in your own bed," Alex said to Charlie. "I'll take you home and stay with you tonight. Then I can take you to school tomorrow, okay?"

"Okay," he answered. "When is Daddy coming home?"

Alex said, "He called me when I was coming home from work and said he will be here tomorrow afternoon to pick you up. He might have to go back to see your grandma in a day or two, but that's all right. CJ or I will come and get you, okay?"

"Okay," he said again, rolling his meatball around the edge of his plate.

When dinner was over, Alex went into their bedroom to pack an overnight bag. CJ got Charlie settled with a picture book and followed her into the bedroom.

"I'll go with you," she offered.

"There's no reason," Alex said. "No point in both of us having to manage Nic's guest room."

CJ frowned. "The point is you and me being together."

"Look, it's one night. I'll take what I need for tomorrow and see you at work in the morning, okay?"

CJ watched her pack for a moment, and finally asked, "Are you sure you don't want me to go with you?"

"CJ, my day was awful, and so was yours. Tomorrow will probably be worse. Let me go deal with Charlie, and you go and take a bubble bath or something. I'll call you when I get to the house, okay?"

CJ kissed her goodbye, unhappily.

CHAPTER FOUR: WEDNESDAY

CJ got to the main conference room on the first floor of the Colfax Police Station just before nine. There was a low platform set up at one end, flanked by the American flag on one side and the Colorado State flag on the other, the wall carefully draped with a dark blue cloth. CJ detected the artful staging by Allen, the department's public spokesman.

There were three television camera setups in the back of the room, and seven or eight reporters in the chairs set up in front of the three microphones. CJ looked for Alex, but she was apparently still with Chief Wylie, ready somewhere in the hall to make an entrance.

CJ stood at the rear of the room, her back against the wall near the door, behind the cameras. Just before nine, the door beside her opened, and she caught a flash of light blond hair.

CJ got to her quickly and grabbed Chris Andersen's arm. Chris whirled on her angrily. "What the hell…"

CJ said firmly, "Don't. Come with me, right now."

She hustled Chris out the door and down the hall into the ladies' room before the detective could resist. When the door was safely closed behind them, CJ released her arm. Chris snarled, "What the fuck do you think you're doing?"

"What are you doing here?" CJ asked. "You're suspended, remember?"

"Does that mean I can't show up for a press conference about me?" Chris barked at her.

"Tell me what you're doing here," CJ demanded again. "How did you even know about this?"

"How do you think? You may be trying to screw me over, but at least my boss has my back."

CJ was momentarily disoriented. "Alex called you?" she asked.

"Yeah, last night. She told me how very helpful you were yesterday, digging up a witness to call me a murderer."

Still reeling from the fact that Alex had called her, CJ responded with, "Chris, I just found the woman. I didn't tell her what to say. It's not as if I liked hearing it."

"You know what, Inspector? I just don't fucking believe you!"

CJ snapped, "It's actually irrelevant whether you do or not. But let me tell you, Detective, going in there is a really lousy idea. Chief Wylie and Captain Ryan are going to do whatever they can to try to protect you, but if you show up in this mood, the press is going to turn on you with a hundred questions you can't answer."

"You're full of shit. All I have to do is tell the truth. You just don't want my side of the story out there."

CJ tapped her fingers and said, "Really? Try this. 'Detective, tell us about how you knew the victim.'"

"I never saw him before..." Chris began.

"That's not true. You arrested him three years ago. And perhaps you can explain why his alleged victim says the deceased never carried a knife, that it was just an excuse to blow some innocent civilian away."

Chris blinked at her in confusion. "I...I don't know what..."

"Exactly," CJ said shortly. "You'll look like a fool at best, a liar at worst. Get out of here and let us do our jobs, all right?"

Chris didn't say anything, just glared at her. CJ could see that Chris still thought she was manipulating her somehow, but didn't have a way of responding that would make sense. She shoved past CJ without another word. CJ followed her out until she saw her push her way out of the front doors of the building.

Sighing in relief, CJ slipped back into the conference room.

Police Chief Nathan Wylie had completed his statement, and was taking questions. Allen was standing behind him, to one side, and Alex was standing on the other, hands folded in front of her. The chief was in uniform, and Alex was wearing a navy blue suit with a subtle pinstripe, complete with hose and low heels. CJ always thought of it as Alex's "court suit," even though she hadn't testified more than a couple of times since getting promoted.

CJ could see the smudges under Alex's eyes, even from the back of the room. Under the bright lights of the cameras, she actually saw a little more gray in Alex's dark brown hair, just at the temples.

She wished she could go up to the platform and fold Alex into her arms. She hated it when Alex was stressed, or exhausted, and she knew part of the reason was selfish. Alex was her anchor, and when she was troubled, it made CJ anxious.

Alex glanced at her, and CJ thought she could see a note of relief at her presence, even though Alex's expression didn't change. CJ nodded reassuringly, but she couldn't help but wonder about the reason for Alex's phone call to Chris.

She saw Alex casually shift her jacket sleeve up a moment, and CJ saw a brief flash of precious stones from the bracelet on her wrist. CJ couldn't help but grin at her across the room as Alex carefully adjusted the jacket back into place.

One of the reporters was asking about the investigation. CJ heard Wylie say, "We have referred the case to an outside investigating agency for a determination of whether criminal charges are appropriate. This is our usual procedure in cases involving an officer-involved shooting…"

He was still talking, but CJ saw Alex flinch ever so slightly. What was going on?

Finally, one of the reporters asked about Carlson's former accusations of excessive use of force by the Colfax PD. In his question he mentioned the upcoming press conference from candidate Robert Carlson, and CJ knew why Alex was looking deeply unhappy. As they'd feared, Carlson was already on the scent of another excessive use of force allegation. CJ watched Wylie tap-dance his way around the question.

It was finally over, and the chief left, trailed by Allen and Alex. CJ went back the way she'd come in, then went around to the stairwell. She trotted up one flight to the Investigations squad room, and got to Alex's office just after she did.

Alex looked up wearily when she entered, and CJ closed the door behind her. There was a large window from Alex's office into the squad room, but although they could be seen at least the conversation wouldn't be overheard.

CJ ached to go and kiss her, but she just said, "Did you sleep at all?"

"Not a lot. Everything all right? You were late."

Sighing, CJ answered, "I intercepted Chris going in just before you started. I managed to convince her to leave."

Alex flinched and said, "God damn it."

Her voice carefully neutral, CJ said, "She told me you called her last night."

Alex leaned back and shut her eyes. "Yes," she admitted. "The chief called my cell last night and told me about Carlson, so I called Chris. I thought she should know about both press conferences from me instead of hearing it on the news at noon."

Still cautious, CJ asked, "Do you think that was a good idea?"

Alex opened her eyes and fixed CJ with an intense stare. "You're not suggesting that my calling her compromised the investigation in some way, are you, Inspector?"

CJ felt trapped by the question, but tried to feel her way out. "We don't normally keep suspects informed of everything we find out as we're completing the investigation," she said coolly.

"Suspects?" Alex lashed out. "Now she's a suspect?"

"She's a suspect until we clear her." CJ stood her ground. "You know that."

"I was not going to let her hear it on the news," Alex repeated harshly. "She deserves more consideration than that."

CJ dropped into the chair in front of Alex's desk. "Alex, it will be all right."

Alex gazed at her for a long minute. Then she shut her eyes again, and said, "Will it?"

***

An hour later, Alex was reviewing one of Morelli's open files. There had been four armed robberies in the Colfax office district in the last two weeks. All the victims were women returning to their cars in various underground parking lots after work. There were two perpetrators, one of whom brandished a shotgun. Fortunately, no one had been hurt yet, but Alex knew that armed robbers usually ended up using their weapons eventually, and she wanted to find them sooner rather than later. Morelli and Andersen had interviewed the victims, but hadn't yet gotten any real clues. Alex began to make notes about parking garages that hadn't been hit yet, and thought about how to cover the possible sites.

Her cell phone rang. She checked the caller ID, but didn't know the number. She debated briefly whether to answer, then punched the talk button.

"Ryan."

"Captain. It's Chris Andersen."

Alex put the file down and said, "Chris. How are you doing? Inspector St. Clair told me she got you to leave the press conference this morning. I think that was good decision."

Chris said bitterly, "Yeah, she was very persuasive. Look, Captain..." She hesitated.

"What?"

"Do you have a few minutes? I know it's early for lunch, but I'd really like...I'd like to talk to you."

Alex wondered what the request had cost her. She said, "I could do that. Where are you?"

"I'm across the street, at Jersey's. I thought it would be easier if you could just walk over."

"Yes, okay." Alex checked her watch and said, "I'll be over in five minutes."

"Yeah. Thanks."

***

When Alex walked into the deli, she saw Chris sitting at one of the small tables in the back. Jersey's did a brisk takeout and lunch business, but at eleven a.m., there were only a couple of other people in the place.

Alex crossed the black and white tiled floor to stand by the red table, edged with chrome, and asked Chris, "Did you order?"

Chris shook her head. "I wasn't sure if you had time to eat," she answered hesitantly.

Alex was struck by the difference in her demeanor from Monday. In Alex's office forty-eight hours ago, she'd been brazen and provocative. On the phone last night, she'd been angry. Today she looked younger, more vulnerable.

Alex said, "I have time. Let's go order."

They went to the counter. Alex got broccoli cheese soup and half a turkey sandwich, and Chris had pastrami on rye.

"Oh, the metabolism of youth," Alex grumbled good-naturedly, and insisted on paying.

"You don't have to buy me lunch," Chris flared, back to her old self for a moment. "I invited you."

"You can get it next time," Alex responded calmly.

When she reached for her change, her sleeve rode up momentarily, and she exposed the bracelet on her wrist. It flashed with emeralds and sapphires, green and blue catching the overhead fluorescent lights.

They sat down to await their meal, and Chris said, "Nice bracelet. I don't think I've seen you wear it before.

In fact, I don't think I've seen you wear any jewelry other than earrings."

Alex blushed a little. "I usually save it for the good suit," she said, brushing imaginary lint from the navy blue jacket.

Chris asked, "May I see it?"

Alex, a little reluctantly, pushed her sleeve up and offered her wrist. Chris took her hand gently and traced the design with one fingertip. The bracelet, while almost austere in design, looked both beautiful and expensive, the emeralds and sapphires woven together in fine gold wire, the effect remarkably delicate.

"It looks custom," Chris said.

"You a jewelry expert, Detective?" Alex asked dryly.

Chris laughed. Alex realized she'd never heard her laugh before. "No, but I've never seen anything like it," she answered.

Alex took her arm back and said, "It is custom, as it happens. It was a gift. My taste is not even close to being this good. Not to mention my bank account."

Watching her, Chris finally said, "I guess I shouldn't ask what you did for the guy to get it, then."

Alex leaned forward suddenly and glared at her. "You just like trying to piss me off, don't you, Andersen?" she snapped. "Because that remark is both offensive and so full of wrong assumptions I wouldn't know where to start correcting you."

Chris swallowed. "I wasn't trying to be offensive, Captain…"

"Save it. Of course you were. If you wanted to know about it, you could ask instead of trying to needle me into telling you. Maybe that works on suspects, but it won't work on me. Clear?"

"Clear."

The food arrived, and Alex picked up a spoon. "Why did you call me?" she asked.

"Always direct, aren't you, Captain? Look, I appreciate you phoning me last night. But when I got to the press conference this morning…"

"I told you about the press conference so you wouldn't be surprised. Not so that you could show up."

Chris muttered, "It was about what I did, wasn't it? I thought it made sense to hear what was being said about me."

"You could have heard that on the noon news. You really shouldn't have come."

"You sound like St. Clair. She grabbed me and hustled me out of there so fast you'd have thought the room was on fire or something."

"She was trying," Alex said carefully, "to protect you."

"That's bullshit!" Chris barked, earning them both a glance from the customers at the counter across the deli. "I don't trust St. Clair, I'm telling you. First she digs up a witness to call me a murderer, then she doesn't want me in the room while you're discussing the case."

"Chris…"

"I know you used to be partners, and she saved your life, and all that shit, but she's IA now and she's going to hang me out to dry, I know it!"

"Stop it!" Alex interrupted her sharply. "She's doing her job."

Chris stopped and glared at her. "How the fuck do you know she's not out to get me?"

Alex tore at the crust of her sandwich. If I tell her, she won't trust me, either. She'll think it's all some kind of conspiracy. And if I don't tell her, she'll find out anyway, from Frank or someone else, and wonder why I lied to her. Hell.

"Chris, listen to me," she looked into Chris's eyes, the clear color of a cloudless sky. "I wouldn't let IA or anyone else treat you unfairly, and you don't have to worry about

Inspector St. Clair. She wasn't my work partner. She's my life partner. We live together. I know she's not out to get you, believe me."

Chris looked at her, lunch forgotten. "Partner," she repeated blankly. "She told me she was with somebody, but I didn't know…you?"

Alex nodded.

Dazed, as if it somehow made Alex a liar, Chris said, "She wears a ring. You don't."

Alex shrugged. "I don't like rings. I didn't wear one when I was married before, which my ex-husband hated very much. CJ is a lot more forgiving."

"She gave you the bracelet."

"Yes," Alex acknowledged. She didn't explain the significance of the emeralds and sapphires, symbols for the colors of CJ's eyes, and her own.

"Sorry, I just…I didn't know you were gay," Chris managed.

Alex wasn't going to discuss that, either. "The point of this conversation," she said, finishing her soup, "is that I think I can assure you Lieutenant St. Clair's sole objective is to find out the truth, and be able to prove it. She's not after your scalp, I promise you that."

Chris put her head in her hands, fingers thrust through the fine blond hair, so pale it was almost white. "Why is that asshole Carlson going to hold a press conference, too?" she asked miserably.

Alex sighed. This was going to be much harder than explaining CJ's motives. "Look, Chris, it's just politics, and it's bullshit. Carlson's campaign is pretty much based on his made-up allegations of police brutality and the current administration of the DA's office covering it up, and he's going to try to twist this for his own purposes. You'll be cleared eventually, we just have to wait for the storm to blow over."

Chris looked at her, openly disbelieving.

Abruptly, Alex changed the subject and asked, "Do you want to go running in the morning?"

"What?" The suggestion clearly caught Chris by surprise.

"I usually run before work, and since you're off, I figured we could run together. I try to do three miles. What do you think?"

Chris seemed to think it over for a few seconds, then she said, "Sure. Where shall we meet?"

***

As Chris drove home, she still was scrambling mentally. Good news, and bad, in the same revelation. Great, she likes women. Fuck, she's, like, married, whatever the hell that means.

She had liked holding Alex's hand, she realized. Not that surprising, really. Chris considered every woman she met a potential bed partner, and Alex was attractive to her in a serious way. Really, really too bad she's my boss.

Her thoughts turned involuntarily to the shooting. Living through the actual event was bad enough, but now, with all this political crap going on, God only knew what would happen.

Maybe it will all just go away. Yeah, and maybe the sun would rise over the mountains in the west tomorrow.

***

"And this is just confirmation of the serious cancer eating away at justice in our district, a disease of police brutality condoned and facilitated by the cowardice in the present administration of the District Attorney's office…"

Chief Wylie, still watching candidate Carlson's press conference on his office television set said to Alex, "I think that's a mixed metaphor, isn't it?"

Alex listened to Robert Carlson pontificate about police use of excessive force. Carlson had a face made for television, a large head of silvery hair carefully swept into what was almost a pompadour, large intense eyes and a deep cleft in his chin. His suit looked custom fit, maximizing his narrow shoulders and minimizing his wide hips.

He was a skilled speaker, she had to give him credit for that. He didn't use notes, knew how and when to gesture for emphasis, and modulated his deep voice for the best effect. Lots of practice before judges and juries, she thought. But the content of his speech was making her queasy.

Poor Chris. She didn't deserve this.

***

CJ was sitting alone in her office, staring out the window. The lights had already come on in the parking lot, the sensors reacting to the early twilight. She didn't mind the thought of the coming winter. She actually liked snow, and cold, at least until New Year's. January and February were the tough months in Colorado, and snow could fall as late as May. She wished Alex would come downstairs and take her home.

As if by wishing it she had made it so, Alex's voice from the doorway interrupted her thoughts.

"You sure you don't need a front-end loader to help you with the stuff in this office?"

CJ turned her swivel chair back from the window and answered, "I don't need machinery. Just a spare weekend and the help of a loving spouse who suffers from obsessive-compulsive disorder."

Alex had her navy suit jacket over her arm, and her white cotton blouse, so crisp at the press conference this morning, looked creased and tired. CJ longed to unbutton it, slide it from Alex's shoulders, and enjoy what was underneath.

"Ha," Alex said. "You're just jealous because I can actually locate my file folders without a bloodhound."

"I keep telling you, I know where everything is," CJ said loftily.

"And I keep telling you that you're full of it, Red." Alex dropped wearily into CJ's lone visitor's chair.

"Not a good day?" CJ asked gently.

"Started lousy, got worse. How was yours?"

"Same answer."

"Shit." Alex rubbed a hand over her cheek. CJ saw the tiny smudges of mascara under her eyes, deepening the dark circles under them. "I'm not surprised, I guess, but still…"

"I know. Did you see the Carlson press conference?"

"Unfortunately, yes. I got back from an early lunch in time to watch with Wylie."

"Oh, that must have been fun."

"Not so much."

Alex had clearly given up any pretense of staying away from the case, and CJ wondered briefly why. Not that she didn't trust Alex, of course. "So what's your plan for tomorrow?" Alex asked.

CJ sighed and said, "I'm going out to interview Marina Nero again, first thing. Something's not right there, and I'm going to find out what it is."

Alex said wearily, "Okay. Can we go home now? I'm just beat."

They walked out of the building. The stars seemed hard and bright, like tiny spotlights against the cold night sky. CJ asked, "Why didn't you call me about lunch? You said you ate early."

Alex hesitated a moment, then said, "Chris called me, so I met her at Jersey's."

CJ stiffened, involuntarily, and then forced herself to relax. Mildly, she said, "Really?"

"Yeah. She's under a lot of strain, and she's got no one to talk to."

"Really?" CJ said again.

Alex continued, "We're going running tomorrow at six thirty, at the track at Pine Ridge High School. I thought it might help her cope with all this."

"Sounds like fun," CJ said, trying to conceal that she was lying.

"Want to come?" Alex kidded her. "We'll try to go slow and limit ourselves to ten miles."

"You are so hysterical. I think not. I need my beauty sleep."

Alex bumped her, hip-to-hip, gently. "Nah. You're pretty enough already."

"Flattery will not convince me to get up and go running with you in the morning."

"Will it convince you to eat out tonight? I was thinking Indian."

"Sounds good," CJ said, wearily. "I'm too tired to cook, even for you."

As CJ stopped by her car, she watched Alex get into her truck. She looked at Alex's profile a moment, lit by the dashboard lights as she turned the key. She was trying to remember the last time Alex went running with anyone else but her.

CHAPTER FIVE: THURSDAY

CJ was heavily asleep when the phone rang. She groped for it. Both the phone and the clock were on Alex's side of the king-size bed, and she had a long scramble to get to the far nightstand.

The sheets were still warm from Alex, who had left minutes ago to meet Chris for their run. CJ mentally cursed the phone, for ringing, and Alex too, for being gone.

She managed to find the talk button and punched it. "St. Clair," she said. It had to be a work call. No one else would call at this hour.

"Uh, CJ. It's Tony. Is Alex there?"

She slumped back on the pillows. Lord. The day could not start any worse, could it?

"She's not here, Tony," she answered, trying to sound civil.

"Oh?" The bastard actually sounded hopeful, she thought.

CJ actually briefly considered saying, Yeah, it's amazing she could stagger out of bed after our passion-filled night, but decided to take the high road. "She just left to go running," she explained calmly. "You could try her cell."

She heard him growl unhappily. "I just wondered if she'd seen the morning paper."

"I imagine not," she said, wondering what was going on. If Tony Bradford was desperate enough to have a conversation with her, he must be in real distress.

He growled again. "There's a story. Front page of the *Post*. The wife of the guy the detective shot gave an interview. With her attorney."

CJ was fully awake, her stomach beginning to feel like tightly knotted rope. "Her attorney," CJ repeated. "That was fast. She didn't have one when I interviewed her yesterday."

"She's got one now," he snarled at her. "They say they're suing the city for wrongful death. She claims the cop, what's her name…"

"Andersen," CJ supplied, trying not to sound as angry as she felt.

"She says Andersen never said she was a cop, and that Andersen shot the guy in cold blood. Claims to have seen the whole thing. Says there was no knife."

The knot in her belly was pulled tighter, but she said, "Tony. We've got the knife, okay? Don't worry." She didn't really feel much like reassuring him, but she decided to try to be polite, for Alex's sake.

Tony demanded, "You're investigating this, aren't you? What the hell is going on?"

Fighting her urge to snap at him, CJ said, "Yes, we're investigating, and no, I can't tell you what's going on yet."

"Can't or won't?" He was almost shouting. "What the hell are you people doing over there? Are you trying to ruin this for me, you…" He stopped abruptly.

Furious, CJ snapped, "What name are you going to call me this time, Tony? Oh, I forgot. You don't have the balls to say anything to me directly, you just enjoy tormenting Alex."

"You listen to me!" he began, screaming, but she cut him off.

"No, you listen to me," she said, her voice low and threatening. "You want to discuss this case as a deputy district attorney, call me at the office, during business hours, and act like a professional, or at least as close to one as you can get. But stop calling Alex, do you understand me? She's got enough to do without listening to your bullshit."

"Listen, you bitch!" he raged. "You can't tell me what to do! I'll call her whenever I…"

She was beyond angry. This had been a long time coming, and fury iced her words. "No, you won't!" she spat at him. "I've had enough. I don't give a rat's ass what you think of me, or my relationship with Alex. It's none of your goddamned business, do you understand me? I used to feel sorry for you, Tony, because I thought you loved her once, but for the love of God, get a clue! She doesn't love you, she's not coming back to you, and you're not going to convince her to leave me by calling me names. Just stop it!"

She heard him breathing heavily into the line. Finally he said, "Or what? What kind of threat are you making?"

Now she laughed at him unpleasantly. "You're an idiot, Tony. You really have no idea, do you? I guess you'll just have to wait and find out if you don't stop acting like a moron."

She hung up without another word and threw the phone on the bed, shaking with anger. She felt half ashamed of herself for losing her temper, half gratified for finally telling him off.

CJ was glad Alex hadn't heard the conversation. She could only imagine what description of it Tony would be providing Alex with later.

She didn't care. There would be no more sleep for her this morning, so she got up and read the *Post* article online, shaking her head in disbelief.

Everything Marina Nero had told her before was repeated, with a few embellishments. And the pending claim against the city meant that CJ shouldn't talk to Marina without her attorney present, or the city attorney would have her badge.

CJ made a note of the name of Marina's attorney, and just shook her head again. Could the case get any worse?

***

Chris let Alex get a little ahead of her as they rounded the last lap. They were actually compatible runners, going at about the same pace. Chris was impressed, as she figured she was a decade younger at least, but Alex had no trouble keeping up. Chris dropped back a few paces, not because she was particularly winded, but because she wanted to improve her view.

The morning was bright with fall sunlight but cool, and Alex was wearing a white long-sleeved shirt and black running tights. The tights did an excellent job of providing

Chris with an outline of Alex's legs and ass, and Chris wanted to enjoy the sight.

Chris had her mind, not on the run, but on the best way to proceed with what she hoped would be a successful seduction. After lunch the day before, she realized how much she wanted to sleep with Alex. She considered the possible impact on her career, but figured that, if anything went wrong, Alex had a lot more to lose by having sex with a subordinate than Chris did by having the affair with her boss. And the pursuit would distract her from all this crap about the shooting.

The real problem, as Chris saw it, was Alex's relationship with St. Clair. Chris wasn't remotely interested in breaking them up. She wanted to go to bed with Alex, not have an emotional relationship with her. She didn't care about hurting St. Clair, of course, but she was more than a little worried about St. Clair's reaction if she found out, because she was clearly a smart woman. Chris strongly suspected she was not going to tolerate Alex having extracurricular activities.

She'd just have to be a little careful, Chris thought. The challenge actually added to the excitement of it. Not that she needed any added motivation. Just the thought of getting Alex between the sheets was incentive enough.

She considered whether Alex was the top woman in her partnership with St. Clair. In a way, she hoped so. There was nothing hotter than a power struggle in the bedroom, and Chris felt confident in her ability to flip Alex to the submissive role, if it came to that.

She had a sudden daydream of Alex in her hands, her head thrown back in surrender as Chris moved over her...

Jesus, I have to stop thinking about that. The vision of Alex under her made her legs start to wobble. Back to strategy.

If Alex likes to be in charge, maybe the best approach is just to play it as if I'm a little insecure. That wouldn't be hard, not with the damn investigation hanging over her head. She'd have to be careful about what she said about St. Clair, though. Alex had seemed defensive of her partner yesterday.

They finished the run, and Chris caught up as they slowed to a walk, cooling down.

"You okay?" she asked Alex, smirking. "I didn't wear you out, did I?"

Alex shot her a look. "You want to do another mile, smart mouth?"

Chris lifted her hands and laughed. "No, no, I'm good."

They finished walking it off, then went to a bench to do some stretching. Chris admired Alex's legs again, and had some trouble keeping her hands to herself.

Alex said, "Thanks for this. I enjoyed it."

Glad to hear that. "You usually run alone?"

"Yeah. CJ's good for about once a week, on the weekends."

It took all of Chris's self-control not to ask if they were still talking about running, or some other activity.

Alex continued, "The rest of the time she prefers the gym, the bike or elliptical."

Chris did a hamstring stretch and asked, "How'd you meet, anyway? On the job?"

Alex nodded, and Chris could see her make an effort to have a real conversation. "Yes. It was hard for me, at first. For her, too."

"Talked her into it, did you?" Chris asked, beginning her probe for information about the relationship.

Alex laughed a little. "Well, sort of. I had to talk myself into it first. I'd never been with a woman before."

Chris almost fell out of her stretch. "What?"

Alex flushed a little, but said, "Yeah. I'd been married, I'd only dated men."

Chris was gaping at her. "You're not telling me she's the one who brought you out?"

Alex was a little puzzled at her surprise. "What's the big deal?"

"It's just…you have no idea how rare that is."

"What?" Alex asked, still confused by her reaction.

Chris said carefully, "Nobody ever stays with their first woman. You're still in that 'wow, this is so hot' stage, so you have to get through that to find somebody you really want to be with."

Alex said calmly, "I found the somebody I wanted to be with the first time, that's all." A little amused, she continued, "Is that what you're doing? Trying to find somebody you really want to be with?"

Now Chris had to be careful. The honest answer would have been, Hell no, I'm just trying to fuck as many women as possible, but that wasn't what she was going to say. The question was: what answer would most likely make her attractive to Alex?

Cautiously, Chris answered, "Yes. It's just harder than it looks."

Alex nodded and Chris was pleased. She'd gotten it right. She asked, "Do you have time for coffee?"

Alex checked her watch. "Afraid not. I've got to go home and shower before work."

Chris nodded, trying to look sad because she didn't have a job she could go to.

Alex caught the look and something apparently nudged at her. She said, "I can have lunch today, if you want. I think it's your turn to buy."

Chris figured she was feeling guilty, or maybe that she was worried that Chris was too isolated to fully recover from the trauma of the shooting without a little support.

She kept the triumphant look from her face. Either way, this wasn't going to be as hard as she thought it might be.

"I'd like that," she answered shyly. "Jersey's at noon?"

***

Alex was reviewing the parking garage armed robbery case file again. She noticed that all the robberies were later than the usual five o'clock quitting time. The earliest robbery had been six thirty, the latest almost eight o'clock. Were the robbers waiting for a nearly deserted garage?

Her office phone rang. As she picked up she glanced at the caller ID first to see that it was an internal number from the DA's office. She sighed and said, "Ryan."

Tony said, "Alex. Got a minute?"

She was a little surprised—he rarely bothered to ask. She carefully capped her pen and replaced it on her desk. It was sterling silver, a fountain pen because Alex liked to write with one, carefully cushioned and beautifully balanced. Alex looked at it fondly for a moment. It was, as were all the material luxuries in her life, a gift from CJ, a woman who loved beautiful things.

"I have some time," she answered Tony. "What's up?"

He said, "I assume you read the morning paper."

He sounded subdued, and Alex wondered why he wasn't already screaming.

"I glanced at it," she acknowledged. "The city attorney called me this morning and told me Nero's attorney has already sent a notice of claim to the city, and I know the lawsuit will follow. The city attorney won't let us talk to Nero's widow without her attorney's permission, so we're kind of stuck. The detective we borrowed to do the criminal investigation will talk to her, or maybe already has, but with her attorney there, I'm sure. When we know more, we'll tell you."

She heard him breathing into the receiver a moment. He still wasn't yelling, and she was deeply baffled.

"Is CJ still working this case?"

"That would be her job, yes."

"Alex, tell me something. Honestly."

Her bewilderment continued to grow. "Sure, if I can. What do you want to know?"

"Be objective. I mean, I know you…that you're with her, and all, but is she any good?"

Now Alex's head was spinning. "Tony, what the hell are you asking me?" she demanded sharply.

"Jesus, Alex, calm down. I'm talking about her as a cop. Is she a good investigator? Because I'm telling you, we're all up shit creek here. I am, the DA's office is, the department, Wylie, even you. This case is a disaster, and we're pretty much having to rely on St. Clair to pull our asses out of the sling."

Now she had to take two deep breaths to relax. "You forgot Andersen," she said tersely.

"What?"

"Chris Andersen. My detective. The one who had to kill a guy, remember her?"

"No, I didn't forget about her," he said, defensively.

"Tony, what the hell is the matter with you?"

He didn't say anything for a few seconds, and then said, "Maybe you should ask your girlfriend."

Three deep breaths. "Okay, Tony. I'm not playing games. For the record, CJ is not just my girlfriend. She's my partner, we're as married as we can be in Colorado, and you know it. Second, she is a really good cop, smart and hard-working, and she is, hands down, the best detective I've ever seen in the interview room. Now, what the hell are you talking about?"

A longer pause from him this time, so long Alex thought he'd put the phone down. Finally he said, "I called the condo this morning to talk to you. CJ and I had...a conversation. I wanted to talk about the case and she ended up screaming at me. About you."

Anxiety tightened through her like a boa constrictor. CJ screaming at him? Not that she hadn't had more than enough provocation, but that didn't sound like CJ to her.

"And what did you say to set her off, Tony?" she asked, trying to sound calm.

"I didn't say anything." He sighed, and she recognized his tactic. He was playing the victim. This was supposed to trigger Alex's anger at CJ, and enlist her sympathy for him. It wasn't going to work, yet she was still worried.

"I doubt that," Alex said coolly. "I have a tough time getting her to raise her voice, so you must have worked really hard to get her mad. What exactly was it she said to you?"

"She told me to stop calling you. Alex, she's jealous, pure and simple."

Alex laughed, although she felt far from happy. "Tony, please. What on earth would she be jealous of?"

"Alex, you're just not being rational here. She's jealous of me, of our relationship, the fact that we were married. She knows she could never compete with that, with me."

Alex held the phone receiver away from her ear and stared at it, in disbelief at what she was hearing. She returned the phone to her ear and said, "Whatever is going on, she is not jealous of you, believe me. She's got nothing to be jealous of."

"You're not thinking straight, hon."

That's true, she thought dryly, skipping the joke he wouldn't appreciate.

"Come on, Alex." His tone was wheedling. "She's just desperate to keep me out of your life so you won't—"

"Come back to you?" she cut in. "Tony, I've run out of different ways to tell you this. I'm not coming back to you. Ever. If CJ, God forbid, walked out on me tomorrow, I would still not be coming back to you. Is that clear enough?"

"Honey, I know this…thing with a woman is temporary. She knows it, too, that's why she's jealous. I'm a man, she knows you like men."

She'd already been with CJ about as long as her marriage to Tony had lasted a decade ago, and he thought it was "temporary."

There wasn't enough air in the room to calm her down from that, so she counted to ten. Twice.

"Okay, that's it," she said, amazed at how calm she sounded when what she wanted was to reach through the phone line and strangle him. "When we find anything, I'll call you. Until then, Mister Bradford, do not call me at home, do not call me at the office, do not call my cell phone."

"Alex—" he began again.

"No," was all she said, and hung up.

She sat, motionless for a few minutes, staring out across the parking lot without seeing it. If the conversation had made her this furious, she could only imagine what it must have been like for CJ.

Having lost both parents in her teens, she always thought of herself as self-sufficient, independent, not needing anyone else for comfort. After CJ, whenever things got bad, when the pressure started to tighten her shoulders, she tried to think about CJ and let the sensory memories wash over her like a soft blanket, wrapping her in a cocoon of love and security. Red hair like silk slipping through Alex's hands, the rich springtime scent of her skin, the warm vanilla taste of her mouth…

Alex laughed at herself. Yeah, some tough cop you are, Ryan.

She wanted nothing more than to clear Tony Bradford away from her brain. All it would take would be for her to go downstairs, wrap her arms around CJ, and breathe the same air with her, inhale her. But it was noon, and she had to go meet Chris Andersen.

***

CJ and McCarthy had worked together all morning, going over other cases, trying to clear the decks as much as possible.

After a couple of hours, CJ dropped her pen, sat back in her chair to stretch, and ran a hand through her hair. One strand caught on her diamond and she had to tug it free. "Ow!" she exclaimed.

McCarthy, seated across from her, laughed. "Your own damn fault," he kidded her. "What the hell are you doing wearing a rock that size anyway? Just showing off?"

CJ plucked a single red hair caught in the prong of the ring and grinned back at him. "Darlin', when somebody you love buys you a ring like this, you wear it all the time, believe me."

McCarthy looked at her. She was one damn fine-looking woman, and he figured she could have just about any guy she wanted. He still couldn't quite figure out the whole lesbian thing.

CJ caught the look and said, "Question, Sergeant?"

He blushed a little, but said, uncomfortably, "Sorry, Lieutenant. I know you're, like, with Captain Ryan and all, but I mean…you just really don't like guys?"

"I like guys fine. I just don't want to sleep with any of them. No offense."

"None taken. I don't really get it."

CJ shrugged. "It's simple, darlin'. I presume you like women, you're attracted to them? You think they're beautiful, and sexually appealing?"

"Hell, yeah," he smirked.

She grinned at him again. "Me, too," she said simply.

He stared at her silently, rubbing a hand over the small bald spot on the crown of his head. He'd always thought of gay women as being from some other planet. She could see that he actually hadn't thought about it that way before, that they had the attraction in common. She suspected he was tempted to ask her if she was more of an ass woman or was into tits, but decided he probably shouldn't be having that discussion at work.

"Look, we're in pretty good shape here," CJ observed. "I'm going over to talk to Rod Chavez this afternoon—he's handling the criminal investigation on Andersen, and I'm hoping he's had a chance to talk to the widow."

"Especially since we can't," McCarthy said.

"Yes. And in the meantime, see what you can find about this attorney, Raymond Elliot. He's Marina Nero's lawyer. I need to figure out if he's going to let me talk to her again, and I'd like to know more about him first." She stood up and stretched more completely.

"Will do," McCarthy answered. "Want me to get you lunch?"

"No, thanks. I need to walk. I think I'll get something across the street and bring it back. Can I bring you something?"

"Nope, I brown-bagged it today. I suspected we might be just a little busy."

"Good thinking. I'll see you in a few minutes."

***

Chris was waiting for her when Alex arrived. Jersey's was full, but Chris had snagged a two-top near the back.

As Alex wove her way through the crowd, Chris checked her out. Alex was back to her usual workday attire. Today it was dark blue button-fly Levi's, white oxford blouse and a gray wool blazer.

Chris had decided on a pair of black herringbone trousers that fit her particularly well, and her deep blue silk shirt had a couple of extra buttons undone. No bra, in case Alex was into that. She couldn't compete with St. Clair in cup size, but she figured she could effectively display what she had.

Alex smiled when she got to the table. The smile seemed forced, Chris thought, but at least she was making an effort. She said, "I got here early, figured it was our only shot at a table. I ordered, too, I hope that was okay."

Alex lifted an eyebrow. "Ordered for me too, did you?"

Chris ducked her head shyly. "I just figured you might be pressed for time, and didn't want you to wait. If you don't like what I got you, you can have my lunch instead."

Another smile, more natural this time. "I'm sure it'll be fine. I'm not a fussy eater. When I was single, I used to eat cereal for dinner a lot."

She sat down across from Chris, and Chris took whatever opening she could get. "I don't really cook," she said. "Sounds like you don't, either."

Alex laughed, and Chris began to congratulate herself. From cranky to laughing in thirty seconds flat. It had been quite a while since she'd bothered with any flirting more difficult than a casual pickup at a bar, and this was fun.

Even without considering what she hoped to gain. Damn, Alex looked better to her every time she saw her. Chris liked intense, repressed women because they were usually unbelievable in bed once they let go, and she was sure Alex would be worth the trouble.

Alex said, "I couldn't cook anything more complicated than a piece of toast before I met CJ. She's gotten me to the point that I can at least make a decent omelet now."

Chris grinned and said, "Good, maybe you can teach me," but she was kicking herself. She wanted to talk about anything except CJ St. Clair.

Their food came and Alex contemplated her chicken salad sandwich and cup of baked potato soup.

"Okay?" Chris asked, trying to sound anxious.

"It's great," Alex said, and dug in.

Chris smiled into her corned beef on rye.

"So," Alex said between bites of sandwich, "tell me what you've been doing."

Chris swallowed and said, "Well, my apartment has never been cleaner. Yesterday I washed my Mustang within an inch of its life, and I have no dirty clothes left. Pretty soon I'm gonna start having to look at college catalogs and figure out how long it would take me to get a bachelor's degree. I've just got the two-year degree from Douglas Community College."

"Good for you," Alex said, blowing on her soup to cool it. "I'm still a good eighteen months away from finishing a four-year degree myself."

Chris was surprised, and said so. "I started college when I was eighteen," Alex explained, tasting the soup. "But I had to quit after a year."

"Money?" Chris asked sympathetically.

Alex shook her head. "No, I had a scholarship. My father was killed when I was nineteen, and my mother had died years before, so I had to quit and take care of my younger sister. I joined the department, and just never got around to finishing up."

"Sounds like a tough time."

"It was. He was a patrol lieutenant, died in a hit-and-run while at an accident site. We never found the driver."

Chris shook her head. She'd never really had a family, but wondered if it would be worse to have had one and then lose them.

Aloud she asked, "So you went back to college?"

"Yes. It's been tough going, but I can see the finish line now, and I'm glad I did it."

"Why'd you finally decide to go back?" Chris thought she was doing a good job getting her captain to talk about herself. It was almost like a real date.

Alex caught an escaping chunk of chicken breast before answering, "That would be CJ's fault. After we started living together, I could afford the tuition. I'd always been sorry I hadn't had a chance to finish, and she encouraged me to go."

Jesus, are there any topics of conversation that don't lead back to how fucking wonderful St. Clair is?

"Do you like being the captain?" Chris asked, abruptly changing the subject. "I mean, it must be a lot different from having your own caseload."

"It is," Alex agreed, sitting back in her chair. "I do like it, actually. It's a lot of paperwork crap, but I'm actually good at paperwork, as it turns out. I like being able to help with cases without having to be back on the street. I mean, I miss it sometimes, but I was in a couple of shootings, and I certainly don't miss that."

"You were in a shooting?"

Alex blushed a little, but answered, "Yeah. The first time I was in uniform, traffic stop. Guy started shooting at me when I was on my way back to my unit. I returned fire. As with most situations like that, neither he nor I hit anything. We caught him about two miles down the road. He had seven outstanding warrants, if you can believe it. The second time..." She hesitated.

"Yeah?" Chris said encouragingly.

Alex took a breath. "The second time a man came to my house to kill me," she said. "CJ was there."

She'd already heard that story, Chris realized. St. Clair, again. She felt like waving her white napkin into the air to surrender. Next, Alex was going to tell her that the woman had hung the moon and the stars, no doubt. Talk about something else, anything else.

Chris started in on a story about one of her classmates at college, a guy who desperately wanted to be a cop but couldn't grasp any of the required physical skills—driving, shooting, self-defense. By the time she described his antics at the "shoot-don't shoot" simulator, she had Alex smiling again. Chris leaned forward carefully to make sure Alex could see well down her blouse.

Alex glanced down at the unfettered cleavage on display, then brought her gaze back up to Chris's face. Her expression wasn't readable, at least not by Chris, but she was pleased to note that Alex noticed, anyway.

"So he actually managed to blow away every single one of the innocent civilians," Chris laughed. "And when the instructor was chewing him out, he kept saying, 'But I hit them all dead center!'"

Alex laughed out loud.

***

At the pickup counter across the room, CJ turned around at the sound of familiar laughter. Alex's back was to her, but CJ knew her at once, even without the sound of her voice. Across from her was Chris Andersen, flashing a lot of skin, laughing with her at whatever the joke was.

CJ watched them a moment, an unpleasant flutter in her stomach. She couldn't see Alex's face, but her partner didn't laugh easily, and Alex must have been enjoying herself.

But it was Chris that caught her focus. Her pale skin was flushed, and she had her hand on Alex's arm. And several buttons undone. CJ knew flirting when she saw it.

They hadn't seen her, and she debated briefly whether to go over, but she didn't want to interrupt the hilarity by looking like a jealous spouse, like a woman who didn't trust her partner.

CJ picked up her sandwich and went back to her office. *I trust Alex. Even if Chris is flirting, it doesn't mean anything. I do it all the time. Well, not like that, exactly.*

***

When CJ got back to her office, McCarthy said through a bite of ham and cheese, "Visitor for you, Lieutenant. Put him in the filing cabinet you use as an office."

"Funny man," CJ said, and went in to find Rod Chavez in her visitor's chair.

She dumped her lunch on her desk to hug him. "I was just going to call and come see you, darlin'," she said.

He returned the embrace. "No point in you coming all the way out there when all the people and evidence are here," he said. "Good to see you, CJ. It's been, what? Couple months since you and Alex came out to the house."

She went around to her desk chair and said, "Yes, Alex reminded me that we owe you dinner. Have you eaten? I'm willing to share with you if you like roast beef and swiss."

"I'm good. Had a chile relleno before I came over."

"Sounds great. I keep thinking I have to learn how to make good Mexican food. It's a cuisine missing from my repertoire. Didn't have it a lot in Savannah. Maybe Ana would teach me a couple of things."

He chuckled. "My wife will not be sharing any recipes carefully memorized from her *abuela*, but you can give it a try."

"I'll look forward to the challenge..." CJ smiled, biting into her sandwich. "Goodness, I love real sourdough."

Chavez laughed again. "You are such a foodie," he kidded her. "Great cook, rich, and good-lookin', too. Jesus, did Alex hit the trifecta or what?"

She chewed happily, swallowed, and said, "Believe me, darlin'. I'm the one who got lucky."

He sat back in his chair to chat, letting her eat before getting down to business. "You remember that first time you told me about her, during your investigation of her? I knew you were goin' to get together then."

"Rod, I thought she was a murderer. You knew no such thing."

"I did. I never heard you talk about anybody like that before. You had it bad."

CJ snorted at him. "You're brilliant in hindsight, Lieutenant Chavez. Let's see how good you are before we know the ending."

He rubbed a finger across his mustache. "I talked to the Widow Nero this morning, at her attorney's office."

"That was fast."

"No grass growin' under my feet. She said some pretty serious shit about your detective, including a rather nasty accusation that she shot an unarmed man. She volunteered that she thought it was because Nero was Hispanic. Her slimy lookin' lawyer looked kinda happy about that."

CJ flinched. "I don't know Andersen very well," she admitted, "but as she's in a protected class herself, I don't sense that she's a bigot."

"Andersen doesn't exactly sound like a minority name. Is she black?"

"No, she's a blonde. And a member of the family."

He lifted thick black brows in surprise. "Really? You guys out recruiting lesbians?"

"No, darlin', no recruiting necessary." She leaned forward and dropped her chin, whispering, "We're everywhere."

He laughed, then reached across her desk and snatched her dill pickle.

"Hey, I was going to eat that," she protested.

He crunched down on it and said, "You snooze, you lose. So what do you think about Andersen? Assumin' you can separate out any influence she may have on your libido."

"No problem there," CJ said calmly. "Not even a flicker. I think she's a bit of a cowboy, maybe a little immature, but I don't think she's a bigot and I really don't think she's a murderer."

"Not even a flicker?" he asked, finishing the pickle.

"Are you attracted to every woman you see?" CJ asked, amused.

"Nah, I'd say no more than eighty-five, ninety percent, tops."

"I'll be sure to mention that to Ana. Well, I'm not attracted to every lesbian I meet, either. She is not my type."

"Lemme guess." Chavez grinned at her. "Your type. You like skinny blue-eyed brunettes who are compulsively neat, intense, and don't have a sense of humor."

"She most certainly does have a sense of humor." CJ rose loyally to Alex's defense.

"She must have a helluva sense of humor, if she's still living with you. I notice you didn't deny skinny, intense or compulsively neat, by the way."

She folded the sandwich wrappings into an untidy square and dropped them into her trash can. "Could we maybe get back to the case? You can harass me about my choice in a life partner later."

"Okey-doke," he said easily. "Let's go look at the physical evidence, okay? And let's pass by the vending machines on the way. I could use a Twinkie."

CJ snorted in a distinctly unladylike manner. "You are a Twinkie. Come on, Chavez."

***

The evidence clerk on duty was a good-looking black man, his hair in neat dreadlocks.

"Hello, Munro," CJ greeted him. "This is Lieutenant Chavez, Roosevelt Sheriff's Office. He's doing the criminal investigation on the Nero shooting. We'd like to see the evidence bin on that."

"Sure," he answered easily. "Let me look up the number."

He punched a few keys on his terminal, then wandered down a nearby row, where most physical evidence was kept in various sizes of plastic bins stacked on open metal shelving. He pulled out a small gray container and brought it to the counter.

"Just the one," he said. "Must not have been much."

Chavez pulled off the plastic lid and looked inside. "Can we just take this over to the table?" he asked. "It shouldn't take long."

"Sure," the clerk responded, and Chavez took the bin to the metal table on the other side of the room and carefully dumped out the contents.

"Have you seen this stuff?" he asked CJ.

"No," she answered. "Are you looking for anything in particular?"

"Nah, just tryin' to get a feel for it," he answered.

There were two spent casings in a plastic baggie, carefully labeled. Chris's gun was also tagged and Chavez automatically checked to make sure it wasn't loaded. There was a bloodstained shirt, and the dead man's personal effects.

"Where's the knife?" Chavez asked.

CJ poked around the objects on the table. "I don't see it," she answered, frowning. "Wilson, is this all?"

"Yeah, just the one bin," he repeated. "Why?"

"Check the list. There should have been a knife."

He returned to the terminal and punched the keys with two index fingers. "It's listed," he said. "Rivera checked it in. Are you sure it's not there?"

"Look for yourself."

The three of them went through the tub without success. "Oh, shit," Wilson grumbled. "The damn thing must be misfiled."

Chavez shot CJ a look. "I think we oughta look for it, don't you?"

"It'll turn up—" Wilson began to explain but CJ interrupted him.

"We need to look now," she said tersely.

"Lieutenant, there must be a couple hundred bins down here," he complained.

The Colfax evidence room was a single medium-sized room, not a huge warehouse, but the shelving looked pretty full.

CJ exchanged another look with Chavez and answered, "Then we'd better start right away."

***

Alex thought she'd misheard. "What?"

"You heard me. I went down to check the evidence out this afternoon with Rod, and the clerk couldn't find the knife. It was logged in on Monday by the crime scene tech, but it's not there. Anywhere. We tore the place apart for two and a half hours. It's gone."

Stunned into silence, Alex could only stare at CJ. She'd been glad to see CJ in her office, she was normally glad to see her any time, but this... Finally she managed, "What in the hell is going on?"

"I have absolutely no idea, but I'm going to find out," CJ said grimly.

"The clerks are civilian employees, not cops. IA doesn't usually..." Alex began.

CJ snapped, "The missing weapon is evidence in an ongoing IA investigation. And we can investigate any department employee. It sure as hell is my case."

CJ cursing aloud was rare enough that Alex said dismally, "Oh, my God. CJ, what is going on?"

"I have no idea, darlin'," CJ confessed again.

Alex shook her head miserably. "This is a complete disaster. No weapon and a witness who said Chris shot the guy in cold blood. We're about to get ourselves crucified, and Chris is gonna be the first one nailed to the cross."

CJ tried not to frown. Was Alex really more worried about Chris Andersen than the case?

***

There were three civilian employees who usually worked the Colfax property room, and CJ saw them all by the end of the day. She interviewed Wilson first, saw Rivera when she came in at four p.m., and had McCarthy call Calvin in early before his midnight shift. She also had McCarthy pull their employment records and she went over them in detail.

Jack Calvin was forty-seven, thin and graying, and he had worked the graveyard shift for eight years. Elizabeth Rivera was twenty-two, and had been working some day shifts and some evening shifts for two months. Munro Wilson was a thirty-year-old perpetual art student who had been with the Colfax PD for almost two years.

CJ gave each clerk a Garrity advisement and questioned each of them, separately, for over an hour. All three denied any knowledge or involvement in the disappearance of the knife.

Not only upset at being called in early, Calvin was angry at the accusation. Rivera was quickly reduced to tears, and

Wilson was calm but annoyed. CJ spent hours and her considerable interrogation skills on the three, and by six p.m. had no more information than she had started with at one o'clock.

She asked McCarthy to thoroughly search the evidence room again while she was questioning the clerks, and, as she and Rod had discovered before him, the knife was nowhere to be found. Before he left for the day, she instructed him to have the evidence bin fingerprinted, and the prints compared to the three clerks, Rod Chavez and her own prints to see if there were any others that didn't belong.

Staring out her window at the dark sky, CJ again considered the possibility of the knife simply being misfiled or mislabeled, but discarded it. If the weapon had been there, at least one of them would have found it. No, they didn't find it because it wasn't there to be found.

Yet Alex, and the crime scene tech, and presumably Chris, had all seen the weapon, so it must have existed.

CJ rechecked the evidence log. Elizabeth Rivera had signed in the knife, and the rest of the evidence from the crime scene, at 8:34 a.m. on the morning of the shooting. She thought about the three evidence clerks. It would have been very difficult, though not impossible, for someone other than one of the three of them to have taken the knife, but one of the three was very likely involved. Rivera had been the clerk most upset by CJ's questioning. CJ had stopped twice to let her compose herself. Rivera had also been employed the shortest time, which tended in CJ's view to make her a more likely suspect.

But Rivera claimed she had no knowledge about what had happened to the knife. Neither did anyone else. Seventy-two hours after it was checked in, it had vanished as if it had been vaporized. It could not be a coincidence, she thought grimly. It simply could not. Her earlier opposition to talking about the case with Alex disappeared for a moment. She wished Alex were here to discuss the case with her. CJ had never worked with anyone as good at developing the theory of a case as her partner.

"Hey," Alex said from her doorway.

CJ swiveled around. "Perfect timing again. I think about you and you appear."

"Good thing it doesn't work the other way," Alex said dryly.

CJ frowned. "Because as often as I think about you, you'd never get any work done," Alex added. "You'd just be popping in and out of my office all day."

"Nice save." CJ smiled a little.

"Any headway on our vanishing weapon?"

"Three property clerks whose stories may be summarized as 'It wasn't me, man.'"

Alex picked her way carefully around the piles of folders and perched on the edge of CJ's desk. "I'm guessing you haven't talked to Wylie today."

"I've been in the interview room nonstop all afternoon, darlin'. What's going on?"

Alex heaved a sigh. "Carlson issued a press release and gave the local stations a lovely thirty-second sound bite in time for the evening newscasts."

CJ was afraid to ask. "Saying what, exactly?"

"Saying, essentially, that Eddie Nero was a nice boy and the police murdered him, with an assist by the DA to cover it all up. Only this time, he insisted that we produce the quote alleged weapon unquote."

"You're kidding."

"Somebody tipped him. Could one of the clerks have called him?"

CJ pushed fingers into her hair. "I have no idea. It's a good question. All we have are questions, apparently."

Alex's face hardened into a familiar grim mask. CJ knew what was happening, and didn't like it. Alex was about to become obsessed with the Nero shooting, and that wouldn't make CJ's job any easier. Alex asked, "You think somebody paid one of them to make the knife disappear?"

"I was just sitting here wishing for you to come in and give me a better theory. Got one?"

Even with the stress, and the fatigue, CJ could see her relax a little. Alex replied, "Not yet. I'll work on it." She sighed again and said, "My brother-in-law called me just before I came downstairs."

"How is David's mom doing?"

"The good news is she didn't break a bone, by some miracle. The doctors don't think it was a stroke, but some inner ear problem caused by…I can't remember what David called it, but it means they have no idea."

"Idiopathic," CJ supplied.

Alex gave her a twisted smile. "I should have realized you'd have a two-dollar word like that committed to memory. Anyway, the schedule is that they're planning on releasing her on Saturday afternoon, so David is going to drive down tomorrow night, stay Saturday and get her settled at home, then come back Sunday."

"So does this mean that Charlie's at the condo for the weekend?" The thought cheered her.

But Alex shook her head. "No, he's got some playdate or something on Saturday morning, and a birthday party in the afternoon, so there's no point in driving him back and forth. I'll go down tomorrow night, stay Friday and Saturday, get him to Sunday school and then come home."

"All right," CJ said. "Then I'll come with you to the house."

Alex said, "We'll talk about it. Let's go home, okay?"

CJ gathered jacket, purse and keys, trying not to worry. What was there to discuss?

***

"Are you sleepy?" CJ asked as she lifted the sheet for Alex to climb into bed that night.

Alex answered, "Tired, but not sleepy. All this has got me really wound up. I hate not knowing what's going on."

CJ said gently, "Or maybe you don't like not being able to do anything about it."

"Are you calling me a control freak?" Alex said grumpily.

"Um…yes?" CJ said lightly.

Alex turned to face her. "So why did you want to know if I'm sleepy?"

"Bet you can guess," CJ said, in her best sultry tone, running one hand easily down Alex's arm.

"Yeah, you're so hard to read." Alex smiled a little. "Are you sure? It's not even Saturday night." She lifted her fingers to CJ's hip and let them rest there lightly.

"Ha. Bad news. Comedy Central called, and you're not getting your own show."

"I'll work on my disappointment. Are we allowed to make love on a school night?"

"No," CJ whispered. "But let's break the rules."

She slid closer and laid a kiss in the gentle valley between Alex's collarbone and the top of her shoulder. Alex made a soft noise.

CJ kissed her again and Alex made another noise, deep in her throat, and brought her hands up CJ's back.

She coaxed Alex over to her. When Alex was tied up in knots, CJ knew she needed to let Alex take the initiative, and she gave herself happily over to her mouth and hands.

Alex's mouth caressed her, soft as angel's wings. Being with Alex was like her favorite jacket, when new leather over time shaped itself perfectly to her body, as if it had always been made for her. And, as with the jacket, CJ knew every smooth spot, every crease, every curve.

Now the jacket was warm, soft, comfortable. Perfect. Alex had been created, molded, shaped, just for her.

Alex kissed CJ's throat, her fingers mapping the faint scar between CJ's breasts, caressing it with her fingertips. Then she moved her mouth down, kissing gently along the raised line of skin.

CJ murmured, "When they opened up my chest, and saw my heart, it had your name written on it."

Alex smiled against CJ's breast. "You are such a romantic. We'd hardly even been together then."

"Didn't matter, Irish," CJ answered, her voice low and husky. "I was already yours."

Alex navigated the familiar hills and valleys of her lover's body, the breathtaking curve of waist into hip, her beautiful breasts, the tender skin at the top of her thighs.

Then Alex claimed what CJ had given her, what was hers to have. She loved CJ until she came apart in Alex's hands.

CJ took a long time to recover from the intensity of her climax, feeling warm and completely connected to Alex again. When she could move, she whispered to Alex, "I do love you, darlin'."

Alex nuzzled her but said nothing, and let CJ ease onto her.

CJ made love to her gently, tenderly, but Alex still seemed tense, with desire or anxiety, she couldn't tell. When CJ finally brought her mouth down to Alex, she sensed Alex fighting her release. CJ could feel the spiral building, then felt Alex go away. CJ persisted, heard Alex gasping above her. Still Alex seemed to fight against the climax.

CJ stopped moving, lifted her head. Laying one cheek on dark curls, she said softly, "Darling. It's all right. Let go."

Alex said quietly, "CJ. Stop."

"Alex, relax."

"No," Alex said firmly. "Stop. Come here."

She rose to kiss Alex's shoulder. "What is it?"

Alex muttered, "I'm sorry, I just can't. Let's go to sleep, okay?"

CJ was stunned into silence for a moment. Alex had never stopped her lovemaking before.

"Talk to me," she demanded of Alex.

"There's nothing to say," Alex said with finality. "I'm just too wound up. Just hold onto me, sweetheart, okay?"

She shifted onto her side, let CJ curl around her from the back. Alex brought CJ's hand up to her waist and put her own hand over it. CJ felt her relax after a few minutes, and soon Alex was breathing deeply and slowly.

But CJ lay awake, anxious. What had she done wrong? What hadn't she done right? CJ had spent plenty of time lying warm in Alex's arms, feeling as if the hours were flying by like minutes, wishing the night would never end.

Now she held onto Alex, watched the clock, and worried, her earlier comfort vanished. Was Alex telling the truth, or was something else going on?

CHAPTER SIX: FRIDAY

By late morning, CJ and McCarthy were going over the bank records and credit reports from the three property clerks, courtesy of the releases CJ had asked them to sign the day before.

"What have you got?" CJ asked him after they'd both been at it for close to an hour.

McCarthy looked at her in appraisal. She knew she looked a little haggard this morning. Apparently he knew better than to say anything. "Calvin's in trouble.

Two ex-wives, three children, all coming complete with support payments. He filed bankruptcy a couple years back, but that didn't help him with the child support."

"Right," CJ said, tapping a pen thoughtfully on her desktop. "He can't get rid of child support in bankruptcy. Any sudden and unexplained increase in his bank accounts?"

"Nah, but if somebody paid him off, it would have been cash. God knows he needs the dough."

"Sounds like it," CJ agreed wearily.

"Wilson is another matter," McCarthy continued. "I can't figure out what he's working here for. Somebody's got money. He deposits a check every month for a tidy little sum."

"Same amount? I wonder what it's for," she mused.

"Blackmail payments?" McCarthy suggested. "He's pushing drugs on the side? Or maybe those paintings of his actually sell?"

"It can't be drug money or sale of his art, because the payments are too regular and all for the same amount," she mused, glancing at the account records. "Could be blackmail, I suppose, but that seems unlikely. Who pays their blackmailer with a check?"

"Okay, but if he's got this kind of money from his family, I ask again: why's he working here?"

She shrugged again. "You could ask me the same question. I don't have to work for money. I'm here because I like the challenge. I like feeling as if I'm making a contribution. Maybe he feels the same way. Best way to find out is to ask him."

"What about Rivera?"

She looked down at her own notes. "Just about the most ordinary report you could find. Only deposits her paycheck, no sudden burst of income. Payouts for rent, a car payment, I imagine, regular bills. Credit history shows almost nothing. Not too surprising, she's just twenty-one."

He sighed. "What now?"

"We interview them again. Who's on now?"

"Wilson's on until four, Rivera works four to midnight, Calvin midnight to eight."

"Okay." She checked her watch and said, "I have an interview with Marina Nero and her lawyer at eleven. Set up Wilson for one o'clock. I'll see Rivera when she comes in at four, and Calvin when he starts his shift."

"You're coming in at midnight? On a Friday?"

Might as well, she thought. Alex will be at Nicole's house tonight, and she made it clear that she didn't want me there. She tried again to push worry away and said, smiling a little, "I'd rather come in late than be here before eight in the morning. I'm not a morning person."

He laughed. "I'd noticed, Lieutenant, believe me. Sometimes I even feel sorry for Captain Ryan."

CJ lifted an eyebrow at him and said, "Don't you worry about Captain Ryan. She manages just fine."

"Oh, I'll just bet she does," he leered.

"Stop it, Sergeant," she ordered pleasantly. She wished, not for the first time, that he would get a girlfriend rather than continue to show so much interest in her sex life. "Any word on the prints yet?"

"Amazingly, they found prints from the following people: Wilson, Rivera, Calvin, Lieutenant Chavez and you," he answered her question. "Nobody else. I'm thinking you and Chavez aren't really suspects."

"Thanks for the vote of confidence," CJ said dryly. "Call Captain Robards and see if he'll lend us a uniformed officer to cover the evidence room while we're doing the second round of interviews."

"Should be interesting," McCarthy remarked.

"We can only hope so," CJ answered.

***

Marina Nero's bruising had begun to turn sickly colors of pale green and yellow. The rest of her looked better than the last time CJ had seen her, however. She was wearing black double knit slacks and a fisherman's knit sweater. Her lipstick was a bright pink too garish for her dark coloring. It made her lips look as if she'd been eating pink cotton candy.

Her attorney, Raymond Elliot, had handed CJ his business card when they arrived, and spent the first ten minutes reminding her that Ms. Nero had filed a notice of claim with the city for Eddie Nero's death.

"I'm aware of that," CJ said. "The purpose of my investigation is to establish whether there was excessive use of force or other wrongdoing by a Colfax police officer."

Marina said, "Wrongdoing? Is that your word for murder?"

Elliot lifted a hand to stop her. "Marina, please. Let me handle this. Inspector, as I'm sure you know, Ms. Nero witnessed the shooting of her husband by your off-duty police detective. As she told you, your officer was in plain clothes and didn't identify herself as law enforcement. She had no reason to pursue Mr. Nero, and certainly no reason to use her weapon."

CJ looked at him. His dress shirt was so blindingly white and starched that she was tempted to ask him the name of his dry cleaner. Still, there was something off about him. He was a little too well-groomed, his nails buffed to a shine, his tie sporting a gold pin. With a jolt, she realized he reminded her of Tony Bradford.

"I'm not here to argue with you Mr. Elliot," she said. "I certainly could point out that Mr. Nero's assault on his wife was more than enough reason for Detective Andersen to intervene, and that his refusal to put down his weapon when she confronted him would indicate that use of force would be appropriate in the situation."

"There was no knife," Marina said flatly, then glanced at Elliot.

CJ's mouth tightened. "That would be a different story than you told me Tuesday."

Elliot shifted in his seat as Marina retorted, "That's exactly what I told you."

"No. You said you didn't see a knife. That's different from saying there was no knife."

"Well, there wasn't," she said flatly, looking at Elliot again.

CJ read the situation, and she didn't like it. Elliot had prepped Marina carefully, making sure his lawsuit against the city was as strong as possible. The disappearance of the knife was too helpful to be coincidental. But how on earth could Marina, or her lawyer, have arranged the disappearance without the cooperation of an evidence clerk? One of the clerks had to be involved.

As she leaned back in her chair, CJ asked, "How is it, Ms. Nero, that you managed to find an attorney so quickly? Were you concerned about the possible criminal charges against you?"

Elliot said quickly, "I'm not here to represent Ms. Nero on any criminal matters. What are you talking about, Inspector?"

"The items in Mr. Nero's car were stolen in several vehicle burglaries that took place the night before his death," CJ told him. "We're still investigating whether your client had any involvement in those thefts."

"I had nothing to do with that," Marina said quickly.

"Yet you told me that you'd been out late with Eddie that night," CJ said. "Were you his lookout, perhaps?"

"Don't answer that," Elliot instructed his client. "If you think you can prove her involvement, Inspector, charge her.

Otherwise, this is just a smokescreen to cover up the police department's culpability in Mr. Nero's death."

"I don't believe we've established any culpability yet," CJ replied. "Ms. Nero, would you like to make any additions or corrections to the statement you gave me on Tuesday?"

She looked confused and Elliot gave her an encouraging nod. "Just that we didn't know she was a cop," she said, "and Eddie didn't have a knife. That's all."

Elliot looked satisfied and CJ felt only dismay. This interview had been a waste of time. Marina had either contacted Elliot because she thought she could get a financial windfall from the city, or he had seen the news reports and initiated the call to her first. Either way, the lawsuit was going to keep Eddie Nero's death in the news, and cause Chris Andersen and the Colfax Police Department a lot of grief.

She had to find out what had happened to that damned knife.

***

Munro Wilson leaned forward and put his arms on the gray table in the interview room, his dreadlocks swaying forward gently.

"I told you yesterday, and I'll tell you today: I didn't take the damn thing, and I don't have any idea what happened to it."

CJ searched his face. He was telling the truth, or else he was a very, very good liar. "Your prints were on the evidence bin," she said calmly.

"Well, hell, of course they were! I handed it to you, Inspector, remember?"

"Who deposits five thousand dollars a month into your checking account?" She switched topics abruptly.

"And what the hell business is that of yours?" he replied evenly. He still seemed, as he had yesterday, more irritated than angry.

"Let me help you out. Somebody stole the weapon from the evidence room, a location where you are responsible for the preservation of the property. You either screwed up, Wilson, or you're on the take."

"What crap is this? There are two other people responsible, too, and lots of others who go in and out of there all day and all night, for all I know."

"You're the one who gave me an evidence bin with missing property," CJ pointed out, as if it mattered which clerk was on duty.

"Well, that doesn't prove shit."

"Is somebody paying you regularly to pass interesting bits of evidence along?" she persisted.

He sat back, his dark eyes narrowing. "No," he answered flatly. "And if they were, you'd have missed something by now, and probably something a lot more interesting. There was the cocaine dealer they got a couple months back. That stuff alone would be a lot more valuable than some knife. We get cash in, sometimes. That'd be a lot easier to steal, now wouldn't it?"

CJ looked him over thoughtfully. "Who's paying you the five thousand, Munro?" she asked again, gently.

He sighed and said, "My father."

She made a note and said mildly, "You know I'll check that out."

"Yeah. We made a deal when I started painting. He'd support me so long as I had what he called a real job, and I could go to school and paint until I got it out of my system."

Wilson smiled and added, "Eight years later, and he's still waiting, but he's gonna be surprised. I'm showing at the Cherry Creek Arts Fair next spring, and then I can quit this shit job. But I'm not gonna screw it up this close to the finish line. I didn't take the knife, okay?"

CJ wondered why parents always thought children should be able to give up who they were in order to make their parents happy. What would her own mother have given if CJ could have gotten her sexual orientation "out of her system"?

She mentally shook herself and said, "All right, Munro. I'll verify what you've told me and let you know if I need to see you again. You can go back to work now."

He slid his chair back and said, "I hope you find the damn thing, Inspector, I really do."

"Yes," she agreed. "And Munro? Send me an announcement about the Art Fair, okay? I'd love to see your work."

He favored her with a brilliant smile.

***

She was surprised to see Jack Calvin appear at four o'clock. "I thought Rivera came on at four," she told him.

Calvin scowled, and CJ saw that his face settled organically into the expression, as if perpetual discontentment was his natural state.

"The girl called me this afternoon, asked me to cover her shift. Said she's sick or something. I'll be on until eight in the morning."

She said, "Give me a minute." Stepping out of the room, she called to McCarthy.

"Did you talk to Elizabeth Rivera to set up the appointment?" she asked him.

"Yeah. Isn't she here?"

"No, Calvin showed up instead. Did she sound all right? Not ill, or anything?"

"She didn't sound happy about it, but otherwise she sounded okay."

"Call her again, at home, and see how she's doing, will you? I'm going back in to talk to Calvin."

"Will do."

She returned to the interview room. CJ looked at Calvin and said sympathetically, "I'm sorry you have to cover for Rivera. A double shift is tough."

He shrugged, the scowl still firmly in place.

"Yeah, it sucks, but I could use the overtime."

"Has Rivera ever done that before?"

He rubbed a hand over the three remaining hairs on top of his head and said, "Nah, but she's only been here a couple of months. The guy before her, Arnold, he was a real motherfucking pain in the ass. I got called every other week to cover him because he just didn't show. Surprised it took them so long to fire his sorry ass."

CJ asked, "You do need the money, don't you, Jack?"

The frown deepened. "Hell, yes. I'm sure you know why by now. I've got three fucking jobs and I still have to live in a dump so my ex-wives and ex-kids can live in comfort. Husbands really get fucked over in court, y'know?"

CJ lacked sympathy for any man who referred to his children as "ex-kids," but asked only, "Did you take the knife, Jack?"

He all but spat at her. "I don't know where the hell it is, but I didn't take it. I'm not that much of an idiot. I need this motherfucking job." He looked at her sharply. "Is that what this is, just some excuse to fire me? White guys like me who actually work are a vanishing breed, y'know, everything these days is blacks and Mexicans and queers."

Now she was mad. Carefully, she said, "So, now I'm curious. Was the remark about blacks a reference to Munro Wilson? Maybe Mexicans includes Elizabeth Rivera? Or were you perhaps referring to me?"

"What the fuck? Inspector…" He stopped suddenly, realizing what she meant.

"Get out, Calvin," she said, her fury carefully controlled. "I've got your denial of any involvement in the theft on record. If I find out you did take the weapon, I'll do everything I can to see that you are prosecuted for it. As it is, I think a transcript of this interview might be useful to Chief Wylie."

His face went brick red, and he barked, "Why, you little—"

"Don't finish that sentence," she said sharply. "Or your suspension and mandatory diversity training will turn into a termination before you can say 'motherfucking bigot.' Go back to work."

He slammed out of the interview without another word, the banging door loud in the small room. CJ sat for a minute, feeling exhausted. She tried to breathe her anger away. She still had no idea whether Calvin was involved in the theft, but she found Rivera's absence suspicious.

Maybe I'm going about this the wrong way. Instead of focusing on who took the knife, perhaps she should be thinking about the motive instead. Ideas that had been tumbling around in her brain since yesterday began to line up nicely.

***

CJ was surprised to see Alex's SUV in the parking lot at the condo when she got home. She ran up the stairs, eager to see her. "Hey," she called out when she unlocked the door. "Where are you?"

"Bedroom," came the answer.

CJ kicked off her shoes and had a brief flurry of hope that Alex had changed her mind. Instead she found her in jeans and sweatshirt, packing her overnight bag.

Hiding her disappointment, she asked, "Where's Charlie?"

"Dinner at the home of a classmate," Alex answered. "I'm picking him up in an hour, assuming I can get through the Tech Center traffic."

"Rush hour is usually early on Fridays," CJ remarked. She ran her hand down Alex's arm. "Are you sure you don't want me to come with you?"

Alex said, "Your week was brutal, and next week will probably be as bad. You don't need to do babysitting. He's my nephew."

That stung a little. CJ said, "He is my nephew, too, Alex."

She heard the hurt in her own voice and Alex said quickly, "Sorry, you know I didn't mean it like that. It's just with all this crap with the shooting, and being shorthanded, I'm just lousy company. Call Vivian and go to lunch tomorrow, or something. Relax. I'll be back Sunday afternoon. We could do a late brunch, if you wanted."

"Could we?" CJ felt sad that Alex was leaving, and she made an effort to cheer up. Alex and food—her two favorite activities.

Alex leaned over and kissed her. CJ could feel how distracted Alex was from the brush of her lips.

"Yes, we could," Alex answered. "You decide where and make the reservation somewhere nice, okay?"

"Okay." She watched Alex get her toothbrush and sighed. "I'm going to miss you, darlin'. I really like sleeping in the same bed with you."

Alex smiled. "The feeling is very mutual. Just think how nice Sunday night will be. How was your day?"

CJ sat down wearily on the bed. "I think dreadful is a good word," she answered. "I've been giving you that answer a lot lately, haven't I?"

"Too much. No progress on the missing knife, I take it?"

"Honest to God, Alex. For all I can tell, I'd swear the stupid knife was imaginary. I just can't believe Chris Andersen would shoot an unarmed man."

As soon as she said it, she saw Alex freeze. "CJ," she said, her voice dangerously calm, "Chris did no such thing. The tech saw the knife. So did I."

"I know you did," CJ said quickly. "But between Marina Nero's story and the fact that we can't produce the weapon, this looks really bad for Chris. Add to that the fact that she'd arrested him before, but said she didn't know him, and—"

Alex stopped packing and said harshly, "I know how it looks. Bad enough if things were normal, but with the DA's race…we're completely screwed. And Chris cannot only kiss her career goodbye, she'll be really lucky if she doesn't end up going to prison. It's some kind of damned conspiracy. Christ!"

CJ had rarely heard Alex so impassioned in anyone's defense. She had wanted to discuss her theory about the motive with Alex, but instead she looked at Alex's fierce expression and said carefully, "I still don't know what happened to the knife, but maybe the witness was right. Maybe Chris didn't identify herself. You know how adrenaline affects people's judgment."

Alex glared at her. "What the hell are you saying?"

"Just that I don't believe that this is a conspiracy, just some bad luck. And maybe some poor judgment on Chris's part."

"God damn it," Alex snarled. "She's a good cop, and she's all alone on the end of a short stick."

She couldn't understand Alex's reaction. The scene from Jersey's replayed itself in her memory for a moment. Had Alex's friendship with Chris caused her to lose her objectivity?

"Alex, you said yourself you worried about her, you thought she might be too reckless."

But Alex slammed her suitcase shut and said, "I saw the damn knife, CJ. She didn't screw this up, all right? Just do your job and she'll be all right."

She could see in the grim set of Alex's mouth that Alex knew she'd gone too far, but CJ was angry and didn't back down.

"I'll do my job," she snapped. "I always do. Maybe you should consider the possibility that your detective may not be quite as perfect as you seem to think." She didn't know how to rewind the conversation so that they weren't both wrong.

Alex said abruptly, "I'm going to pick Charlie up. I'll call you when we get to the house."

"Fine." CJ bit off the word angrily.

She couldn't see her way back to a calm discussion, and she was miserable. She hated fighting, especially with Alex, and Alex was leaving. They wouldn't have a chance to make up tonight, and that made it much worse.

Alex, on the other hand, looked as if she was glad to have an excuse to get away from the fight, though CJ suspected she would be upset about it in a couple of hours.

"I'll call you," Alex repeated.

Alex didn't kiss her goodbye, and CJ didn't offer.

***

"Why does Eeyore's tail keep coming off?" Charlie asked.

Alex closed *Winnie the Pooh*, got up from Charlie's bed and answered seriously, "I think the tack he uses to keep it on must be loose."

"What's a tack?"

"It's like a little nail."

"Oh." Charlie considered thoughtfully. "Doesn't it hurt?"

Alex put the book down on the bedside table, and rearranged the covers securely around her nephew. "No, it doesn't hurt. He's made of sawdust on the inside, so it doesn't hurt him one bit."

"What is sawdust?"

Alex thought it might be time for *The Velveteen Rabbit* by next Christmas. She answered, "It's a kind of stuffing made up of really little pieces of wood. And you don't hurt wood when you put a nail in it."

"Okay. What does gloomy mean?"

She smiled down at him. "You wouldn't be trying to keep from going to sleep, would you?" she teased.

"No," he said solemnly. "I really want to know."

"Gloomy means he's really sad."

"Okay." He looked thoughtful again, and Alex had a sudden jolt of bittersweet sadness. She thought of her parents, and how delighted they would have been with this grandson.

"So why is he really sad all the time?"

That was a more interesting question, Alex thought. She sat down on the edge of his bed and said, "I'm not really sure I know. But I think maybe it's because he doesn't have a special friend. Kanga has Roo, Pooh has Piglet and Christopher Robin. Everybody should have at least one someone who thinks they are the best, most wonderful person in the world, and I think Eeyore doesn't have anybody like that."

His lower lip quivered a little and she smoothed his dark hair back and kissed his forehead.

"It's okay, Charlie," she said softly. "I think Eeyore will find someone."

"I have Mommy and Daddy," he said. "And you and Aunt CJ."

"Yes," she reassured him. "And we all think you're wonderful. You have so many people who think you're wonderful."

"What about Mommy and Daddy?" he asked, still worried.

"They have each other. And they have you."

"Okay." His deep brown eyes gazed up at her. "What about you?" he asked, genuinely worried.

Alex tried not to tear up. "Your mommy is my sister, and we've been each other's special friends our whole lives. And now I have you, too, don't I?"

"Yes," he said. "What about Aunt CJ?"

Now she had to actually blink the tears back in earnest before he saw them. "Your aunt CJ has you, too. And she has someone else who thinks she is the best, most special person in the whole world."

His eyelids were drooping, but he persisted with, "Is it you?"

She leaned down to kiss him again. "Yes, Charlie," she answered tenderly "Your aunt CJ has me. And I have her. Now go to sleep."

Alex turned out his light and she left his door ajar so she could hear him if he woke in the night. She retreated to the guest room and undressed. Grabbing a long T-shirt, she padded into the bathroom to brush her teeth and scrub her face.

When she came out, she looked on the nightstand at the book she'd brought with her but didn't reach for it. She just felt wiped out. She hated fighting. CJ had looked so miserable when she left that Alex still felt a little guilty.

She decided to give it up and go to bed herself. Once she was under the covers, she picked up her cell phone to call her sister.

"Hi," Nicole answered, her tone weary.

"Hi, yourself. You sound beat. What is it, only an hour earlier there?"

"Yes, but a week of eighteen-hour days is catching up with me."

"I've never known a judge to go past five o'clock in my life."

"It's not just being in the courtroom, though that's exhausting enough. It's all the craziness in between. Breakfast is prep for the morning testimony, lunch is prep for the afternoon, dinner is a complete debrief of the day and panic about what the jury is thinking. And I've got at least another week of this. Believe me, being mother of a first grader is a cakewalk by comparison."

"How is the trial going?"

"Honestly, Alex, I really can't tell, and if you don't mind, I'd like to talk about anything else. How's my boy?"

"He's fine. We read *Winnie the Pooh* tonight, and I received many questions on all things Eeyore. Kid has already got your flair for cross-examination," Alex kidded her gently.

"Does he? Frankly, I'd rather he had more of his father's qualities. What did he ask you?"

"We discussed the attachment of Eeyore's tail and the exact makeup of sawdust." She paused and added, "He also wanted to know why Eeyore was so sad."

"Oh. When Dad read the books to us, I don't really remember ever wondering why Eeyore was such a grump, did you?"

"No, I just thought that was the way he was. Thoughtful little boy."

Nicole asked softly, "Alex, what's wrong?"

"Everything's fine. Did you talk to David?"

"Yes, he got to Trinidad just fine. I'm not asking about David or Charlie. What's wrong with you?"

"I'm fine, Nic," Alex repeated. "It's just been hell at work this week. One of my detectives shot a guy off-duty and the political fallout has been messy."

"That son-of-a-bitch Tony," she said acidly. "Is he giving you shit again?"

"He always gives me shit. I'm used to it. It's my penance for having been so stupid as to marry him." She hesitated before adding, "Apparently he called the condo after I left yesterday morning and he got into it with CJ."

"With CJ?" Nicole sounded alarmed. "What the hell did he say?"

"I'm not sure I really know. His version is not believable, and she didn't mention it."

"What do you mean? You haven't talked about it with her?"

This was the discussion Alex wanted to have, because she knew she could trust Nicole and she wanted to talk about the situation with CJ. She also wanted to avoid talking about it, because she wasn't quite sure she was in the right. She didn't know what else to say, so she said simply, "We're not in a good place at the moment."

She could sense Nicole's alarm ratchet up another notch. She knew that Nicole cared about CJ, but she also knew that Nicole believed in the transformation that CJ's love had made in Alex's life.

"What the hell does that mean?" Nicole demanded.

"It's not a big deal. Everybody fights, Nicole. We'll work it out."

"Work what out? Is this about Tony?"

"No. We're having a…a philosophical difference about how this shooting case should be handled, that's all."

"Whose case is it?"

"Damn it, don't you start cross-examining me!"

Her defensiveness answered the question. Nicole said, "Alex, if it's her case, you have to let her handle it, don't you?"

Whose side are you on? Alex wanted to ask, even knowing how immature that would sound. Instead she said, "It's not that simple."

"Isn't it? She doesn't interfere in your job, does she?"

"Nic, it was one of my detectives who shot the guy. She's going to get eaten alive by the press, probably sued for a million dollars, not to mention what's going to happen in the criminal investigation. She doesn't have anyone else on her side."

Nicole was silent, and Alex heard herself for the first time. How could you let Chris Andersen get between you and CJ?

It's not like that, she told herself, trying to push the image of Chris leaning over the table at Jersey's away. She knew Chris was coming on to her, but it didn't matter because she wasn't interested. It was just the way Chris was reacting to the stress of her situation, Alex told herself.

Into the silence Alex said, "It'll work out. I'll go home Sunday, and we'll talk, and it'll be okay. Just get some rest and don't worry about anything here."

"If you say so," Nicole said wearily. "But call me tomorrow, okay? I want to talk to Charlie, and I want to make sure you're all right."

"Of course."

"And Alex?"

"What?"

"Don't be an idiot about this. Call CJ. Don't let things fester."

"Thanks for the advice," Alex said.

CHAPTER SEVEN: SATURDAY/ SUNDAY

"That was pretty good," CJ said to Vivian Wong as they left the restaurant and joined the Saturday afternoon shoppers.

"Yes," Vivian agreed. "I'm always pleasantly surprised when I can get a decent meal in Denver from a place in a mall."

Glancing around at the upscale shops around them, CJ commented, "Now you have to admit this is a very nice mall."

"True. Notice how many spaces are vacant, though? Retail is struggling, and high-end stores are being hit harder than usual."

CJ linked her arm through Vivian's and said, "It's just so handy to have a best friend who's in the mortgage industry. I learn so much about real estate."

Even for a casual Saturday shopping expedition, Vivian was immaculately dressed in designer jeans, a bright red blouse and a matching set of beautiful jade earrings and bracelet. The jade enhanced her smooth skin and black hair. She remarked skeptically, "I thought your best friend was some Irish cop."

CJ laughed. She was trying hard to cheer herself up after last night, and Vivian always helped. "You are the best friend I've got that I'm not sleeping with," she corrected.

"God knows you had your chances," Vivian remarked, her voice dry.

CJ glanced at her, wide-eyed. "Well, that would have screwed up the friendship, wouldn't it?"

"You seemed to have managed it with Alex," Vivian observed.

"Not always," CJ said, without thinking.

Vivian's flawless eyebrows lifted to vanish under her bangs. "You're not having trouble with Miss Perfect, are you?"

"She's not perfect, Viv," CJ said. "Neither am I. We have problems like everyone else does." She glanced at Vivian again and added, "Except you. You never hang in there long enough. One disagreement and you're out the door."

"One disagreement and she's out the door, you mean," Vivian corrected.

"Viv, have you actually ever considered the advantages of monogamy?"

"And what would those be?"

"Well, the more you're with someone, the better you are together. I know Alex, what she wants and needs, and she knows me, everything. We have memories, and dreams."

"That's a good thing?" Vivian demanded. "Sounds boring."

"It's not boring," CJ said indignantly.

"I'm not interested in comfort sex," Vivian said bluntly. "Give me good old-fashioned pleasure every time."

CJ looked at her friend and said, "Pleasure's fine, Viv. But it's transitory. Pleasure doesn't last. Joy lasts. And the only way you get joy is with love."

"I know a lot of people in love who aren't getting any joy out of it," Vivian said cynically.

"Not all love gives you joy," CJ acknowledged. "But without love, you can't get joy, believe me. You just have to risk it."

"You be my guest," Vivian said. "I'll stick with sex for fun." Then she changed the subject. "That was actually good sushi. I really miss the food in San Francisco sometimes. You could get anything, seafood, dozens of ethnic cuisines. You can keep New York, I'll take the City by the Bay."

"All right," CJ teased her, "but where is the shopping better?"

"Speaking of shopping…shoe sale at three o'clock," Vivian exclaimed.

"Right behind you."

Vivian got open-toed sandals at the end-of-season price, CJ found some sling-backs in her hard-to-find ten and a half size. As they exited, CJ resumed the earlier conversation.

"I wonder why you left San Francisco," she said. "It's got to be a great city to be out and proud."

"It is," Vivian acknowledged. "It just happens to be the city my parents are living in."

CJ frowned a little. "I thought your parents were all right. You said they took you coming out to them calmly."

"They were calm, but not happy," Vivian admitted. "They weren't setting me up with men or anything like that, but they were always watching me, hoping for a miracle conversion to guys."

"I'm sorry," CJ said, meaning it. She had never been sexually interested in men, but Vivian would have scored a six plus on the Kinsey scale for women. The thought of Vivian sleeping with a man was too ludicrous to contemplate.

"It's just easier to be gay a couple of states away from them," Vivian explained. "I go home a couple of times a year and manage celibacy for a week or so."

CJ chuckled. "What a strain that must be."

Vivian heaved a theatrical sigh. "You have no idea. Or," she added, pursing her lips, "maybe you do."

CJ replied, "Single people always think married people are getting more sex than they are. Married people always assume singles are getting more action. It's funny to me."

"That's not really an answer."

"You didn't really ask me a question," CJ countered.

"Gee, you really want to discuss Lesbian Bed Death in the middle of Cherry Creek Mall?"

CJ rolled her eyes. "Please stop. There is no such thing. Didn't you say you needed a new piece of luggage?"

"Yes. Damn United Airlines."

They went in to the Coach store and ordered a replacement bag for Vivian's set. As they left, Vivian said, "I want to go upstairs. Elevator?"

"I'll bet you can manage one flight of stairs. Come on."

On the second level, Vivian walked purposefully down the mall until she reached Victoria's Secret.

CJ said, "Does your lingerie supply need replenishing?"

"It's not for me, kiddo. Come on, let's find something the little woman will like."

CJ followed her in reluctantly. "Viv, this is not necessary."

"Oh, come on. You refuse to discuss the down-and-dirty details, at least let me assist with the wardrobe."

CJ fingered an ivory silk camisole and finally admitted, "Alex is not really a lingerie kind of girl."

"Ah," Vivian said, seizing on any morsel of information she could get. "Tell me more. You guys using those handcuffs you carry around?"

"Stop it."

"Help me out here. Leather? Wife-beaters and boxer shorts? Latex?"

She had CJ flushing a bright pink. "Viv, knock it off."

A salesclerk approached them. "May I help you ladies find something?"

Vivian gave her a quick, assessing glance. CJ could read Vivian's mind: Nice looking blonde, but straight. Pity.

"No, thanks," Vivian answered. "We're just getting to the kinky part of the conversation."

"Viv, for heaven's sake…" CJ blurted.

Vivian watched the embarrassed clerk walk away, then turned back to CJ and said, "Give me something here. Maybe it's not the clothes. Three-ways? Because I could make myself available…"

Suddenly, all CJ could think about was Chris Andersen. Stung as if Vivian had slapped her in the face, she turned on her heel and left abruptly. Vivian ran after her.

She caught up with her and said, her voice stunned, "CJ, I'm sorry. You know me, I was just kidding."

CJ wouldn't look at her, and kept walking. Vivian had to trot to keep up with her. She exclaimed, "Christ on a life raft, CJ, you have to talk to me. I'm your very best friend, remember? Why are you so mad?"

CJ finally slowed down, then stopped. "I think," she said quietly, "you should buy me a cup of coffee."

"Yes, of course, okay."

Vivian got CJ settled at a table with a latte and sipped at her cappuccino. "Okay," she said. "Spill it."

CJ glanced away and finally said, "You remember Steph."

"Well, of course. I introduced you, which I was happy about when you started dating, ecstatic about when she moved in, and pissed off about when she moved out. What does this have to do with her?"

"She moved out because I refused to invite another woman to bed with us."

"Oh. Fuck. I'm sorry, I didn't know."

"I know."

They were quiet for while, until Vivian said, "Is something really wrong between you and Alex? Because that would piss me off, too."

"Why?"

"Because you and Alex have the best relationship I've ever seen, and some tiny part of me uses it to keep open the possibility that a lifetime commitment to someone is actually possible."

CJ felt vague shock. "You? Settle down?"

"I imagine I'll be getting around to it eventually. When I'm about sixty or so, maybe."

They drank coffee for a while, then CJ blurted, "Buttons."

"What the hell are you talking about?"

"That's what you wanted to know, wasn't it? You want to know what we're into, now you know. Buttons, okay?"

"Buttons," Vivian repeated stupidly. "Um, I have no idea what you are saying."

"Blouses that button. Levi's, sweaters, whatever. Buttons can be unbuttoned. Zippers are okay, too. Anything that comes off slowly. That's it. I'm not judging you or other people, different strokes, and all that. I just don't need anything else, and neither does Alex, apparently. I just need her, Viv." She was close to tears.

"Okay, what the hell is going on?" Vivian demanded. "Did you guys have a fight?"

"Yes, sort of," CJ admitted. "It wasn't that big a deal, I just hate fighting with her. She takes everything so seriously, she's so darn…intense."

Vivian took another sip of her cappuccino and said, carefully, "But that's what you love about her, too, right?"

CJ looked at her thoughtfully. "Yes," she admitted. "It's true. Really, everybody's best quality is their worst quality, too."

"What?" Vivian was confused again.

"Whatever you have a lot of, that's what attracts someone to you. And because you have so much of it, it can get wearing, too. I love Alex's intensity, it just gets to be too much sometimes."

Treading cautiously, Vivian said, "So tell me something good about Alex's intensity, what you like about it."

CJ's gaze softened and she glanced away, over the Saturday crowds jamming the mall. She looked over at the children playing in the kids' play area which was dotted with a giant plastic Bugs Bunny and Daffy Duck for them to slide on and climb.

"When we're together," she began, "I can feel her focused on me, just on me. She makes me feel beautiful, and sexy, and smart, and like she can't live without me. I've seen her look at me as if…if she doesn't kiss me right that second, she'll just implode. When we make love…"

She stopped, still looking away, and Vivian didn't move or say a word, afraid to break the spell. Finally, after a minute Vivian prompted her with, "Go on. When you have sex…"

CJ said, "We make love."

Vivian couldn't help it. "Isn't that the same thing?"

CJ looked at her directly, her expression filled with longing. "Oh, no," she answered softly. "It looks the same, but it feels different."

Vivian had to swallow hard. CJ could tell that she'd never actually heard anyone say anything like that before.

"When we make love," CJ continued, looking away again, "I'm the only person in the universe for her. I can feel it, in the way she kisses me. And when I touch her, she's always with me, right there, with me…"

She stopped, sad again. Except for Thursday night, when Alex had stopped her.

Vivian impulsively reached across the tiny table to grip her wrist. "Then think about that," she said firmly. "Whatever else is going on with you guys, just remember what you really love about her, and it'll all work out."

CJ blinked at her. Vivian was right. Reflecting about Alex like this, remembering what she loved about her, was helping, giving her back the warm feeling thinking about Alex always gave her.

"When did you get so wise about relationships, Ms. Love-'em-and-leave-'em?"

Vivian released her arm and sat back with her cappuccino. "I've been watching the two of you, of course," she answered lightly.

***

Alex had Charlie settled in bed, at last. He'd been pretty wound up after the birthday party, and it had taken her a while to get him to sleep. She was exhausted, and wondered how Nicole and David did it, working full-time and managing an active four-year-old.

Going to the kitchen, she began to scavenge for something to eat. Charlie had had plenty at the birthday party: hot dog, ice cream and cake, but for some reason, she hadn't been hungry.

She stood in the middle of Nicole's spotless kitchen, hands on the cool brown granite countertop, and contemplated: Scrambled eggs? Cereal? Frozen dinner? Her cell rang and she dug it out of her pocket. She was expecting CJ, but the caller ID surprised her. "Hi, Chris," she answered.

"Alex," Chris said. "Am I, um, interrupting you?"

"No, not at all. What's up?"

There was loud music in the background, as if she were outside a club or bar. Chris half-shouted, "Look, have you got time to meet me? I'll go wherever you want."

Alex heard distress in her voice and asked sharply, "What happened?"

She said, "I just got a call from some asshole reporter, wanting to ask me a bunch of shit about the case. Some prick from Carlson's office put him onto me, I think, but I have no idea how he got my number."

"What did he ask you?"

Chris laughed bitterly. "He wanted my side of the story, but he kept asking crap like whether I called the guy a name before I shot him, and whether there was really a knife at all."

Alex took an involuntary sharp intake of breath.

"What?" Chris demanded.

"Chris, I'm not at home," she explained. "I'm at my sister's house, babysitting my nephew, and I can't leave. But if you'd like to come down here, talk for a while..."

Chris said, "I'd like to do that, if it's okay."

The pain in her voice was like acid on the wound of Alex's conscience. Alex gave her directions, and added, "Don't ring the doorbell. I just got Charlie to sleep. Just knock quietly and I'll hear you, okay?"

"Yeah, okay. And Alex? Thanks for this."

***

Chris stared at her with ice-blue eyes from the black leather couch in Nicole's family room, incredulous.

"What? You're not serious!"

Alex said, "That's what I said when CJ told me. But it's true. The knife was taken out of the property room."

"I do not fucking believe this!"

"Quiet," Alex said, with a glance toward the bedroom. "I don't want to have to get Charlie asleep again."

"Sorry, I just...sorry."

Chris dropped her face into her hands. Her stomach was churning with anger, fear, frustration. She tried, as she always did, to shut her feelings down, but they wouldn't go away this time.

Her distress over the reporter's call had been real enough, but the decision to phone Alex was calculated. She needed to see if they'd come far enough in the friendship that Alex would meet her at night, on short notice like this. It would get St. Clair used to the idea, and the next call would be for an entirely different reason. But this...

"When did you find out?" Chris demanded.

"Thursday. CJ took Lieutenant Chavez down to look at the evidence and it was gone."

"They misfiled it, maybe?" She had a memory of talking to the clerk on Monday morning—Rivera? Elizabeth Rivera. Deep brown eyes, long, shiny black hair. She mentally shook herself.

"CJ tore the property room apart. It's gone."

She couldn't sit still anymore. She jumped off the couch and started pacing in front of the fireplace, running her hand across the mantel.

"What the fuck is going on?" she demanded. "What is your girlfriend doing to me?"

Alex flinched. "Chris, stop it," she said firmly. "Whatever is going on is not CJ's fault."

"Well, it sure as hell isn't mine!"

"No, it's not, but just because you're looking for someone to blame, don't decide this is CJ's doing."

Chris stopped pacing, turned to look at her. "How the hell can you be so sure?"

"I know her," Alex said.

"Yeah? So what is going on, Captain?"

It came out more harshly than she intended, and Chris tried again to calm down. Come on, don't forget this is the woman you want. Don't piss her off.

Alex said, "I think way too much is happening for this to be a coincidence. I think you're being framed."

Chris gaped at her, pushing her fingers through her hair. "Framed?"

Alex shook her head grimly. "I think someone is taking advantage of a random opportunity. There's just too much going on that doesn't make sense: the witness's story, the press conferences, the missing knife. You, and the department, are being set up somehow. And believe me, I know exactly what that feels like."

"Who? Why?"

"I don't know yet. It's probably some kind of shakedown for money."

"A lawsuit," Chris guessed.

"I imagine so. Look, we're going to get to the bottom of this, Chris. It's just going to take some time."

She came over and flopped down on the couch again.

"Time," she repeated. "Meanwhile, I'm getting calls from reporters, my name is spread all over the paper and the news like I'm some kind of mad-dog killer, and Lieutenant Chavez looks at me like a fucking suspect. I have a second interview with him on Monday. Jesus." She looked hopefully at Alex. "I need a drink."

Alex shook her head. "You drove over here. I don't think you need a DUI added to your troubles."

Chris dug into her pocket and extracted her car keys. She handed them to Alex. "I'll stay here. Guest room?"

"I'm in the guest room. You can have the couch."

Chris bounced up and down on the cushions and said, "Sounds good to me."

Alex got up and went to the bar cabinet in the corner. Chris figured that Alex was wondering if it was a good idea for her to stay. But she was genuinely angry, upset, and it wasn't smart for her to be out driving around, maybe drinking too much. At least here Alex would keep an eye on her.

"What do you want?" Alex asked.

"Whatever you're having."

"I'm not drinking. I'm still on nephew duty."

"Fine. Scotch, rocks."

Alex poured out the amber liquid, then crossed back to the kitchen for ice. Chris watched her, wondering what to do. She really, really wanted to make a move on Alex. I mean, Jesus, the woman looked hot in a T-shirt and sweats.

But the timing was wrong, and she knew it. She needed for Alex to be focused on what Chris was going to do with her, not her nephew in the next room. Besides, her own stomach was still twisted in anxiety, not the best preparation for a sexual encounter.

She took the drink from Alex and nodded her thanks. From the other room, a child's voice called out, "Aunt Alex? My tummy hurts."

Alex flashed Chris a tight smile and said, "Probably nothing. I'll be back in a minute."

Chris watched her leave, then downed half the drink in one gulp. Wait, she told herself. It'll be worth it.

***

It took CJ only a little over half an hour to drive to Lone Pine. The traffic was light, but it was never absent, not even at almost one in the morning. It was Saturday night, or early Sunday really, and she'd been a patrol officer long enough to know to watch carefully for drunk drivers.

She hadn't been able to sleep. All she could think about was the disagreement with Alex on Friday night. Their two telephone conversations during the day had been brief and focused on what Charlie was doing: the playdate went well, but Alex was afraid Charlie had eaten too much junk at the birthday party.

After lying wakeful in their bed, CJ decided she wasn't going to wait twelve more hours to see Alex again.

She was still sharply alert when she got off the Valley Highway, feeling happy, and turned toward Nicole and David's house. The suburban streets were dark, but there was half a moon shining, and she felt optimistic. She would wake Alex up, and they would sleep in the same bed tonight, and Alex would hold her. Tomorrow morning they would talk, and it would be all right between them again.

CJ saw Alex's SUV when she rounded the corner, parked in the driveway, a silent presence. What she did not expect was a Mustang parked at the curb in front of the house. In the pale moonlight, the red color looked like dark blood.

She stopped her car across the street and stared at the house. The lights were out, as she would have expected. Whoever was inside was undoubtedly asleep.

Frowning deeply, she got out of her Lexus and walked over to the Mustang. The early morning was almost silent—there was just the faint rumble of traffic from the highway a mile away. As CJ approached the car, a dog barked a couple of times from a yard across the street.

She touched the hood and found it stone-cold. She was sure she'd seen the car before, and a moment's thought reminded her that it had been at the park early Monday. She'd seen Chris Andersen drive away in it from the shooting scene.

Chris Andersen was here. With Alex.

CJ stood completely still, the warm thoughts about Alex from her conversation with Vivian earlier today vanishing completely.

Maybe Chris had come over, perhaps they'd had dinner at the house. Chris was too drunk to drive, so she was staying the night.

But why hadn't Alex told her? And for that matter, why the hell hadn't Chris just taken a cab home?

Stop it, CJ told herself firmly. Her imagination was conjuring all kinds of possibilities, most of them frightening, but she refused to give in to the worst-case scenario.

She would not give in. She turned around and got in her car again. She trusted Alex, completely and implicitly. There was simply nothing happening, she knew that. She trusted Alex.

The problem was, she didn't trust Chris Andersen.

***

Alex took a call from CJ at almost eight o'clock the next morning. The Sunday morning paper had a feature story on police brutality in the Denver metro area, with the Colfax PD and Chris Andersen prominently discussed. Alex hoped CJ hadn't read it.

"Hey," Alex answered. "What are you doing awake at this hour?"

She herself had been up since six after only a couple of hours sleep, pouring enough coffee into Chris to insure that she was awake for her drive home. Chris had said very little, mumbled her thanks, and roared away in the early Sunday morning quiet.

CJ said simply, "I missed you. How did you sleep?"

"Lousy. Charlie was up most of the night. He threw up a couple of times, poor little guy."

"Is he okay?" CJ was genuinely concerned.

"Yeah, it's either what he ate yesterday or maybe a little stomach virus. He's not running a fever, so I don't think it's serious. He's not going to Sunday school, obviously. I'm going to keep an eye on him today."

Alex had decided there was no point in mentioning Chris Andersen's visit. CJ said, disappointment ringing in her voice, "So you're not coming home until later?"

Alex sighed into the phone. "David called before you did. He wants to spend one more day with his mom, and I told him I'd stay, and get Charlie to preschool in the morning. I won't be back today at all. I'll have to see you at work tomorrow."

"I see," CJ said, some unidentified anxiety tightening her voice.

"I'm sorry about brunch," Alex said, genuinely apologetic. "I guess I'll have to make it up to you." Her voice was low and held a note of promise.

To her surprise, CJ didn't respond to the implied invitation. "Don't worry," CJ said shortly. "I'm sure I can find something to do."

Alex frowned and said, "I really am sorry, sweetheart."

"I'm sure you are, Alex." She paused, then asked, "Is there anything else going on?"

The question surprised Alex. "No, I'm...what do you mean?"

"Do you need anything? Clothes, food, medicine for Charlie?"

CJ was acting weird, but Alex didn't know how to find out why. "No, we're fine, really. Did you have fun yesterday?"

"Yes, you know Vivian. She's nothing if not entertaining."

"She is that. I'll call later, give you the update."

"You do that."

CJ hung up before Alex could say "I love you." Alex stared at the phone and figured that CJ was still mad about their fight on Friday.

***

The afternoon was a postcard picture of autumn in Colorado. The sky was brilliantly blue, the perfect backdrop for golden aspen leaves. CJ breathed in fresh fall scents as she climbed the outside stairs to the second-floor apartment. The sunshine was warm on her back, but the air had the promise of a chill that warned that winter would be coming soon, soon.

Alex hadn't mentioned Chris in their conversation, and she wasn't coming home again tonight. Worry was making CJ anxious and restless, so she'd decided a field trip was in order, as much to keep her mind off Chris Andersen as anything else.

She checked the apartment number, juggling a plastic container as she knocked firmly on the door. From within she heard a voice call out, "Just a second."

When the door opened, an astonished Elizabeth Rivera stared at her.

"Hello," CJ said in a friendly tone. "I was worried about you, being under the weather and all. Thought I'd drop by and bring you some of my momma's famous chicken soup."

Elizabeth was still staring at her. "Inspector," she managed.

"May I come in?" CJ asked politely.

"I…of course, of course. Please."

She moved away and CJ stepped into her living room. It was spotlessly clean, and fairly neat. The flowered upholstery on the couch was a little worn, and the plush blue chair didn't match. Neither did the plastic wood-looking coffee table and the battered end table. There was a small television set on one wall, flanked by a metal étagère containing a few photos and knickknacks, a couple of books.

The tiny café table that passed for a dining room table was just to her left, and beyond it was the galley kitchen. CJ smiled and said, "Let me put this away. How are you feeling?"

She had already noted that Elizabeth was wearing a skirt, blouse and cardigan. The morning paper lay folded to the feature story about the Nero shooting. Beside it on the café table lay a worn black leather Bible and a folded piece of paper with a picture of flowers on the front.

"Please, let me take that," Elizabeth said. "It was so thoughtful of you…you didn't have to come over."

She took the plastic bowl and went into the kitchen. While she was gone, CJ opened the paper with one finger and looked at it.

It was a church program, dated that morning, from the huge independent evangelical congregation out west, just off I-70.

Elizabeth returned, standing in the doorway of the kitchen, and looked deeply embarrassed.

"I…I was feeling better when I woke up this morning, and went to services," she admitted. "I go every week."

"I'm glad you're feeling better," CJ said cheerily.

She just stood there, smiling, suspecting that Elizabeth would be unable to resist the pressure of her silence. Finally Elizabeth said, "Can I get anything for you? I haven't had lunch yet, but I could make something."

"No, but thanks," CJ said. "I'd love a cup of coffee, though."

"Yes. Yes, of course. Please sit down."

CJ slung the strap of her purse over one of the chairs and seated herself at the table. She watched Elizabeth try twice to get the ground coffee into the coffeemaker, then fumble with the mugs.

"Do you take milk or sugar?" Elizabeth asked nervously.

CJ was pretty certain that Elizabeth Rivera had neither cream nor half-and-half available, so she said, "No, black is fine." She wasn't planning on drinking very much of it anyway.

She just sat, and waited, until at last Elizabeth returned to the table with the two mugs. CJ accepted hers with a smile, and Elizabeth sat across from her, not quite meeting her gaze.

CJ said nothing. Elizabeth finally asked, "Is it really your mother's chicken soup?"

CJ laughed and said, "No. My momma doesn't cook a lick. My daddy, though, was a doctor, and he always said homemade chicken soup was better than any medicine. For most things, anyway."

"Have they passed away?" Elizabeth asked.

CJ kept the tiny prick of pain from showing on her face. She answered, "Daddy died a couple of years ago. It was very peaceful for him, he'd been sick for a while. My mother...Momma is still alive."

"I'm sorry," Elizabeth said. "My mother died when I was four. I don't really remember her. My father still lives in Wyoming, that's where I grew up."

CJ tried the coffee. It wasn't bad, but it wasn't particularly good, either. "How was the church service?" she asked.

Elizabeth stared into her mug, her eyes almost as dark as the liquid it contained. "Good. It was good. Do you…do you go to church?"

"I did regularly when I was young," CJ said, her voice carefully neutral. "A conservative church in Savannah, where I grew up. I have been occasionally since I moved to Colorado, to another denomination. One a bit more… liberal."

Elizabeth's glance flicked up at her and CJ had trouble reading her look. She said, "My father is a preacher on Sundays, a rancher during the week. We went every Sunday morning, and Sunday night, and Wednesday nights, too. I promised him I would go every week after I moved to the big city."

CJ took another sip of coffee and considered her approach carefully. Finally she said, "I was concerned when you called in sick. I was concerned because I was afraid that you weren't really sick at all."

Startled, Elizabeth said, "I don't know what you mean."

"I think you do," CJ said, firmly but kindly. She touched the newspaper and continued, "I think you're afraid, Elizabeth. I think you should talk to me about whatever it is that's scaring you."

Now her eyes were huge, gazing at CJ as if she had suddenly grown another head. "I don't know what you're talking about," she managed to choke out the words.

The more she denied it, the more certain CJ became that she had guessed correctly. "Yes, you do," CJ said.

Elizabeth was silent for a long time, then blurted out, "You don't know anything. You don't understand…"

"All right," CJ said calmly. "Explain it to me."

Unexpectedly, Elizabeth's eyes filled with tears. "I can't," she whispered. "I can't."

CJ watched her a moment, then asked, "Can you tell me why? What's the reason you can't tell me?"

Her voice was shaking with the effort to keep from crying. "I can't," she repeated. "I just can't."

CJ put down her mug and said, "All right. I'm going to tell you, then. And if I get it wrong, you correct me, okay?"

Elizabeth didn't say anything, just continued to stare at her.

"You took the knife from the evidence bin," CJ said. "Someone asked you to do that, and you did. And you know it was wrong, and you're feeling upset and guilty that you did something wrong. That's right, isn't it?"

Slowly, sadly, Elizabeth Rivera nodded. CJ felt as if the knot that had been twisted inside of her had loosened just a bit. She often felt a sense of accomplishment during an interrogation when the moment of truth arrived, but this time she felt less a sense of triumph and more a profound relief.

"When did you take it?" CJ asked, keeping her voice gentle.

"It was Wednesday. I worked the day shift, and I took it out when no one was there."

CJ was afraid to ask the next question. "What did you do with it?"

If she'd destroyed it somehow, gotten rid of it, not only would the chain of evidence be broken, but no amount of explanation would get Chris Andersen—or the department—any forgiveness in the court of public opinion.

"I have it," she answered, in a voice so soft CJ could hardly hear.

"Where?"

"It's here," she whispered. "He told me to get rid of it, but...I couldn't do it. It was evidence, and I couldn't just... it's here."

CJ was almost dizzy with relief. "Get it for me, Elizabeth."

She rose, and went to her freezer. She handed CJ a large plastic freezer bag. Inside it was the smaller evidence bag, and inside of that was the knife, still labeled. CJ put it on the table and asked, "Was this continually in your possession from the time you took it from the property room?"

Elizabeth apparently knew the significance of the question and answered carefully, "Yes, it was."

CJ released a breath she didn't know she'd been holding. "All right, okay," she said, trying to sound reassuring. "It's going to be all right, Elizabeth. We can deal with this."

Elizabeth dropped her head into her hands, dark hair falling over her face. "No!" she began to sob. "No, you don't understand."

CJ let her cry, struggling with the right degree of detachment. She was responsible for investigating the case, but she felt sorry for the woman. She was so young, and apparently pretty sheltered, and had made a terrible mistake.

But how had Elizabeth been persuaded to take the knife? Was it for money or a man? And either way, the most important question remained.

Who wanted the knife to disappear?

She suspected that she knew the answer, but she clearly wasn't going to get any more information out of Elizabeth Rivera today. Time enough for that tomorrow, in the interview room. She would get the answers she needed.

And she would wrap this up and get back to her life, the way it was before this case had interfered with it.

CHAPTER EIGHT: MONDAY

Frank Morelli sat in Alex's office, drinking his first cup of coffee of the day. "What's up, Cap?" he asked.

Alex answered, "Just a status check. How are you doing? Are the cases you have left manageable without Andersen?"

"I'm fine. You took the worst two off my hands."

Alex waved a hand. "The assault case was no big deal. We're getting a warrant, and should have an arrest in a few hours."

"The brother-in-law?"

"The sister herself, actually."

"You're kidding?"

"Nope. Her husband finally broke."

"I'll be damned. Want me to go with you to make the arrest?"

"No, you've got plenty to do. I'll get a couple of units from uniform. How's the safety deposit box break-in?"

He made a face. "The Feds are being a pain in the ass."

Alex chuckled a little. "That wouldn't be the first time. Got a suspect?"

"Oh, no shortage of people to interview. We have a nice, long list. We'll be pounding the pavement for a while. How are you with the parking lot robberies?"

"The composite sketches of the suspects are finally ready. I'm going to visit the garages in the area that haven't been hit yet, see if security or anybody else has seen our guys, maybe doing some preliminary surveillance."

"Good idea," he said, a little envious of the strategy.

Alex laughed a little at the expression on his face and said, "Don't sound so surprised, Frank. I used to be an actual detective, you know."

"Oh, I know. I've heard rumors." He hesitated a moment, then asked, "Any idea when I'll be getting my partner back?"

Alex grimaced, then said, "Not really. Chavez is seeing her again today. I don't know what he's doing, but I imagine he'll get back to me after he talks to her."

"What about the IA case?"

Alex sighed and said, "I really couldn't tell you."

"You mean you won't," Frank said, nodding a little.

"No, I mean I really don't know what's going on. You know IA cases are confidential. It's CJ's investigation."

"Well, hell, Alex, I mean you are living with the woman. Doesn't she talk to you in her sleep or something?"

He was joking, but at the expression on her face, he said, "Shit, Captain. Are you guys okay?"

Alex rubbed her wrist uncomfortably. "Yeah, we will be. I mean, we are, it'll just be easier after this is cleared up."

He shook his head. "I gotta tell you, you're braver than I am. I don't have what it takes to be married to a cop."

"Good thing Jennifer doesn't feel the same way, isn't it?"

He smiled. "Yes, it is. But seriously, Alex, don't let this fuck with you guys. Apologize or something if you have to."

"What makes you think anything was my fault? You sound like my sister." Alex glared at him a little.

"It doesn't matter, does it? The point isn't about who's wrong. It's about not screwing up the relationship."

Alex leaned back, still frowning.

"I'm serious, Cap," he continued. "I knew you before you met her, and I've seen you after. You gotta know you're a lot better off with her."

Yes, Alex thought. I'm a lot better off with her.

***

When CJ got into her office, her phone was already ringing. She threw her jacket and purse on her visitor chair and snatched up the receiver.

"Ryan here," Alex said. "I have a question for you, Inspector."

"Of course, Captain. What would that be?"

Alex cleared her throat and asked, "Are you still pissed off at me?"

CJ went around her cluttered desk and sat in her swivel chair. She stared out the window across the parking lot. Yesterday's brilliant weather had turned overnight into a dull gray day, the wind lashing at the trees in the park and tearing leaves away from branches to swirl like bright golden confetti.

Am I still angry? CJ answered truthfully, "I'm not mad at you, Alex. I'm a little sad, and more than a little worried."

"Why are you worried, sweetheart?" Alex's voice was low.

CJ knew it was to keep her conversation from being overheard in the squad room, but Alex's quiet tone had the usual calming effect on her. "Because it seems to me that we're letting...this case come between us, somehow."

She'd almost said let Chris Andersen come between us. She was diligently pushing the memory of Andersen's car at Nicole and David's house out of her mind.

There was an explanation for it, and she didn't need to hear it to know that it was nothing she needed to worry about.

Alex answered, "This was my fault. I should keep out of this, let you do your job. The IA investigation is your case, and I shouldn't have interfered. I'm sorry about what I said on Friday. I didn't mean it."

That was what CJ wanted to hear, but she didn't quite trust it yet. "Are you sure?" she asked, her voice still a little cool.

Even through the phone line, she could sense that Alex was a little taken aback. CJ was slow to anger, and usually quick to forgive. "Very sure," Alex said firmly. "I trust you. You will do whatever needs to be done, I know that. Forgive me."

CJ capitulated, as she had known she would as soon as Alex started to apologize. She knew how hard it was for Alex to admit that she was wrong, and she couldn't stay mad at Alex very long anyway. "Apology accepted, Captain Ryan."

Alex sighed in relief. "Friends again?"

"Oh, we're quite a bit more than that, I believe. You are coming home this evening, I imagine?"

"I talked to David after dropping Charlie off at day care. He'll be back after lunch, and I'm off duty. I will definitely be home tonight."

"Good. Then you can apologize again, in person."

"Hmm. Perhaps some nonverbal communication techniques?"

CJ laughed. "Absolutely, darlin'."

"Good. Speaking of lunch, are you available?"

She said, "I'm not sure. I got a lead yesterday on the case, and I may be busy most of the day. Can I call you if I get a break?"

"Of course," Alex answered, and CJ noticed that she was carefully not asking about the new information. "Good luck with whatever it is."

"Thanks. I have hopes."

"CJ?"

"Yes?"

"Don't forget to get something to eat."

She hung up, feeling better than she had in days. She called out to McCarthy and he came into her office, carrying two manila folders.

"Hey, Lieutenant," he greeted her. "I have some good stuff for you."

"Me, too." CJ grinned at him happily. "I had a little chat with Elizabeth Rivera yesterday. She'll be in at ten to make a statement."

He lifted his eyebrows.

"Rivera is the one who took the knife."

"No shit!" he exclaimed. "Have you got it?"

"Checked it back into the evidence room this morning before I came upstairs. Chain of evidence is nice and clean."

"Do you know why she took it?"

"We'll find out in a few minutes. Now, your turn. What have you got for me?"

"I am," he began in a hushed voice, "the finest investigator in the history of the Colfax Police Department. Present company excepted, of course."

CJ, amused, said, "I believe that the current Captain of the Investigations Unit could beat both of us with one hand tied behind her back, but we needn't debate the point. What has the brilliant Sergeant come up with?"

"You want the long version or the short one?"

"Condensed, please. I've got to get ready for Elizabeth Rivera."

"Fair enough. I found a connection between Marina Nero's lawyer, Raymond Elliot, and candidate for district attorney Robert Carlson."

CJ leaned forward across her desk in excitement. "You did not!"

"I did," McCarthy said, clearly proud of himself. "I had to go through a pile of crap to find it, including campaign materials. Elliot is a contributor to Carlson's campaign, and has even done a couple of public appearances for him."

"I seriously doubt this is a coincidence," CJ said, happy that her theories were beginning to work out.

"Me, either. In fact, here's something funny. They actually go to the same church, if you can believe that. That huge evangelical one in Golden."

CJ sat back in her chair. "Rock of Ages Congregation," she said, staring off into space.

He grinned at her. "How'd you know? You haven't been attending there, have you? Not exactly your kind of place, I wouldn't think. They don't exactly take to, um, alternative lifestyles."

Still staring, outside, she said automatically, "Being gay is not a lifestyle, Chad, but we'll have that chat later. And I know the name of the church because I know at least one other person, who goes there."

"Yeah? Who's that?"

"Elizabeth Rivera."

It was his turn to stare in surprise. "That is quite a coincidence," he said at length.

"Oh, no, darlin'," she said. "I don't know what it is, but it is not a coincidence. I don't know what the connection is yet, but I'm about to find out."

***

Alex had her head and her calculator deep into a budget report when there was a tap on her doorjamb. As always, she looked up hoping to see CJ, but instead the doorway was filled with the square, dark figure of Rod Chavez.

She pushed the budget report away and got up to greet him with a hug. Originally he had been CJ's friend, but he and Alex had grown close. They had a lot in common. He'd helped raise younger siblings after he lost his father, and he'd been a dedicated cop for over twenty years. Rod was dressed in his usual polyester dark slacks and a long-sleeved western shirt, complete with snaps down the front of his thick torso.

"Hey, it's good to see you," Alex said.

Chavez returned the hug with solid, strongly muscled arms, and said, "Chica, how are you holdin' up?"

"I've been better," Alex admitted. "How have you been? How's Ana?"

"My bride is lovely and feisty as ever. Woman is a handful, I'm telling you."

"Yeah, and you love it."

"I do, actually." He grinned at her under his mustache.

Alex went back around her desk to sit down, and Chavez settled into her visitor's chair. She brought him up to date on David and Nicole and her babysitting duties.

"So how come you didn't take your personal chef with you to feed Charlie?"

Alex looked away, fiddled with her calculator a moment. "She just needed to have some time to herself, relax a little. This case has been a tough one."

He eyed her carefully, then asked, "You guys all right?"

Mildly irritated, Alex said, "Everybody keeps asking me that. We're fine. What's going on with Chris Andersen?"

He ignored the question and said, "You sure about you and CJ?"

"Rod, we're okay. What's the big deal?"

He smoothed his mustache and said, "You know how some people seem cool on the outside, but they're really all soft and sentimental on the inside?"

"Is there a point to this?"

"I'm just sayin'. CJ is a fragile soul, and she really needs to feel secure. If you guys are havin' problems, you gotta make sure she knows it's gonna be okay. She worries."

No one knows that as well as I do, Alex thought. I should never have made her feel insecure, not for one minute. All the things she does for me, and all I have to do in return is love her, and let her know that.

"And as for you…" Rod continued.

"More psychoanalysis?" Alex asked wryly.

He chuckled. "I know you're not quite the big, tough cop you seem to be."

She met his look. "Are you going to tell me about Chris Andersen?"

He heaved a deep sigh. "We got issues."

"Well, no shit," Alex grunted. "You going to charge her?"

"I gotta tell you, today's interview didn't change anything. She hasn't changed her story, she doesn't know anything about what happened to the knife. She's defensive and pretty hacked off at the world."

"Are you going to charge her?" Alex asked again.

"I'm thinkin' about it. I could go manslaughter, or maybe negligent homicide, around the theory that she thought he had a knife but he didn't."

"Charge her with anything and her career is over, you know that."

"I know. She did kill the guy, Alex."

Alex swiveled her chair away and looked out the window. "Her story could be true. If it is, she acted in self-defense. I saw the knife, Rod."

"Hey, I'd buy it in a minute if we could produce the damn weapon. You know testimony about it isn't the same thing. As it is…" He spread his hands.

"CJ told me this morning she's got some kind of lead."

"She tell you what it is?"

Alex shook her head. "She didn't tell me, and I didn't ask. Me getting in the middle of this case is what caused us problems in the first place."

"Ah," was all he said.

"I'm not telling you what to do, Rod," she said carefully.

"So what are you sayin'?"

Alex turned back around to look at him again. "Give us a day or two, see if CJ can track down what happened to the knife. Let her work her lead and see what happens. It doesn't really matter if you charge Chris today or the end of the week, does it?"

He sat back in the chair and gazed at her. She thought, she hoped, that he respected her request, one cop to another. She wasn't doing anything wrong asking him to wait, just pointing out a legitimate alternative course of action.

"I can wait a little, see if something turns up," he said slowly. "But I gotta tell you, Alex, if we don't get something pretty damn soon, I'm going to talk to the DA."

Alex's stomach sank for Chris, but she said, "Fair enough, Rod. Do what you think is right. But give CJ some time, if you can."

***

CJ had feared that Elizabeth Rivera might fail to show up, but at nine fifty-five, McCarthy buzzed her.

"She's here, Inspector," he reported. "I put her in the interview room."

CJ went into the gray room, smoothing her dark blue skirt as she sat across from Elizabeth. Elizabeth's dark eyes were shadowed as if she hadn't slept much, but she was neatly dressed in a dark brown cardigan and white shirt over a brown skirt. She had her hands folded neatly on the table. She wasn't fidgeting, or twitching nervously.

She looked like a woman facing the firing squad, one who had made her peace with her impending destruction.

CJ said, "Thanks for coming. Do you want anything? Chad made some coffee, and it's better than most police station brews."

"No, thank you," she answered politely.

CJ sat back, trying to get her to relax. "Elizabeth," she said gently, "I want you to know something. I know you did a bad thing, but I also know you're not a bad person. I'm on your side here."

She had expected to make Elizabeth feel better, but to her surprise, the woman's eyes filled suddenly with tears. She had huge, soft eyes, like a deer. CJ felt like a brute, making her cry.

"Oh, hey, darlin'…" CJ began.

"No, I'm all right," Elizabeth said, wiping the tears away. "It's just that…after I tell you everything, I…think you might not feel that way anymore."

CJ could not imagine what this woman thought she had done that was so terrible to cause her this overwhelming guilt. Surely this was about more than just taking the knife?

"Tell you what," CJ said, "I promise you, no matter what, I will still like you when this interview is over. Just tell me the truth, all right?"

Elizabeth nodded, mutely.

Her voice still gentle, CJ said, "I have to give you another Garrity advisement, okay? Then all you have to do is answer my questions, and you can say anything you want. We're recording the interview, you understand that?"

She nodded again, and then said, "Can I ask you a question before we start?"

"Of course, darlin'."

"Am I...am I going to go to prison?" she managed to choke out. "I mean, I know I did an awful thing, and I deserve to go, but I don't know if I could stand that."

"Oh, Elizabeth." CJ reached across the table and put her hand on top of Elizabeth's hands, realizing that they were tightly clenched together. "When this interview is over, I will personally go with you to the District Attorney and we will figure out what happens next. You may have to plead to something, but I'll do everything I can to make sure you don't have a prison sentence."

Right. I have so much influence with the DA's office, she thought wryly. I hope I can keep this promise.

She started the recording, repeated the Garrity advisement, and then asked, "Elizabeth, did you remove the knife from the evidence bin in the Nero homicide case?" She rattled off the case number and evidence tag number.

"Yes," Elizabeth answered softly.

"Tell me about that," CJ asked.

She led Elizabeth through the story, carefully establishing the chain of evidence. "Then can you tell me why you removed the weapon?"

Elizabeth looked away.

"Elizabeth?"

"Someone asked me to," she said, finally.

"Who was that?"

"My pastor. The assistant minister at my church, Rock of Ages Congregation."

"What is his name?"

"Willoughby. Pastor Thomas Willoughby."

"When did he ask you to do this?"

"After our regular counseling session, on the Tuesday afternoon after the shooting. We meet in his office at the church, and he asked me then."

"Did anyone else hear this conversation?"

"No. No one else was there."

Carefully, CJ asked, "Did he tell you why he wanted you to take it?"

She nodded, and CJ said, "Answer out loud, please."

"Yes. Yes, he said that it would help prove that the police were wrong to kill that poor man, and that would help solve the problem of police brutality."

"Did he mention how that would address the problem of police brutality? Did he mention any one's name?" CJ probed cautiously.

"No, he didn't."

Damn. No link to Carlson.

"Elizabeth, is that why you took the knife? Because he convinced you that it would help?"

She shook her head, and CJ had to remind her again to talk aloud.

"No," she said quietly. "I didn't really believe him. How would taking the knife help? It would be trying to prove the truth by telling a lie, and that would be wrong."

CJ approved of her logic, and asked, "Did you tell him that?"

"Yes. It made him angry, and he told me to do it anyway or—"

She stopped, and CJ knew that they had gotten to the core of the issue.

"Or what, Elizabeth?"

She whispered, "He threatened me."

CJ felt a surge of anger. She was going to nail this sonofabitch to the wall and leave him hanging there.

"Physically threatened you?" she asked, keeping her rage out of her tone.

"No, not like that."

"Elizabeth, what did he threaten you with?"

"He…" She swallowed, as if the words were stuck in her throat like a bitter pill. "He said that he would call my father, tell him all about me."

CJ tried not to let her confusion show. "What was he going to tell your father?"

Elizabeth collapsed onto the tabletop, weeping. CJ said, "Interview temporarily suspended at ten forty-one," and cut the recording.

She rounded the table, put her arm around Elizabeth's shoulders and said, "Just take your time, darlin'."

Elizabeth cried almost silently but CJ could feel delicate shoulders shaking under the sweater. After a few minutes, she managed to sit up again, and said, "I'm sorry, Inspector, I'm so sorry."

"Don't apologize. Take a couple of deep breaths. What can I get you? You want that coffee now?"

In a small voice she said, "Some water? And a tissue, maybe?"

"Absolutely," CJ gave her a dazzling smile.

When she returned five minutes later, Elizabeth had pulled strength from somewhere and looked almost calm again. She drank half the water, and blew her nose.

"Thank you," she said. "I'm sorry I just broke down like that."

"Don't be. Do you feel strong enough to continue with the interview?"

Elizabeth stared at her, then asked, "Do you think… could we just talk for a minute? This is really hard for me, and I want to do it right, but I just…"

"Of course," CJ said encouragingly. She could always

get the rest of it on tape later, after the shock of the first telling had worn off.

She sat at the end of the table instead of across from her, to emphasize that they were just chatting, friends. She said gently, "I know this is hard, but if he made you do something wrong by forcing you, it's really his fault, not yours. Can you try to tell me about it?"

Elizabeth took a deep breath and said, "I've been seeing him, Pastor Willoughby, once a week for, um, seven or eight months. I promised my father I would go to counseling when I left Wyoming. I told the pastor all about my job, and growing up and about... about my sinning. He was going to help me, and then..."

The tears threatened again, and CJ said, "You're doing great. Go on."

Elizabeth bit back the tears and said, "He said if I didn't do what he wanted, he'd call my father and tell him I wasn't repenting of my sins. My father would just...I don't what he'd do. Make me come home, disown me, something terrible."

CJ was wracking her brain trying to decipher what she was saying. "Elizabeth, you have to help me here. Is this about money?"

Elizabeth shook her head, fingering the water glass.

"Is it about sex, then?" CJ probed gently. "Did Pastor Willoughby seduce you, or..."

Elizabeth looked at her in horror. "Oh, no, nothing like that."

"I'm sorry, I'm just trying to understand. So it's nothing to do with sex?"

The tears came again, one running down her smooth, round cheek to fall from her jaw onto the table. She managed at last. "It was about sex. He...he was counseling me...trying to get me to repent from my sinful desires."

"Sinful desires," CJ repeated, beginning to understand.

"For sex…" Her voice dropped to a barely audible whisper. "With…a woman."

CJ sat back in her chair in silence, suppressing a strong desire to drive immediately to Golden and use Pastor Willoughby for live target practice.

"You're a lesbian?" she asked, incredulously. *My God. I have got to get my gaydar repaired.*

Now that the dam was broken, words tumbled out of Elizabeth. "I've never actually…but I was kissing my friend Julie, and I knew I wanted to…and I knew it was a sin and I just…I'm trying to get over it, I'm really trying, but he said he'd tell my father."

"Elizabeth," CJ interrupted her firmly. "What your pastor did is called extortion. He forced you to do something illegal for his own purposes by threatening to reveal something you told him, in confidence, in counseling. You're not the criminal here, you're the victim. He will pay for this, I promise you. I promise."

"But then I'll have to tell…everybody what happened, what I told him."

CJ took a deep breath. "Elizabeth, we're going out for a while, you and I. An early lunch. We'll have something to eat, and we'll have a very serious talk."

The doe eyes grew round. "Are you going to talk to me about how it's a sin, too?"

"No," CJ said forcefully. "I'm going to tell you what I believe. And I'm going explain to you why you feel the way you do, and why you can't be talked out of it, or counseled out of it, or threatened out of it. We're going to talk about God, and sinning, and what's right and what's wrong."

"We are?"

"Yes. And let's start with this. People use sex to sin a lot, I know that. But love is never wrong. Love is never a sin. Never."

"How do you know that?" she asked, amazement clear in her voice.

"Because I know what I believe," she said strongly. "I believe in God. I know love is right. And I've loved only women my entire adult life, and I know it's not wrong."

"You..." Her eyes grew even wider until it seemed to CJ that they would swallow her entire face with their astonishment.

"Yes." Clearly it was true confession week. First Andersen, now Rivera. Perhaps she should just post a notice on the station bulletin board and be done with it.

CJ stood and added lightly, "What sounds good? I'm thinking maybe a burger."

***

Alex threw her pen on her desk and sighed. From her office window she could see a bank of dark clouds beginning to gather over the Rockies. There would be rain later, maybe some light snow after dark, when the temperature dropped. CJ called a gathering storm formation "clouds massing for the attack," and Alex agreed. It looked like an organized military maneuver, huge gray tanks getting ready to plow over the peaks.

The conversation with Rod Chavez had left her unsettled. She was worried about what an arrest would do to Chris, what it would do to the campaign for DA, how it would affect the department. Mostly, though, she was unsettled because she hadn't seen CJ. Talking on the phone hadn't been enough.

"The hell with it," she muttered aloud, and got up. She would just go downstairs and see her, just for a couple of minutes. They could close the door and Alex could touch her for a moment, feel her skin. Nothing was more healing for her than CJ's touch.

Alex smiled to herself at the thought as she reached the stairwell. To her surprise, Chris Andersen was standing in front of the door, staring at it.

"Chris?"

She jumped, startled. She looked disoriented, as if she didn't know where she was.

"Sorry," Alex said. "Didn't mean to scare you. You were far away."

"I..." Chris seemed to scramble, trying to organize her thoughts. "I just got finished a few minutes ago with Lieutenant Chavez."

"I know," Alex said gently. "He came to see me. I figured you'd already left."

"I just sat there, after he was through. I couldn't...did he tell you he's going to arrest me?"

"He didn't say that," Alex hedged a little. "Look, continuing to worry about this isn't going to help you. Go home, read a book, go for a run, or something. I'll walk you out, okay?"

Chris's anxiety over what would happen to her career, to her life, was almost overwhelming her, Alex could see it in her face. Alex vividly remembered feeling the same way once before. And she remembered that just one person believing in her innocence had made all the difference.

She said to Chris, "Listen to me. I know you didn't do anything wrong. I know that, okay? Try your best not to worry." She nodded mutely at Alex and they walked silently down the stairs.

When they reached the first floor, Alex followed her through, then laid an arm comfortingly across her shoulders. Chris felt tense as a tightly drawn bow.

"Chris, it'll be okay," she said again, hoping it was true. She was acutely aware that Chris had no one to give her that illogical comfort everyone needed sometimes.

Not for the first time, she was suddenly sharply grateful for everything that CJ brought to her life.

They walked into the lobby to see CJ standing with Elizabeth Rivera, clearly on their way out of the building. Chris saw them, too, and stiffened.

Rivera? Alex wondered if that was the break CJ had mentioned earlier.

CJ saw them, smiling at Alex before registering Alex's arm around Chris. The smile faltered.

Frowning, Alex dropped her arm and approached them. "Hey," she said to CJ.

Before CJ could respond, Elizabeth gave a small gasp and blurted, "Oh, Chris, I'm so sorry!"

Chris stared at her. "Sorry? For what?"

CJ, suddenly alert, said, "We were just on our way for an early lunch. I'll call you later, Alex."

Elizabeth was already shrinking back as Alex saw realization flash in Chris Andersen's face.

"It was you!" Chris hissed. "You took the goddamned knife!"

Alex was about to deny it on Elizabeth's behalf but the guilt was etched into her face. She glanced at CJ and saw the confirmation with a tiny nod.

"Chris," Alex began, when everything happened at once.

Chris lunged at Elizabeth, fury pouring off her.

CJ snatched Elizabeth out of range, putting her body between them.

Chris clawed at CJ, trying to get past her to Rivera, and also venting her anger on the woman who was masterminding her destruction.

Alex grabbed Chris hard by both upper arms, feeling the muscles taut and bunched under her hands.

"Stop it!" Alex demanded sharply.

Chris struggled and wrenched one arm free. She clenched her fist and drew it back.

CJ blocked the oncoming blow with an open hand, then took Chris hard by the wrist.

"Enough," she said, trying to sound calm. "The last thing you need is a charge for striking a superior officer."

Alex made no such attempt to be composed. She said harshly, "God damn it, Andersen! Cool off, or I'll arrest you myself!"

She was furious with Chris for losing her temper, but she was also angry with herself for letting Chris throw even one punch at CJ. Every protective instinct she possessed was aroused, and she consciously tried to slow her breathing.

Behind CJ, Elizabeth kept repeating, "I'm sorry, so sorry."

Alex marched Chris to the front door, keeping a firm grip on her arm.

"Walk it off," she ordered her. "Don't try to drive until you're calmer. Do you understand me, Detective?"

Chris squirmed in Alex's grasp and muttered, "I get it. Lemme go."

Alex released her with a little push through the door. She turned back to CJ and Elizabeth, and didn't know what else to say except, "Sorry about that."

"Not your fault," CJ said crisply. "As I was saying, we're on our way for a little lunch and discussion." Her tone made it clear that Alex was not invited, and she added, "I'll call you later, all right?"

Alex watched them go, feeling bereft, her anger fading.

***

Chief Deputy District Attorney Tony Bradford turned to CJ and said, "Lieutenant, may I see you in my office?" He added to his assistant, "Get Ms. Rivera some coffee or something, will you?"

He left the conference room, walking down the hall to his corner office without turning to see if CJ was following. CJ stared at his back as she walked behind him, trying to figure out what was going through his head.

He had, uncharacteristically, remained mostly silent during Elizabeth's story, letting CJ ask a few questions to clarify points in her narrative, but asking none himself. She wondered what he was about to say to her, acutely aware that their last conversation had ended in the argument about Alex.

Tony waited for her to close the door behind her. Once again she had to admire his good looks—dark blond hair, classically chiseled features, a deep tan she figured he must work on year-round. He dressed well, expensively: designer suit, cut to fit him, cufflinks, Rolex. Too bad the package inside didn't match the wrappings.

To her surprise, he didn't sit behind his desk, but perched on the edge of it, waving her to a chair. She hadn't been in his private office before, and glanced around. Nice furnishings, not that she would expect anything less from Tony. There was a gold pen on the desktop, and the requisite leather-bound law books in the bookcase on one wall. He had a nice view, the same park CJ looked at from across the street, but without the parking lot in between, and from a much higher floor. On one wall were framed photos of him shaking hands with a series of dignitaries. She recognized the governor, a US senator and a federal judge.

She found herself relieved that there was no photo of Alex on his desk. She wouldn't have put it past him to have their wedding picture in a nice silver frame to greet him every morning.

He fixed her with a look and said, "Is this for real?"

She met his gaze and said, "Rivera? Absolutely. It looks like they took advantage of a random tragedy—Chris interrupting the assault, and the shooting—to try to sabotage your campaign."

"You don't think this is some kind of setup? That she made up the story, so I'll falsely accuse him of this?"

CJ blinked, trying not to accuse him of paranoia. After all, the conspiracy had been real enough. "No," she answered him firmly. "If Elizabeth Rivera is lying, I'll resign. Everything I can see tells me that she's telling us the truth."

He pushed his fingers through his wavy hair. "This would be great news, except…"

"I know. There's nothing to tie Willoughby to Carlson, or his campaign."

He gave her a sharp, appraising look. "That's right. We can arrest Willoughby, but Carlson will just disavow any knowledge."

CJ said, "That's why I think we need Elizabeth's help. I want to send her in to talk to Willoughby, try to get him to incriminate Carlson or at least one of his campaign people. I'm sure Carlson had something to do with this, and I want to nail him."

"You want her to wear a wire?"

"Yes."

"You think she'll do it?"

CJ crossed her legs demurely, smoothing the navy blue skirt over her knees. "I do. She feels tremendously guilty about what she did, and I think she'll want to make it right. And," she added, watching him try to tear his gaze away from her legs, "I'm sure you can make her an offer to make the proposal irresistible."

Still watching her, he said, "Are you talking about immunity? What are you, her defense attorney now?"

She suppressed a tiny flare of disgust. You might want to stop ogling me, you big hypocrite, and listen. I'm trying to bail your sorry ass out here. "I'm trying to get the real bad guys, Tony. She's frightened of being incarcerated, and with good reason. She'd have a terrible time surviving in prison, and I'm sure she'd accept immunity in exchange for talking to Willoughby."

He sighed, conceding the point. "It's worth a shot. She's a small fish, and I'd rather let her go and nail that bastard Carlson. Set up the conversation, and I'll get her full immunity. But she'll have to testify, if it comes to that."

CJ thought about Elizabeth's reluctance to disclose the reason Willoughby was extorting her, and said, "I'll explain that to her. I think she'll agree anyway."

She hoped so. During their conversation over lunch, CJ had told her not to be afraid, or ashamed of who she was, but it was easy to say and hard to do.

She stood up and said, "Elizabeth has a session with Willoughby every Tuesday afternoon. We'll get the warrant and I'll get her ready to talk to him tomorrow. In twenty-four hours, you should have what you need."

"CJ, wait." Here it comes. More yelling? Or perhaps he's going to apologize? Yeah, right.

"Look," he said, pushing his hand through his hair again, "we've had our disagreements, I know."

"That's one word for it," she said coolly.

"I…" he seemed unable to organize what he wanted to say. CJ stood still, letting him struggle, not inclined in the least to bail him out.

He straightened his shoulders and finally said again, "Look, it's just hard for me to believe Alex would prefer being with a woman. I can't help thinking this is some kind of…I don't know, phase she has to work through."

"So she will eventually figure it out and come back to you?" she said tartly.

He winced a little at her tone. "I've never made it a secret that I still love Alex. Of course I had hopes that she'd work out her…issues, whatever they were, and consider coming back to me."

CJ went deep inside herself to find a sliver of compassion

for him. She touched his sleeve and said, "Tony. Listen to me, really listen. I am truly, genuinely sorry, but you have got to see that you're stuck in a past that never really existed. Alex doesn't love you, and she never did."

He flinched. "Don't say that."

"It's true. She's told you that, I'm telling you that, and somewhere within yourself, I think you know it, too. This really has nothing to do with me. You need to be done emotionally with Alex, so you can move on, find the person you deserve to be with."

He looked up at her with big, brown, puppy dog eyes. "I don't know…" he began.

"Yes, you do," she said firmly. "We're not in competition, Tony. Let her go. If not for her sake, or mine, for your own sake."

He stared at her miserably. "You're right, I guess," he almost whispered the words. "But I just don't know that I can do that."

"I know how hard it is to let go of someone you love," she said quietly. "I do. You have to know that this would be a good thing for everyone," she said, wondering if he was really ready, even after all these years. "I know Alex would like for all of us to be on friendly terms, but it's impossible when you're like this."

He nodded but said nothing until she turned to leave. "Thanks for this. Rivera, I mean. It's going to really bail me out of a tight spot."

"You're welcome, but I didn't do it for you. I was only trying to find the truth."

He nodded again, and said, "Can I ask you one more question?"

"You can always ask."

He met her look. "Do you really love her? Really?"

She heard the pain in his voice. "Yes, Tony," she answered softly. "I love her with everything I've got."

CHAPTER NINE: TUESDAY

Elizabeth sat in Pastor Willoughby's office, trying not to shift uncomfortably against the body wire she wore. The room, she noticed for the first time, was decorated in fake: fake paneling that looked like wood, fake rug to look like Oriental carpet, fiberboard furniture masquerading as hardwood. A print of a bad painting of Jesus hung on the wall behind Willoughby, next to his framed certificate of ordination.

She looked at him as he sat stunned into momentary silence by her demand. He was the most false element of all, she realized, pretending love and compassion when he was filled instead with self-interest and hatred. How could she have ever thought him wise or kind?

The world had turned topsy-turvy in the last few days. Her pastor could be evil, and a gay police officer could be kind to her. She was disoriented, but tried to focus on the task before her. She knew how important it was.

"What on earth," Willoughby managed, "makes you think I will give you five thousand dollars? I don't have anything like that kind of money."

She spoke carefully, trying to sound as natural as possible. "I told you. I understand that it isn't just you who needed for the knife to disappear. I'm afraid they'll find out I took the knife, and I'll lose my job."

"Are you saying they suspect you?" he asked sharply. Everything about Willoughby was sharp, his beak nose, his jutting chin, his protruding Adam's apple.

"They questioned everybody," Elizabeth answered honestly. "They might fire all of us in the evidence room. I'll need the money, to tide me over."

"I don't have that kind of money," he repeated.

She leaned forward, just a little, trying to keep her hands steady. "We both know who does. It wasn't you who needed for me to take the knife."

Willoughby went a little pale. Elizabeth knew that CJ was outside in the van, listening to the conversation. She had to remember what CJ told her: mentioning Carlson's name might be entrapment, she had drilled into Elizabeth's head over and over again. Let him say it. Come on, Elizabeth urged Willoughby silently.

After a long silence, Willoughby said, "You have no idea what you're talking about."

Elizabeth said, "I think I do, Pastor. And I think you should call him, right now." Don't press too hard.

"You're not in a position to bargain here, young lady," he began, trying to bully her.

"I think I am," she replied.

"I will call your father!" he barked.

"If you do, I'm going to the police," she answered swiftly. "You have as much to lose as I do, don't you, Pastor? Make the call. I think five thousand dollars is a cheap insurance policy, don't you?"

There was another long pause and Elizabeth tried not to fidget.

***

In the van, CJ began to fidget. McCarthy, next to her, mouthed, "It's okay."

She heard the faint beeps of telephone buttons and nodded to the technician in the van with them. They had gotten the warrant for the tap on Willoughby's phone that morning, and the technician checked the number as the call went through.

"Carlson?" McCarthy asked hopefully.

The tech shook his head, and CJ looked over his shoulder at the computer screen at the number. "Next best thing," she said.

The phone was picked up and a man's voice answered, "Elliot."

Willoughby's voice came through the line, thin but clear. "We have a bit of a problem," he said shortly.

He briefly outlined Elizabeth's demand, and ended with, "She wants me to call him."

"Bullshit," Raymond Elliot said. "I'm on my way over. Keep her there."

Willoughby said, obviously for Elizabeth's benefit, "You'll call Carlson, then?"

CJ grinned at McCarthy in triumph. Elizabeth hadn't mentioned Carlson's name, so Willoughby was well and truly caught.

Elliot laughed unpleasantly. "Don't worry. I know how he wants things like this dealt with. She won't be a problem after today. Just keep her there. I'll be there in fifteen."

He hung up.

McCarthy said triumphantly, "A fucking touchdown. How do you want to handle this?"

CJ said crisply, "Get two units over here right now, running blacked out. Have them both wait in the back. When Elliot shows up, you take one of the uniforms and arrest him when he gets out of his car. I'm taking the other and we're going in to get Willoughby."

"Got it," he said, calling as CJ listened to Willoughby talk to Elizabeth in soothing, placating tones, telling her Carlson was on the way with the money.

CJ listened to him lie and muttered, "Keep talking, you worthless piece of garbage. I'm coming for you."

She prayed that Willoughby wasn't armed, but he seemed intent on using persuasion rather than violence.

Elliot was a different matter, that was clear from his words to Willoughby. As she and McCarthy got out of the van when the uniformed officers showed up, she said, "Chad, he's probably carrying. Be careful."

He said, "You can bet on it."

CJ said to the other officer, a short, square man whose nametag said Bennett, "You're with me."

She put on the lanyard with her badge, and walked into the church office, past the secretary who called out to stop her. She opened the door to Willoughby's office and said, "Pastor Willoughby."

He looked up at her and demanded angrily, "Who are you? This is a private counseling session. You have to leave."

"I don't think so," she answered. Her first priority was Elizabeth's safety, so she took her by the arm and pulled her out of her chair. "Ma'am, you go with Officer Bennett. You, sir, please stand up."

Willoughby stood, but demanded furiously again, "Who are you?"

"I am Lieutenant St. Clair, Colfax PD. I am also," she added with a note of grim satisfaction, "the officer who is arresting you."

Now the anger was laced with fear. He took one quick glance at his window.

CJ said, "If you are expecting Mr. Elliot, I'm afraid he's been detained indefinitely."

"I…what are you arresting me for?"

"A number of things, which will be explained at your arraignment. A few highlights would include extortion, obstruction of justice and conspiracy. Put your hands on your head, please. Are you carrying any weapons?"

He was in shock, and she swiftly searched and handcuffed him. Snapping the metal around his wrists gave her as much pleasure as any arrest she'd ever made.

She took him by one arm and marched him out of the office, reciting his Miranda rights to him as they walked. The shocked faces of the staff flashed by as they walked out, and CJ enjoyed every second of it.

"Do you understand your rights?" she finished as they made it to the parking lot.

Willoughby was still dazed. "Yes, yes, but…I haven't done anything. You can't prove anything."

Two entirely different arguments. I'm looking forward to this interrogation.

CJ smiled unpleasantly. "Oh, I think you'll find I can prove everything I need to."

She left Willoughby with Officer Bennett and walked over to McCarthy, who was standing near a handcuffed Raymond Elliot.

"Everything go okay?" she asked.

McCarthy gave her a shit-eating grin. "You'll be absolutely shocked to learn, Lieutenant, that Mr. Elliot here was carrying a loaded weapon without a concealed carry permit."

Elliot glared at her. "You're responsible for this travesty, aren't you? I can promise you your career is over."

"So nice to see you again, Mr. Elliot," CJ said cheerfully. "I'm just curious. Was Marina Nero in on this little conspiracy, or did you just promise her a lot of money if she cooperated to sue the city?"

"Go to hell!" Elliot snarled.

CJ smiled at McCarthy. "Take good care of Mr. Elliot," she said. "We have so much to talk about."

She watched McCarthy put Elliot in the back of the unit. Returning to Willoughby, she said, "Bad news, I'm afraid. I believe we will have to add a charge of conspiracy to commit murder. So much prison time. Very bad."

Willoughby was already babbling as they helped him into the car.

***

"Alex," CJ's voice came through on her office line, warm and excited. "I have a gift for you."

"What?"

"At this moment, fresh from the judge's chambers, I have an arrest warrant that needs to be served in the Nero shooting case. Andersen was being framed, and two of the conspirators are being booked as we speak."

"So who is the warrant for?"

Alex could almost see CJ's grin. "Our good friend and District Attorney Candidate Robert Carlson. He was trying to set us up, using the shooting to get the leverage he needed to win the election."

Alex sat forward in her desk chair. "Oh, my God," she exclaimed. "Why the hell didn't we see that before?"

"It wasn't that easy to see. There were a lot of players: Nero's widow, her lawyer, and, unbelievably, Elizabeth Rivera's minister."

"What the hell?"

CJ laughed, the relief clear in her voice. She gave Alex a brief summary of the day's activities. "Don't worry. I do believe that Mr. Elliot and Pastor Willoughby are going to be very forthcoming in the upcoming interviews. Elizabeth got enough on the tape to nail them both. On the way to the station, Willoughby was talking faster than a used car salesman, and suddenly Mr. Elliot is very happy to assist us. He was carrying a gun into the meeting to use on Elizabeth. Carlson is finished. I thought the Captain of Detectives might want the pleasure of serving the warrant."

"It's your case," Alex said. "Sure you don't want to do it yourself?"

"I've got my hands full with these two characters. Besides, I know you'll have to call Chief Wylie first, and I'm sure he'll want to send in his chief investigator for the honors."

"Jesus, CJ." Alex grinned into the phone. "Have I told you lately you're a brilliant cop? Have you called Rod?"

"Just about to," she answered happily. "Call me when you're done. This deserves a celebratory dinner."

"Yes, sure," she answered. "Look, I'd like to stop by one of the armed robbery possibilities on the way home tonight, is that okay?"

"Of course. I'll go with you, and then we can go out."

Alex tried to remember the last time she'd heard CJ so happy about a case. "See you soon," she said. "Call me if you get hung up."

"I will. Alex?"

"Yes?"

"I love you, darlin'. See you as soon as I can."

Alex walked into the bullpen, almost empty at the end of the day. Frank Morelli was still at his desk, filling out some form on his computer screen. "How about a ride, Sergeant?" Alex greeted him.

He looked up, surprised. "Sure, Cap. What's up?"

"We're going downstairs to pick up a warrant, then we're going crosstown to pick up the man who's made your partner's life miserable. Interested?"

"Hell, yes!" He grabbed his jacket from the back of his chair.

"You drive. I'll be talking to the chief on the way over. He'll want to start getting his press release ready."

Frank switched off his computer. "Press release? A high-profile thing?"

"Oh, yeah. And frankly, I can hardly wait to see the news tonight."

***

Alex's badge did not impress the assistant at "Carlson for DA" headquarters. "I'm sorry," he said firmly. "Mr. Carlson is in conference and is not available."

Frank snorted behind her. Alex said smoothly, "This isn't a social call. Where is he?"

"I can't let you interrupt—"

Frank interjected, "You can either tell us or get arrested for obstruction of justice."

The assistant blanched and said, "Conference Room Two. But—"

"Thank you," Alex said in a friendly tone.

They entered without knocking. Robert Carlson was in midsentence, jabbing a finger at a young woman wearing a button that read "Carlson means Justice." He looked up at them, startled, then rearranged his leonine features into a semblance of friendly surprise.

"I didn't expect visitors," he managed. "Have we met?"

Alex saw Frank roll his eyes. Politicians. "Would you excuse us?" she addressed the young woman. "We have some business with Mr. Carlson."

Carlson looked ready to protest, but Alex showed him her shield. He said quickly, "Wendy, it's fine. I'll see you in a minute."

She left quickly, gathering up a file folder as she went. Alex thought she looked deeply relieved to be going.

"Now, officer," Carlson said in a friendly tone, "what's this about?"

Cool customer. She wondered if Elliot had called him before he went over to see Elizabeth at Willoughby's office. In person, Carlson looked even more oddly shaped than he did on television. He had a large head, topped with the silver mane, and a small body. Alex wondered how the mug shot would look and she smiled inwardly.

Frank moved around the table to stand behind Carlson, and the movement made him jumpy. "What's going on?" he demanded, his voice less welcoming.

Alex laid the warrant on the tabletop in front of him, and said, "Robert Carlson, you're under arrest. Please lean forward and put your hands on the table. Are you carrying anything we should know about? A weapon or perhaps drugs? Any needles?"

He went pale. "What on earth are you talking about? Arrest for what?"

Frank said firmly, "Lean forward, Mr. Carlson."

He frisked Carlson while Alex recited his Miranda rights. She asked, "Do you understand these rights as I have explained them to you?"

He snapped, "Of course. I'm a lawyer, you idiot."

"It really won't help you to call me names," Alex said calmly.

Carlson tried to regain himself. "You've got this wrong, whatever it is. A political tactic by my opponent, I imagine."

Alex said pleasantly, "Did you find his cell phone, Sergeant?"

"I did." Frank handed it over.

Alex took it and mused, "Wonder if there are any recent calls from anyone on this phone?"

"Or maybe," Frank added happily, "there's a voicemail that didn't get erased yet."

Carlson twitched uncomfortably in Frank's grip. "You have no right—"

"Oh, don't worry," Alex said. "We'll wait until we have a warrant to go through your phone. Who knows what interesting calls you might have gotten this afternoon?"

"You'll be hearing from my lawyer!" Carlson spat.

Alex heard her sergeant stifle a tiny laugh. Alex said coolly, "I hope you have someone other than Raymond Elliot on retainer, Mr. Carlson."

"What does that mean?" Carlson's face went even paler as Frank pulled his arms behind his back for the handcuffs.

"I believe you'll find Mr. Elliot will be unable to represent you in this matter," Alex responded, enjoying his dismay. "He'll be a co-defendant, I imagine."

"I—Elliot's lying!"

Alex heard the laugh escape Frank. "What an interesting comment," Alex said. "As you have no idea what he's said, how can you be certain he's lying?"

"I...you're not..." He seemed unable to form a sentence.

"Exercise your right to remain silent, counselor," Alex suggested.

He seemed to shrink, literally, in Frank's grasp. She took one of his arms, Frank took the other, and they strolled slowly through the campaign headquarters in front of as many people as possible.

***

Chris answered her cell phone on the first ring.

"Chris, where are you?" Alex asked.

"I'm actually in my car, about ten minutes from the station," Chris answered. "Why, what's going on?"

"Listen, come up to my office. I've got good news."

"What is it?" Chris demanded.

Alex smiled. "It'll wait until you get here."

Chris pressed the button to disconnect the call and smiled into her rearview mirror. Whatever it was, Alex sounded happy, and she knew just how she wanted to celebrate.

It took her a little longer than she thought to get through the traffic. She crossed a deserted detective squad room and went into Alex's office without knocking.

"Captain," she said. "I could use some good news."

Alex stood and came around the desk, sitting on the edge. She was close enough that Chris could smell a very faint scent of her perfume, and it took some self-control not to reach for her.

Alex said, "I know this has been a nightmare for you, but it's over."

As Alex told her everything she knew, Chris battled her conflicting emotions. Relief, first and foremost. More than a little anger. Gratitude, too, surprisingly.

"CJ cracked this open," Alex explained. "I told you she was on your side. And Elizabeth Rivera took a hell of a chance to try to make it right. They really went to bat for you."

Chris took a step toward her and said in a warm voice, "It was you, Alex. You were the one who got me through this."

Alex shook her head. "You got yourself through it."

Carefully, Chris asked, "Would you mind if I gave you hug?"

Chris could see Alex's relief at how much progress she'd made. A week ago, she'd barely been able to get Chris to talk to her without snarling.

"Sure," Alex said, standing to offer her arms.

Chris stepped into the embrace and hugged her hard, feeling Alex's warmth against her body. It filled her with longing, and when she stepped back a little she saw Alex smiling at her.

Now, Chris thought. It was only a small movement, tipping her head a little to one side.

She heard Alex murmur, "Chris, don't..." as Alex began to release her arms.

Chris ignored her, leaned in, and kissed her, hard.

***

Across the bullpen, CJ opened the door from the stairwell. She saw Alex through the window of her office, saw another woman with her arms around her. CJ shut her eyes for an instant, as if she could make the image disappear from her mind if she just shut it off from her vision.

But it didn't work. She opened her eyes again, and they were still there.

Alex, in Chris Andersen's embrace. Kissing her.

The sight made her blind. She could see, but her mind couldn't absorb what she was seeing.

CJ backed clumsily away, into the door, groped for the doorknob.

Still unseeing, she stumbled down the stairs, almost falling. She grabbed the banister, frantic, spun into a seated position on the stair. No. It wasn't possible.

Everything charged into her head, swirling madly: Alex stopping her lovemaking, Chris and Alex together at Jersey's, the car at the curb in front of the house Saturday night.

Now she understood. She couldn't avoid the truth anymore. Alex was having an affair with Chris Andersen. I never look at other women, Alex had said to her.

Liar.

Every emotion from years ago, when she discovered that Laurel had been unfaithful to her, slammed back into her, a hundred times stronger. Fear, anger, self-loathing, a jealousy so deep it went straight through her. The best relationship she'd ever had in her life, the best love she could ever hope to have, was shattered.

Now the pieces of broken love were shards of glass inside her, cutting, slashing at her heart and mind with every new thought, every new fear.

Why?

What is Chris giving her that I couldn't?

Does Alex want a younger woman? Or just a different woman?

Is Alex in love with her?

It didn't matter, she thought, dizzy with the agony of it. Alex was cheating on her, so it didn't matter whether Alex loved Chris or not. CJ could never be with someone she didn't trust, and she knew she could never trust Alex again.

It was over. All the time, all the promises, all the love she would never be able to give another person.

Broken in an instant.

***

Alex dropped her arms and put them on the front of Chris's shoulders. She pushed firmly and Chris broke away.

"What?" Chris demanded, a little dazed. *Jesus, that was better than I thought it would be.*

Alex said harshly, "No. Not now, not ever. I'm sorry."

Chris simply didn't believe her. She lifted a hand to Alex's lips and said, "I'm getting a very different message from here."

Alex, shaking, stepped away from the touch of Chris on her skin, and said again, "No. Never again, do you understand?"

Chris stared at her. "Why the fuck not?" she demanded. "You want to." She could see the words sting Alex.

Alex said firmly, "Listen to me. You were hurting, and I wanted to help. Maybe I was tempted, but this isn't love, and it's not what I want. And maybe you just want to show me you're grateful, but not like this. I'm your boss."

Chris, seeing what she wanted slip away, said a little desperately, "It's not just that I'm grateful. I want you. I don't care if you're my boss."

"I do care. But even if I weren't your boss, I wouldn't do this."

Chris tried to touch her again. *If she could just get her hands on Alex, she could make her see how good it was going to be.*

Alex stepped away again and said, her voice strong, "I'm in love with CJ. I'm not cheating on her. That's all. Listen to me, Chris. I love her."

Chris dropped her hands in defeat. All this talk about love was making her sick to her stomach. This wasn't about love, it was about wanting and needing and chasing away loneliness.

But Alex wasn't lonely, she realized with a jolt. She wasn't lying. She did love CJ, and she wasn't going to be with Chris. Not for one night, not even for one hour.

"Fine," Chris snapped, bitter in defeat. "Your loss. I would have made it good for you, for both of us. Really good."

Alex gave her a small, tight smile. "No, it wouldn't have been any good. I don't think it would have meant anything to you but sex, and it would have ruined me. I can't imagine what it would have done to CJ."

"She would never have known," Chris said defiantly.

Alex winced. "Yes, she would have. She knows me better than anyone. She'd have known, one way or another, and it would have destroyed everything we have together."

Chris just looked at her. She didn't really understand. Then Alex added softly, "It was my fault, too, and I'm sorry. I should have stopped this earlier." Then she took a breath and said, "Chris, do me a favor."

"Don't worry," Chris was beyond bitter. "I'll never come within ten feet of you again, Boss, believe me."

"I didn't mean that. What I want you to do is go home. Don't go out and pick up some woman you don't know so you can screw her brains out."

"What I do," Chris growled, "is none of your fucking business!"

"And what I'm telling you," Alex said, her voice still gentle, "is that love is worth the trouble you have to go to find it and keep it."

Chris laughed unhappily. "You're the second person to give me that advice recently. I believe her exact words were 'a good relationship beats a one-night stand all to pieces.' Know who told me that?" Chris asked sourly.

"Yeah, I can guess," she said to Chris.

Chris snarled, "Then why don't you go home to her and quit telling me how to run my life?"

She turned, flung open the door and almost ran across the bullpen to the elevator.

***

Elizabeth Rivera sat in her living room, mug of tea cooling rapidly between her hands. She didn't like her tea too strong, so she could see all the way to the bottom of the mug to the tea leaves, but there was no comfort to be found there, no answer to be seen.

It had been the worst week of her life, and it was all of her own making. She had been a victim, a coward, a liar, a thief, all because she couldn't look in the mirror and understand why she felt the way she felt.

Could God really have made her this way? Or was this some kind of trial to test her faith? Was her father, with all of the certainty of his belief, in the right? Or was CJ St. Clair telling her the truth?

She sighed. The battle was still being fought in her mind, in her heart, and she was so tired. She put the mug on the coffee table, deciding to go to bed early. Halfway to her bedroom, there was a sharp knock on her door.

She went to the door and looked out the peephole. When she saw who it was, she hesitated, then opened the door.

Elizabeth stood in the doorway, her hand still on the knob, and said, "Why are you here?"

Chris Andersen lifted her hands and said, "Damned if I know."

"Are you here to scream at me? I wouldn't blame you if you did, but I just don't think I can face it tonight."

"Look, if I promise there won't be any screaming, can I come in for a minute?"

Elizabeth searched her face a moment, then stepped away to let Chris come in. "Do you want some tea?" she asked.

"Um. Okay. Sure."

***

Chris didn't actually remember ever drinking a cup of tea in her life, but it seemed only polite to accept. There was something gentle and timid about Elizabeth that reminded her of a bunny, easily frightened.

"What kind would you like?" Elizabeth called to her from the kitchen. "I have English Breakfast, Earl Grey, Apple Spice."

Chris had no idea. She saw the mug on the table and said, "Whatever you're having is fine."

"Do you want sugar?"

"No, thanks."

"Lemon, or milk?"

Jesus, this was as bad as ordering coffee at Starbucks. "Neither one," she answered, hoping the questions were over.

She wandered around the living room. There were some books on a shelf and she wandered over to glance at the titles. One was a Bible, and next to it were books that seemed to have religious themes. Incongruously, a couple of paperback romance novels shared the shelf.

Elizabeth came in and handed Chris a mug. "I picked Earl Grey. It's my favorite. I hope you like it."

"I'm sure it'll be fine."

They sat at opposite ends of the couch, and Chris wondered if this was the most awkward few minutes she'd ever spent. She had certainly been in plenty of women's apartments, but she had always known exactly what would happen when she got there.

Tonight, she didn't know why she was there.

After she'd left Alex's office, she had driven downtown, to her favorite pickup bar, Regina. She had sat in her car for a few minutes before going inside, trying to tamp down the anger Alex's rejection had triggered.

If she didn't want to, she could have just told me so without all that crap about love.

She went into the bar, but no one caught her attention. Not a blue-eyed brunette in the place. She kept hearing Alex's voice: "Don't go out and pick up some woman you don't know."

"God damn you, Captain Ryan," she growled.

She thought about getting a beer, playing a game of pool, and waiting to see who would turn up on a weeknight, but for some reason she'd asked for a phone book and looked up Elizabeth Rivera's address instead.

Now here she was, blowing on her tea and trying to figure out why the hell she'd come here. Elizabeth sat quietly, watching her with those huge, dark eyes.

Chris cleared her throat and said, "I talked to Captain Ryan this evening. She told me what happened, what you did for me."

Elizabeth said softly, "What happened to you…it was all my fault. I had to try to make it right."

"It wasn't your fault," Chris answered. "The shooting was Nero's fault. Everything that happened after that was Carlson's fault, the bastard. You were just sort of caught up in it, like I was."

"You don't blame me for what happened? You did yesterday."

Chris took a sip of the tea. It tasted of some kind of exotic herb or something. "This is really good," she said, surprising herself. "What's this spice?"

Elizabeth gave her a shy smile. "Some kind of orange flavor. I think it's called bergamot. Anyway, it's what makes Earl Grey tea…well, Earl Grey."

"This guy, Earl Grey. Was he a real earl, or did he just invent this flavor?"

Elizabeth laughed, a quiet chuckle. Everything about her seemed soft and yielding. "I have no idea," she confessed. "I'll have to look it up sometime."

Chris drank more tea, and wondered why she'd never tried it before. She said, "Will you tell me why you did it?"

"What?" Elizabeth asked, startled.

"Why you took the knife. I mean, Captain Ryan told me your minister forced you to do it, said he was blackmailing you, but she didn't tell me what it was."

Elizabeth dipped her head in distress, and Chris backed off. "Never mind. You don't have to tell me. I guess I just wanted to know what would make somebody like you take something that didn't belong to you to get a person in trouble. You don't seem like that type at all."

Elizabeth lifted her chin and said earnestly, "I'm not, really. I've never taken anything in my whole life. But I was just so scared."

Something seemed to pull at Chris. What was it? Chris could see how vulnerable Elizabeth was, and, despite what Elizabeth had done, she sensed honesty as well. And Chris hadn't forgotten how much courage it took to face Willoughby wearing a wire. She asked softly, "Are you still scared?"

Now the dark brown eyes filled with tears, and Chris said, "Oh, hell, I'm sorry."

"No, it's okay, really. I'm just…yes, I'm still afraid."

"Tell me about it," Chris suggested, her voice still gentle. "Maybe I can help you."

Tears were easing down her cheeks. "Why would you want to help me? You were so angry at me when you found out."

"Look," Chris said, trying for a mollifying tone, "I was really pissed off, I admit it. I thought you did it for money or something, and I thought I was going to be arrested. But I understand now, they forced you into it. Just tell me what's got you spooked."

Elizabeth took a deep breath. "I'm afraid my father will find out. He's a…he preaches on Sundays, and he would be so upset and disappointed if he knew about me. Pastor Willoughby said if I didn't take the knife, he would have to tell my father all about my sinning ways."

Chris set her mug down and tried not to show her amusement. "Whatever it is, it can't be that bad, can it? You said you've never stolen anything, and you don't seem like you've got a body buried somewhere."

"Worse than that," Elizabeth whispered.

"Look, you don't have to tell me if you don't want to, but I think you'll feel better if you do. Because people can only hold something over your head if you let them. Tell the truth and no one can ever threaten you with it again."

Elizabeth stared at her, wiping away a tear.

"That's what Inspector St. Clair told me. She told me it would be all right to tell the truth. She was really nice to me."

Will I ever have a conversation again in my life that doesn't include somebody telling me how God damn amazing CJ-fucking-St. Clair is? "Did you tell her—St. Clair—whatever it was?" Chris asked.

Elizabeth nodded. "She told me that I hadn't done anything wrong. I almost believed her."

A tingle started at the base of her spine, and Chris recognized the sensation. She knew, in that moment, and wondered why she hadn't seen it before.

"You're gay," Chris said flatly.

"How did you know?" Elizabeth asked, shocked. "Did the lieutenant tell you?"

Chris almost laughed. "No, we're not exactly buddies," she said, understating the case. If St. Clair knew I'd had my hands on her woman, I'd be lucky to escape with my head still attached. "Besides, I'm sure she'd keep your secret. Did she tell you she's gay, too?"

Elizabeth nodded again. "We talked about it, and about God and sin. She doesn't think it's a sin to love a woman, but I don't know…"

Chris stood up abruptly and said, "Thanks for the tea. And just for the record, it's not a sin and not something to be ashamed of. I'm not."

Elizabeth looked up at her, her mouth forming a circle. "Oh, Chris, I'm—"

"Don't you dare say you're sorry, like I've got a disease or something. I'm proud of who I am. You should be too. You helped them put me through hell for a week because you think being gay is some kind of, I don't know, some kind of fucking character flaw. If you don't get over it, you're going to be pretty damn miserable the rest of your life. Goodbye."

She moved toward the door, but Elizabeth leaped up and stopped her with a hand on her arm. Chris looked down at her hand, then back up to meet her gaze.

The tingle shot up Chris's spine, the familiar sensation of sexual attraction. Beyond that, a fierce protective instinct seemed to rise up in her, a feeling she'd never had before for anyone, ever.

"I was going to say," Elizabeth murmured, "that I am truly sorry for everything I did to you. It's not easy for me,

but I'm going to try to feel differently about this. About…
about being gay. I'm going to try."

Chris blurted, "Good. Go out with me on Friday
night."

Elizabeth dropped her hand and stepped back. "What?"

"I'm asking you out. I figure you owe me one date,
don't you? One condition: we don't talk about Carlson, or
Willoughby, or the case. Okay?"

"Chris, I don't know if I can do this. I'm still—"

"You said you were going to try. It's one date, dinner. I
promise to behave myself. Do you like Italian?"

"Chris, I…I don't think…" she stammered.

"What's the matter? Never been out with a girl before?"

"No."

"What?"

"No, I really haven't."

"You…" Chris let that sink in, and then said, firmly,
"Then it's time you started. Seven o'clock, okay?"

"I don't know if I can do this."

"Yes, you can. I'll come by and get you."

Then, without planning it, Chris leaned over and kissed
her, lightly, on the lips. She half-expected Elizabeth to push
her away, as Alex had done earlier, but Elizabeth surprised
her. She let Chris kiss her, returning a slight pressure against
her mouth until Chris stepped away.

"Friday, okay?" Chris asked, her anger suddenly melted
away, replaced by a light feeling she couldn't remember
having before.

"Yes, Friday."

***

"What the hell is the matter with you?" Alex demanded
of CJ as she got out of the car. She was baffled. CJ had
been so happy on the phone when she called to say they'd

arrested Willoughby and Elliot and would be picking up Marina Nero. Since they'd gotten in the car, CJ wouldn't look at her, would hardly speak.

CJ slammed the passenger door, and the thud echoed through the underground parking garage, bouncing off the concrete support columns and the walls.

The garage was almost empty at this hour. The pillars and walls looked like Stonehenge, gray and solemn in the garish overhead lights. Alex got the sketches of the armed robbery suspects out, still watching CJ, trying to figure out what was wrong.

***

CJ didn't trust herself to say a word. The agony was too new, too raw. What was she going to say, anyway?

Why did you cheat on me?

Why did you throw away everything we had together?

Do you love her?

Alex persisting, began again with, "CJ, for God's sake, talk to—"

Across the garage, they heard someone yell, "Give me your purse, bitch!"

CJ saw them: two men, hooded sweatshirts pulled over their heads, confronting a woman next to a car. One of the men was pointing a handgun at her.

Alex's view was blocked by the concrete pillar in front of them, but she froze at the words and looked across the car at CJ.

Alex whispered, "Wait till they move away from her."

But the victim was resisting. CJ could see her trying to pull away. The man with the handgun raised his arm, preparing to strike her. Or shoot her.

"Alex!" CJ yelled, pulling her weapon free. "Police officers! Freeze!" she shouted.

She was running toward them, gun up and ready, trying to scare them away from the victim.

CJ saw the man with the handgun shove the victim away, then look in their direction.

The second man was raising something he held in his arms and CJ remembered what Alex had told her: shotgun.

"Alex, get down!" she screamed.

She dove for the concrete pillar.

An explosion.

The blast filled the garage like a sonic boom, and the windshield of the SUV shattered with a deafening crash.

CJ looked anxiously under the vehicle to see Alex on the ground on the other side of their car.

"Alex!" she yelled, frantic.

Her partner gasped, "I'm okay. You?"

"Yeah. Go, I'll cover."

CJ leaned carefully around the pillar, her gun up, as Alex made a dash to join her.

Alex yelled, "Police officers! Put your weapons down!"

CJ couldn't see the two men, or the woman.

They waited, backs to the concrete column, hoping the angle put the barrier between them and the shooters. They heard nothing.

"Damn it!" Alex spat.

"Did you see where they went?" CJ had her Sig Sauer in her left hand, safety off, barrel pointed to the ground.

Alex shook her head. "But I'm pretty sure we're between them and the outside exit."

CJ calculated the angle of the shots and said, "I think you're right." She slid her cell phone out and shook her head. No reception, not surprising since they were a couple of stories under a building. Maybe someone had heard the shotgun blast.

Alex took a deep breath and said, "Active shooters, CJ. You know we have to go after them."

"I know."

Alex said, with quiet intensity, "Here's the plan. I'm going to try to get behind them, between them and the stairs. I'm going counterclockwise. Stay put and keep them off me, and we'll pin them."

"Why are you the one going?" she hissed, angry that Alex was deliberately choosing the more dangerous job for herself.

She hated Alex, and she loved her. How could she feel both, so strongly, at the same moment, in this moment?

Alex flashed her a look, blue-gray eyes sharp. "Because I'm a smaller target, I'm faster than you are, and you are a much better shot than I am."

"Alex," she began, anger beginning to overtake her again.

"And because if one of us is going to get hit," Alex said tightly, "I want it to be me. I'm not going to live through you getting shot again."

"That's the worst reason I've ever heard."

"Okay. Then try this. I outrank you, so do what I tell you."

CJ was heartsick, but said nothing.

Alex yelled to the victim, "Ma'am, wherever you are, stay down. Can you hear me? Stay down."

A woman's voice floated across the garage. "Yes. Yes, okay."

Alex took a deep breath. "On three," Alex said softly.

She nodded quickly three times, giving CJ no chance to say anything: to tell her to be careful, to tell her goodbye, to tell her that she hated her, to tell her that she still loved her. Alex half ran, half dove for the next pillar over.

CJ rolled smoothly, bringing her gun to the firing position and bracing against the pillar. She searched for any movement.

When she saw the barrel of the shotgun coming up across a car hood yards away, she squeezed off four shots in rapid succession. Her bullets sang off the car he was hiding behind, and the shotgun barrel rapidly disappeared.

She rolled back behind the pillar and looked across her left shoulder at Alex, safely behind the next support. Alex caught her breath a moment, then nodded sharply to CJ once again.

As Alex took off, CJ moved back to the side of the concrete column, her concentration locked on the previous spot where the shooter had appeared. For an instant, she saw nothing, then saw heard a blast erupt from farther to her right, closer to Alex's position.

She couldn't see him. A little panicked, she shifted away from her protective barrier until she could spot him, crouching behind another car. Furious that she'd let him get a shot off at Alex, she peppered his position with another four shots until he retreated.

She slid back behind her barrier and immediately turned her head again, seeking Alex.

Her partner was crouched three pillars away, and CJ could see she was breathing hard. But she looked back at CJ and nodded.

She'd been holding her own breath. The next move would take Alex out of her line of sight. They wouldn't be able to talk without giving away Alex's location.

No time to say anything anyway. Alex rose to a running position, still catching her breath.

Damn you, Irish, CJ cursed silently. If you get yourself killed...

She took a deep breath to steady her hands. Eight bullets fired—that left her five in the Sig Sauer's magazine.

She carried one spare magazine, and had a backup .38 with six bullets if things got that far.

Alex gave her the sharp nod again, and CJ moved back into firing position.

Where is the second man? CJ asked herself a little frantically, and the answer came in the next moment.

From off to her left, three bullets crashed into the pillar just above and in front of her. A chip flew from the concrete and clipped her cheek.

CJ flinched, ducked, and dove to her left just as another shotgun blast tore into the pillar she'd just been beside.

CJ scrambled frantically, trying to find a safe haven, her mind busy with the vaguely comforting thought: At least they're shooting at me and not her.

She got between two cars, trying to figure out their positions. The second shooter, somewhere to her left, fired in front of her, and she couldn't tell if he was aiming at Alex or trying to hit her.

Either way, it gave her some idea of his position. She put a shot in his general direction and was rewarded with a loud "Motherfucker!"

She didn't know if she'd hit him or not, but at least he wasn't shooting any more for the moment. For good measure she pivoted and fired twice in the general direction of the shotgun, then moved before they could get a clear fix on her.

She made it to a pillar one over from her original spot, gasping by the time she'd made it. I'm getting too old for this.

Two bullets left in this clip. She had to tell Alex where they were, even when it meant revealing her own position.

Assuming Alex was still in the fight. Don't think about that.

She tried to plan her next move. Alex was moving counterclockwise, so CJ figured she should go the other way. Once she called out, she had to be ready to move.

CJ felt for her spare magazine, then mentally measured the distance to her next position. She took a deep breath and yelled, "Alex! Second shooter is ten o'clock from me!"

Amid another shotgun blast and bullets flying, she rolled and scrambled to a column in the other direction. When she had safely reached the barrier, she put one bullet apiece toward the shotgun and the pistol.

She ejected the empty magazine and slammed the spare in, then waited. Bad news was the pistol shooter was still active. Good news was that she herself was still alive, unhurt.

She wished to God she knew if Alex was all right. A single bead of blood eased down her cheek, like a teardrop. She brushed it away and tried to listen, as if she could hear Alex's heartbeat somehow, beyond her own racing pulse in her ears.

After a moment, she heard muttered curses, somewhere off to her left, the guy with the handgun. Had she hit him?

As far as she could tell, he hadn't moved. Maybe he couldn't move?

Both shooters were focused on her. Alex hadn't fired a shot yet. If they couldn't tell where Alex was, then they could only come after her. The knowledge comforted her a little.

CJ went to one knee, and carefully scanned under the cars around her. She spotted him, the second shooter, or his legs, at least.

Could she get behind him? Not without exposing herself if he was mobile.

Carefully, CJ lowered herself onto her stomach, bracing her gun with both hands. If the shotgun was coming toward her, she was in an incredibly vulnerable position, but she thought she had to take the chance.

Forcing herself to focus on the shot she had, she tried not to feel the hairs on the back of her neck rising.

She aimed, and pulled the trigger twice.

The screams told her she'd hit him. The legs lurched away, out of her sight, and she rolled smoothly back to her feet. She sprinted in a circle away from him, until she judged she was behind him.

A bullet shattered a passenger window in front of her. She shifted quickly to the other side of the car, then brought both arms across the hood, her gun aimed at him.

"Police!" she yelled at him. "Drop it now!"

He was sprawled on the cement floor, gun in hand, head turned away, still looking for her. She saw him freeze at the sound of her voice.

CJ saw the instant of indecision as he weighed his chances of turning to fire at her. He was bleeding heavily just above one knee, so there was no chance he would be able to run.

If he moves his hand, I'm going to blow him away.

He turned his head to look at her. All he saw was the barrel of her weapon. His gun hand seemed paralyzed.

"Put the gun on the ground, now!" she barked.

He carefully laid the gun down and put his hands in the air.

She stood and began to come around the front of the car, crouched down. "If you move," she warned him, "I will kill you."

He stopped breathing very well. She cuffed him, frisked him, picked up his gun, and then risked calling out, "Alex!"

There was a lifetime of silence before she heard, "CJ. You're all right?"

Sick with relief, she called back, "Guy with the handgun in custody."

She heard another shotgun blast, then the sound of a heavy door slamming shut.

"Alex!" she screamed, panicked.

"He's in the stairwell!" Alex yelled at her. "Stay there, I'm going after him!"

CJ stared down at her suspect. He wasn't armed, and he wasn't going very far, not handcuffed and with a bullet wound. It was a violation of procedure to leave him, and she just didn't care.

She was not going to let Alex go alone after a man with a shotgun. She sprinted to the stairwell doorway, dodging the few vehicles, catching up with Alex just as she had her hand on the doorknob.

Alex snarled at her, "What the hell are you doing?"

"I am going with you," she said. "Don't you dare argue with me."

"CJ," Alex began harshly.

"Alex, shut the fuck up and open the damn door," CJ hissed. "I'm covering you."

In the dim fluorescent lights of the garage, she saw the fire behind Alex's blue eyes. She said nothing except, "Stand over there."

CJ took position to the right side of the door as Alex eased it open from the other. Alex stepped into the doorway, gun up, and then said, "Clear."

She ran up the first half flight of stairs to the landing and pivoted, gun pointed upward. "Go," she said, and CJ joined her on the landing.

"Ready," CJ said, her turn to point her weapon upward as Alex sprinted up the next half flight. Then Alex covered CJ as she went up the stairs.

Alex gingerly tested the doorway marked P1. "Locked from the other side," she muttered. "The stairwell must be exit only."

CJ met her look. "Limits his options. How tall is this building?"

"Eight stories, I think."

"Okay. Let's go."

"CJ, listen to me—" Alex tried one last time.

"Alex, we're not talking. Go."

They went up the stairwell, pausing at every landing to listen and cover their ascent. On the second-floor landing, they found a pair of boots.

Alex stepped carefully around them and said, "That explains why we haven't heard the son of a bitch."

"He's either got to come down or go to the roof, if that door's unlocked," CJ thought out loud. Every door they'd tried so far had been locked. "Does your cell phone work yet?"

Alex flipped it open and made a face. "No such luck. Ready?"

"Yes. Go."

They got to the next-to-last landing. CJ tried to get her breath back, tried to slow her pounding heart.

Alex glanced at her. "You all right, CJ?"

Aside from the deadly danger and a shattered heart, I'm fine.

"Sure," she answered. She started up the next flight.

Then there was a sudden shadow moving above her. Alex screamed, "Down!"

CJ dropped, flattening against the concrete steps as an ear-splitting blast tore into the wall just over her head. Alex fired twice at the shadow.

An instant later there was the sound of another door slamming shut.

Alex got to CJ, one hand on CJ's back, the other hand still holding her gun upward.

"Are you hit?" she demanded breathlessly.

"Okay," CJ murmured. "I'm okay. Holy God."

CJ tried to find enough air. Her ears were ringing from the gunshots in the closed area of the stairwell.

"He's on the roof, I think," CJ finally said.

"Fine," Alex said, grimly. "There's nowhere for him to go. There's no building taller than three stories for half a mile, and I don't remember an exterior fire escape he can access from here. Let's go get the bastard."

There was no point in trying to talk her into just guarding the roof door until they could get help. CJ said, "Yes, okay. But once you get a signal, for the love of God call for backup, will you?"

Alex stared at her. "Are you sure you're all right?" she demanded again.

I'm not. I'll never be all right again. "Let's just go," CJ said tersely.

Alex tested the doorknob and it turned gently in her hand. CJ said, "My turn to go first. Open it and I'll dive right, you go left."

"All right," Alex conceded with ill-grace, "but stay down, for God's sake."

"You, too. Go…now!"

Alex jerked open the door and CJ got into the darkness as quickly as she could. As long as they were silhouetted against the bright light from the stairwell, they made excellent targets. She felt, rather than saw, Alex dive after her, scrambling away to the other side. There was no shotgun blast this time.

CJ tried to get her night vision. There were some lights from a nearby store parking lot, but the roof seemed bathed in moonlight rather than totally dark. CJ's gaze swept the roof. Where could he be?

There was the stairwell entrance behind her. To her right was some kind of ventilation unit, and what looked and sounded like an air-conditioning unit in front of her. She turned her head, tried to see Alex.

Alex silently pointed to herself and then to the A/C unit. CJ nodded, pointed to her own chest and then to the ventilation vent. They circled their targets separately.

They timed it perfectly, rounding their targets at almost exactly the same moment.

For an instant there was nothing to see, then CJ felt the brutal explosion of weight against her upper back.

He came down on top of her from his perch on the ventilation unit, slamming the barrels of the shotgun into her. As she went down, CJ thought: He must be out of shells. At least I hope he is.

She was rolling with him, trying to free her gun hand while trying to grasp the shotgun, desperate to keep him from hitting her again.

Suddenly he stopped moving. Above her, she heard Alex snarl, "If you move an inch, I'm going to blow your brains out!"

CJ slid out from under him, grabbing the shotgun away. Alex had the barrel of her Glock against his head and even in the dim light, she could see the whites of the man's eyes, his body rigid with terror.

CJ aimed her gun at him and said to Alex, "My cuffs are busy downstairs. He's all yours."

Alex handcuffed him and hauled him to his feet. "Are you hurt?" she demanded of CJ.

CJ put her gun away. It felt as if she'd been holding it for hours. "Just bruised," she answered. And destroyed.

***

It was almost one in the morning before CJ unlocked the front door of the condo. Alex closed it behind them.

CJ tossed her keys on the table in the entry hall and turned back.

She had to speak to Alex now, finish this. "Alex," she began. "We have to talk."

"No," Alex said hoarsely. "We'll talk about whatever it is later. Or tomorrow. Not now."

She lifted a hand to CJ's face. Her thumb carefully stroked the bandage over the tiny wound on CJ's cheek. CJ closed her eyes briefly against the touch, then said, "I have to know before—"

"No," Alex said again, fiercely. "There's nothing you need to know that you don't know already."

She lifted her lips to CJ and kissed her, once, twice. CJ kicked off her shoes, as she always did, to lessen the height difference between them, then opened her mouth to the kiss.

She pulled away. She stared at Alex in the dark hallway. They were standing as they had on the night they had first kissed, in the first moment of desire fulfilled.

CJ remembered every feeling she had had at that moment. Time had not dimmed her memory of the first taste of Alex on her lips, the feel of Alex in her arms.

But there were cracks in the mirror of her memory, flaws she wondered if she should have seen before.

"I have to know," CJ whispered. "I have to know…"

She was afraid Alex coming to her was only a reaction from the shooting in the garage. The aftereffect from the surge of adrenaline could mimic desire, she knew, and there was so much unresolved between them. She couldn't be with Alex, not anymore.

But Alex wanted to prove that they were alive, coming down from the fear she'd had, the fear of dying, and the greater fear from the terrible moment when she thought she was going to have to watch CJ dying in front of her. Again.

Alex said in a low, harsh voice, "You already know everything. I love you. I need you."

She took CJ by the shoulders and kissed her again, more urgently than before. CJ was still afraid, but she could not resist Alex wanting her.

Alex pushed CJ's coat off her arms and it dropped to the floor with a soft whoosh. The heat from Alex's hands felt like fire through the fabric of CJ's blouse.

They kissed each other into the living room. Alex lost her own coat, pulled off her sweater. She was unbuttoning CJ's blouse as they stumbled into the bedroom, and she threw the blouse down. She slipped one hand inside CJ's bra, cupping her breast, feeling the nipple respond instantly, stiffening against her fingers.

CJ groaned. They fell onto the bed together, side by side, tugging at their remaining clothes as they continued their frantic kissing. CJ's skin was burning where Alex was stroking her, caressing her. CJ was beyond caring what this meant between them.

CJ turned, pushed Alex down, palms on her shoulders. She rose above her, stared down into Alex's face, and saw nothing in her but need. Me, CJ thought desperately. She wants me.

She got one leg between Alex's thighs, then lowered herself into the kiss. Alex moved upward to meet her, hands gripping her back.

CJ kissed her hard, tongue probing, reaching down with her fingers to find the soft skin of breasts, filling her hands. Alex moaned, and murmured, "Yes, sweetheart, yes."

CJ kissed her neck, then got her mouth on one hard nipple, pulling it into her mouth. Alex pushed against her, fingers digging into the muscles of CJ's bare shoulders. CJ felt a surge of pleasure and satisfaction, that she could bring Alex from calm control to this frantic wanting.

She tasted, she nuzzled, she suckled. Then, returning to Alex's mouth, she held her wrists down, kissed her hungrily again and again, until Alex gasped, "CJ, please, I need…I need…"

Her hips were already moving hard against CJ's leg. CJ released her hands and slid down her body. Alex was so wet. CJ felt another flutter of pleasure, stroking Alex, caressing soft petals of flesh. She wants me.

As she brought her lips where she wanted them to be, she heard Alex groan above her. CJ knew how to make it last, caressing her softly with her tongue, but Alex didn't let her linger. Alex gripped CJ's head firmly and thrust her hips upward to meet her mouth.

"Now, sweetheart, harder. Harder!" Alex pleaded.

When Alex came against her mouth, CJ felt the spasms twitching in her own body.

She returned to Alex's side, holding her, feeling her breathe. I can make her feel this way. She loves me, she wants me.

After a few minutes, Alex turned and got her arms around CJ, shifting her weight into her, CJ rolling onto her back. CJ was throbbing with her need to be touched, to be taken by Alex, to know that Alex still wanted to make love to her. She laced her fingers into dark hair and pulled Alex to her, her kisses desperate. She pushed away the thought that Alex had been unfaithful, that Alex had had her lips on another mouth, her arms around another woman.

CJ knew she shouldn't forgive Alex, couldn't forgive her. She could not live her life with someone she couldn't trust. Yet she had to have Alex, kissing her, taking her away from fear with her hands and her body.

It was wrong. Alex had hurt her beyond pain, yet nothing but Alex loving her could make the pain go away, if only for a little while.

She pushed Alex's head to her breast, and Alex covered her with wet kisses. It was wrong to need someone like this, to need one person so much. "Go inside me," she heard herself begging Alex.

Alex entered her and CJ felt her world shift back into place with every thrust. She loves me, she loves me, she loves only me…

She shattered in Alex's arms, breaking into a hundred pieces. Then Alex embraced her, putting each piece back again with gentle strokes, soft kisses, words of love murmured low into her ear.

CJ realized she would forgive Alex. If she couldn't, she would lose what still was left between them forever. But could she stay with Alex, wondering if she could be trusted?

Yes. Not because she wanted to, but because she had no choice. She needed Alex, loved her too much to give her up.

At any price.

CJ turned her head into her pillow, so that Alex couldn't see how much she wanted to weep at her weakness, and her pain.

CHAPTER TEN: WEDNESDAY

CJ was sitting at her desk, reading a new complaint filed against a patrol officer by a citizen who'd been stopped for speeding. The citizen claimed the officer had used foul and abusive language.

Not an uncommon complaint, CJ thought, sighing, and it was usually unfounded. This time, though, she knew the officer in question had previously been disciplined for the same type of allegation and CJ wondered what it would take for Robards to take the man off patrol duty.

There were two other new complaints waiting. Cases had piled up since she'd been concentrating on the Andersen case, and it was going to take a while to dig out.

She realized that she was still staring at the file but was no longer reading it. Andersen. The case had been cleared by the arrests of Willoughby, Elliot, Carlson and Marina Nero. But that meant Chris Andersen was back on duty one floor above her, in the Investigations Division, sitting twenty feet from Alex.

CJ closed her eyes, but the picture of Alex in Chris Andersen's arms wouldn't go away. Would it ever?

What was she going to do? she asked herself for the hundredth time. Confront Chris, warn her off? It was a ludicrous idea, but CJ found herself still considering whether it would work.

It wouldn't work, and she knew why. She and Alex were together because they wanted to be. If Alex didn't want her anymore, nothing she could say to Chris could change that.

The knife twisted in her chest again. Alex did want her, hadn't last night proved anything? Alex loved her, she knew it. Whatever was going on with Chris wasn't serious, it couldn't be.

She thrust both hands into her hair. Alex was unfaithful to her, wasn't that all that mattered? If she had one bit of self-respect, she'd be upstairs, telling Alex to pack up and move out.

It had been easier with Laurel, all those years ago. It had hurt like hell, but the choices were clear, sharp.

You want to be with someone else? Fine, go. Why couldn't she say that to Alex? She knew the answer to that, too.

A timid knock on her open door prompted her to lift her head. "Yes, what?"

Elizabeth Rivera stood there, hovering uncertainly. "I'm sorry, Inspector. This is a bad time."

Oh, God, yes. It's a bad time. "It's all right," she managed. "Come in."

Elizabeth carefully sidestepped the haphazard piles of paper and said, "I just wanted to thank you. For everything."

CJ tried to focus on her. "Elizabeth. You can sit down."

"No, I just stopped by to tell you…I'm resigning. I don't think I can work here anymore, not after what I did."

CJ was going to say something soothing and try to talk her out of it, but changed her mind. It was probably for the best, and she respected Elizabeth for making the hard choice. I wish I could.

CJ said, "You're probably making a good decision. What are you going to do?"

"First, get another job, somewhere. Then I'm going to college. I've been meaning to do that anyway, I just didn't get around to applying for this semester. I'll start in January."

"What are you thinking about?"

"Nursing, I think. I liked volunteering back home, at the hospital."

"You'll probably be good at it," CJ said sincerely. "If you need a personal reference while you're trying to get work, please use me. I'll be happy to vouch for you."

To her surprise, Elizabeth approached her around the desk and said, "You've been really, really wonderful to me. I want you to know that I'm going to try very hard to, um, just be myself." She blushed a little, but leaned down and gave CJ a hug.

"Thank you," she whispered again in CJ's ear.

CJ found herself a little teary. "You keep in touch now, all right? And Elizabeth?"

"Yes?"

"You're welcome."

***

Chris looked skeptically down at her desk. "What's this?" she asked suspiciously.

Morelli grinned at her from his desk across from her. "That, Hans, is a homemade blueberry muffin made by my lovely wife."

Chris lifted an eyebrow. "And why," she asked, "would Jennifer make me a muffin?"

His grin broadened. "Because she's very, very glad I've got a partner again and she's hoping I'll actually start working normal hours again."

"Hmm." Chris set down her coffee and took a tentative bite. "Holy shit," she murmured. It was still warm, bursting with fresh, tart berries and sweet, moist cake.

"Seriously, is that not, like, as good as sex?"

She munched happily and mumbled through her chewing, "Hey, it's good, Frank, but I'm not going that far. Maybe it's as good as straight sex, but it's not as good as a woman who's..."

He lifted his hands to his ears. "Oh, God, stop. Do not even think about going there."

"Hey, you brought it up. Aren't partners supposed to talk about all that shit, or haven't we been partners long enough yet?"

"We will never be partners long enough to discuss our sex lives. Period."

She'd missed him, she thought, surprised. He was really a good guy, and the muffin was to die for. *I wonder if Elizabeth can cook.* Then she wondered how that random thought had gotten into her head.

"Frank, can I ask you a question?" she said suddenly.

"Sure, as long as it's not about sex."

"It's not. Well, not really."

"What's the question?" he asked warily.

"Why are you cool with me being gay? I'd have figured a guy like you, nice altar boy type and all, wouldn't be happy about it."

He looked as though the question surprised him. When Chris had told him that first day with him, she'd been almost defiant. This time she felt almost relaxed, genuinely curious.

"Look," he said, "if I did everything those guys in Rome told me I should do, I would never have divorced my first wife who was drinking and sleeping around on me. And I would never be married to Jennifer, have two great kids. And I wouldn't use a condom, either. So just because I believe in God, and go to Mass, doesn't mean I think they're right about everything. I may not be the brightest guy in the room, but I know love when I see it, and you're not gonna convince me God doesn't approve of people loving each other."

He shot a significant look toward the captain's office and Chris swallowed a bite of muffin that threatened to lodge in her throat.

She was licking the last crumbs from her fingertips when Alex approached them and said, "Welcome back, Detective. You two come into the office a second, will you?"

Chris followed Morelli, wondering how Alex would treat her this morning. At least she's not ignoring me entirely.

Alex handed Morelli a case file. "I'll need for you to finish up the paperwork on the parking garage robberies."

"What?" Chris said, surprised. "You've been holding out on me, Morelli?"

"I'm as out of the loop as you are," he exclaimed. "Cap, what's happening?"

"I cleared the case last night. Arrested both perps, during the commission, actually."

"You showed up while they were sticking somebody up?" Chris demanded incredulously.

Alex laughed grimly, and Chris relaxed a little. She's not going to be a bitch about yesterday, looks like. "Yes, perfect timing. The victim is fine, but we'll need a full statement from her, and an identification of our perps from the other victims."

"Okay," Morelli said. "Our suspects are in county?"

"One's in detention, the other one's in the hospital recovering from a gunshot wound."

"Jesus!" Morelli exclaimed. "You hadda shoot the guy?"

"They were shooting at us first," Alex responded calmly. "Fortunately, I was on my way home and had my favorite partner with me at the time. And I didn't shoot him. CJ did."

Frank said, smiling, "Way to go, Inspector St. Clair. Guess IA is good for something after all."

Of course, Chris thought. The Holy Goddess of all things Wonderful. Fucking CJ St. Clair, again.

But there was something in Alex's voice, something in her eyes. What was it? Pride, relief, remnants of fear? Chris saw it, whatever it was, and surrendered. Alex hadn't been lying to her. St. Clair really was all she wanted, all she needed. Chris found that she could let go of the thought of being with Alex, without pain, only a hint of regret.

Alex was still telling Morelli what happened, then he said, smiling, "Nice job, Cap. Any other cases you want to clear for us, you just let us know."

Alex laughed again. Morelli left with the file, and Chris was on his heels when Alex said softly, "Chris, stay for a minute."

Chris turned around. Here it comes. She tried to steel herself. Alex said gently, "Are you all right?"

"Me? Fine. Great. Super. Back at work. Anything else you need to know?"

Alex sat back in her chair and said, "No, but there are two things you need to know from me. First, last night is not an issue. You do your job, I'll do mine, nothing else. Clear?"

"Very clear, Captain," Chris said stiffly. "You are not interested. It's done."

"Good. I'm never going to hold anything against you, I want you to know that. It won't be a problem for you, professionally."

Chris relaxed a little. "I appreciate that, Captain."

Alex leaned forward, her gaze pinning Chris to the spot. "I mean that. I also mean this. If you ever say a word or do anything, anything, to hurt CJ, I will not forgive you for it. Are you very clear about that?"

Chris blinked. She was indeed very clear. "I wouldn't do that, Captain," she said softly.

"That," Alex said, "was the right answer. Don't forget."

"I won't, believe me."

***

Alex watched Chris Andersen return to her desk. She sat back in her chair in satisfaction.

It had been a rough couple of weeks, but it was over now. Last night, with CJ in bed, had mended everything for her.

Nothing healed her like being with CJ. Everything was all right now.

CHAPTER ELEVEN: FRIDAY/ SATURDAY

When the knock sounded on her door, Elizabeth took a deep breath, trying to steady her hands. She didn't want Chris to think she was some kind of scared teenager, going out on her first date.

But it was her first date with someone she actually wanted to go out with, and her nerves were getting the best of her. It was worse than the terrifying week she'd had, first talking to Lieutenant St. Clair, then having to face the district attorney, and then, most frightening of all, having to meet with Pastor Willoughby.

Still, the lieutenant had told her she'd done well, and she didn't have to be afraid of going to jail. The DA would let her testify, and wouldn't prosecute her. The relief had been overwhelming. It was finally over, with Willoughby and the rest in custody.

Now she was so worried, afraid that Chris was taking advantage of the situation. Or that Chris just wouldn't like her.

The knock sounded again, and she forced herself to open the door, even managing a shy smile.

"Hi," Chris said, smiling and relaxed. "I was afraid there for a minute you were going to back out on me."

"Did you want me to?" Elizabeth asked tentatively.

"Hey, don't be nervous," she said, trying to sound reassuring. "We're just going to dinner, okay? We'll talk about stuff, and then I'll bring you home, and then I'll go home. Don't worry, I promised to behave."

She gave what looked like a reassuring smile. Elizabeth brushed her hands down her modest dress, one that covered her knees. Chris was so cool, she thought, so relaxed.

Chris helped her with her coat and said, "You look nice."

Elizabeth looked up and said, "I'm glad you like it. I changed outfits four times."

Chris laughed. "Next time, don't worry about it. You'll be fine in anything. You notice I really didn't go overboard."

She gestured at her dark wash jeans and blue turtleneck. Elizabeth hardly noticed, her mind busy with the implied promise: Next time.

Chris walked her downstairs, and Elizabeth saw the bright red sports car under the parking lot light. She exclaimed, "What a beautiful car!"

Chris grinned. "See, you're already getting on my good side. This is my baby."

On the drive to the restaurant, Chris prattled on happily about the Mustang, Elizabeth listening as if she actually cared about turbocharged engines and horsepower.

Finally Chris said, "Okay, I think you've suffered enough car talk. Your turn."

Elizabeth's nervousness returned. "I don't really know what you want to know," she began.

Chris parked the car and came around to help her out. Elizabeth had been on a few dates in high school, with boys of course, and had never been treated so well. "Let's start with something easy," Chris said. "Elizabeth's a great name, but it's got like a million nicknames. Eliza, Liz, Betty…help me out. What do you like to be called?"

The shy smile returned. "Beth," she said. "My friends call me Beth."

"Beth it is, then," Chris said easily.

***

When CJ awoke, she was holding Alex. She breathed in the warm nighttime scent of Alex, then lifted her head to look at the clock across the bed on the far nightstand.

Three eleven a.m. She'd been asleep for less than three hours. She lay still in the darkness, trying to go back to sleep, trying to forget about the pain in her chest. Unwillingly, she thought again about Alex and Chris Andersen until she could hardly breathe.

She could not bear this. She wasn't strong enough to leave, she wasn't strong enough to stay. It was impossible.

Carefully she managed to slip out of bed without waking Alex, who was heavily asleep. Alex turned and sighed deeply, then CJ heard her breathing become even again.

CJ crept out of the bedroom, gathering clothes as she went. She closed their bedroom door carefully, padded silently away.

***

Alex woke at her usual time, a little after six, without the aid of the alarm. She glanced at the clock, then closed her eyes again. It was Saturday, and she didn't have to get up yet.

She could not remember a more exhausting week in her life. The fight with CJ, the elation of the Nero case getting resolved, the painful confrontation with Chris in her office, then the sheer terror of the minutes in the parking garage.

Alex sensed something was wrong still, and she couldn't get CJ to talk to her. She had to understand whatever it was, she decided, and rolled over to seek out CJ's body in the bed, ready to surrender her morning run for snuggling and a conversation, followed by what she hoped would be a delightful session of slow, weekend morning lovemaking.

But CJ wasn't there. The sheets were cold, her pillow still dented from where her head had been.

Bathroom, Alex thought, still drowsy. She was still amazed at how much she wanted her partner, how good and right it felt being with her. The mystery of their attraction was one Alex couldn't solve, and she'd given up trying, satisfied to simply appreciate it.

After a couple of minutes she called out, "Sweetheart, you okay?"

No response. More sharply, Alex said, "CJ?" She got up. As she lifted the sheets, she could still smell the scent that the two of them made, together. She went into their bathroom. It was cold and empty in the gray light.

Alex frowned, worried. Pulling on sweatshirt and jeans, she went to the door, wondering why it was closed.

She found CJ sitting on the couch in the living room, with no lights on, doing nothing but staring at the wall. Dim predawn light showed through the blinds, striping the floor in pencil thin grays. "Hey. What are you doing in here? Are you all right?"

CJ lifted her eyes to Alex's face and Alex felt her heart jump painfully.

"My God, what is it?" Alex demanded.

She had not truly seen misery before. CJ said dully, "I thought I could do it, but I can't."

"Do what? What is going on?"

"I thought I could leave you, but I can't."

Alex's mouth went dry, her mind spinning with disbelief. "Leave me? What in God's name are you talking about?"

CJ stood and began to pace in her bare feet. "I wasn't going to ask you," she said. "I didn't want to know, but I have to know. Tell me why, Alex."

"Why what?" Alex was half-baffled, half-frightened. She'd never seen CJ like this before.

Her voice shaking, CJ demanded, "Tell me why you slept with her."

"Why I—" Alex stopped, a horrifying glimmer beginning to reveal itself.

"I want to know. Tell me. Did you just want to see what it would be like with another woman? Or is it me, is this supposed to be my fault somehow?"

Her voice started to rise as she continued, "Are you just incapable of being faithful, Alex? Or are you going to tell me you're in love with her?"

Alex stared at CJ, her expression tense. "Who are you talking about?" Her stomach was already knotted with the answer.

"Who? Are you fucking more than one other woman?" CJ was yelling at her. "Chris Andersen! Don't deny it! Bad enough you cheated on me, for God's sake don't lie about it!"

Alex was stunned. "CJ, sweetheart, listen to me. I would never do that to you, to us."

Guilt nipped at her with sharp teeth. You kissed her, her conscience reminded her.

CJ had gone from pain to anger. She was furious, angrier than Alex had ever seen her. But beneath the anger, Alex saw her hurt and fear.

"I'm not an idiot, Alex! I saw you at lunch with her, at the deli. I saw how she looked at you. I know she spent the night with you at Nicole's. Don't fucking lie to me, God damn it!"

Alex was frightened. CJ really believed that she had been unfaithful. She knew CJ would never stay with her if she thought she had cheated, never.

Trying to stay calm, Alex said, "I'm not lying to you. I didn't sleep with her. I wouldn't do that."

CJ just stared at her, her body coiled in fury, fists clenched, green eyes blazing. Her cheeks were stained bright red, and she was breathing hard. Alex thought, with a jolt, how much anger and arousal looked alike.

Alex took a deep breath, trying to gather herself, terrified of saying the wrong thing. If she couldn't fix this, make CJ believe her, if she couldn't make this right...she couldn't bear to think about what would happen.

"Sweetheart, please listen to me," she pleaded. "Chris was frightened, and alone, and she thought she wanted me, that's all. She was flirting with me at the deli, and I should have stopped it. She came to the house Saturday night. She was upset. I gave her a drink, she gave me her car keys and I told her to sleep on the couch. Why were you there? Were you checking up on me, or something?"

Alex tried not to make the question sound like a challenge, but CJ snapped, "If I had been, it sounds like I had a good reason. The funny thing is I wanted to surprise you, tell you I was sorry about...everything that had been happening. When I saw her car, I understood what was happening, but I didn't believe it. I didn't believe you would..."

She moved her arm up, then jerked it down again. Alex saw that CJ was trying not to slap her. Alex almost wished she would hit her, it would have been easier to bear than the slashing words.

"I didn't sleep with her," Alex repeated desperately.

CJ exploded again. "Shut up! I don't believe you! I saw you, in your office with her! You had your arms around her. You were kissing her!"

Oh, God, Alex thought, in terror. She's really going to leave me. "CJ, please! I need to tell you what happened." To her own ears she sounded pathetic, pleading.

She didn't care how it sounded. There was nothing she wouldn't say, nothing she wouldn't do, to keep CJ from leaving.

CJ hissed, "I don't want to hear about it! I don't want to hear about what you did with another woman, what it meant to you or what it didn't mean. I don't care. I don't care whether you love her or not!"

If CJ left her, she knew she would have nothing left. If CJ walked out the door, she would take everything with her. Everything.

Oh, God, oh, God.

***

"I don't care whether you love her or not!"

CJ knew when she said it that she was lying to Alex,

lying to herself. She still cared, desperately, whether Alex loved Chris.

And she hated herself for caring. The tears came, suddenly. She hated Alex, she couldn't trust her. Jealousy filled her with a bitter taste—and she still loved Alex.

It hadn't been like this before, with Laurel. That love had turned to hatred in an instant, the anger clean and sharp. This time the lines were blurred—love and hate, trust and doubt, need and want and revulsion jumbled against each other in her heart.

Alex said, in quiet, frantic desperation, "Please, CJ, for God's sake, listen to me! I never slept with Chris Andersen."

CJ wanted to believe her, but could not. "Fuck you, Alex! You threw everything we had away, you ruined everything!"

She had to escape, she couldn't stand here and look at Alex anymore. Alex grabbed her arm, to stop her, and CJ lost the control she'd been trying to exercise.

She wrenched away violently, and said, "If you touch me again, I swear I will—"

"Go ahead," Alex challenged her. "But you have to listen to me. I'm telling you the truth. She made a pass at me. She kissed me. I let her kiss me for a moment, I admit it. And then I told her to stop, that I loved you, that I would never cheat on you. That was all, I swear to you!"

CJ stared at her, not believing, wanting to believe. "But you wanted to," she said. "You wanted to be with her."

"No! No! I never wanted her, and I would never do that to us. For the love of God, CJ, please…"

Suddenly Alex went to her knees, as if her legs wouldn't hold her anymore.

Alex was weeping, crying like a child. CJ had never, ever seen her do that before. CJ dropped to her knees as well.

Alex choked out, "I swear I'm telling you the truth! Ask Chris. She was so angry with me for rejecting her. She'll tell you the truth. Please, CJ, please…"

CJ couldn't bear it anymore. Anger and jealousy poured out of her in a flood. She got her arms around Alex and said, "Hush, now. Enough."

Alex sagged helplessly into her shoulder, still crying. "Sweetheart, I swear. I wouldn't do that to you."

"Hush," CJ said again. "I believe you."

And she did, she realized. She didn't have to ask Chris about it. Alex wasn't lying to her. It was a momentary temptation, a ripple. It wasn't the end, after all.

The powerful tidal wave of relief almost made her dizzy. "I believe you," she said again, softly into Alex's hair.

Alex whispered, "Thank God. Thank God."

Now all she wanted was to touch Alex, to have Alex touch her. She dropped her head, seeking Alex's mouth. Alex lifted her face to meet the kiss, her lips hot and salty with the taste of tears.

Alex murmured, "Sweetheart, please. I only want you."

CJ lifted her up, kissing her again and again. They stumbled back to their bed with CJ's mouth still on Alex.

The tidal wave turned steaming hot, boiling in her veins. CJ reached around and pulled off Alex's sweatshirt. She got both velvet breasts in her hands, feeling the stiff swell of nipples against her palms. She kissed Alex fiercely, pushing her lips apart as she squeezed hard, and was rewarded with one of her favorite sounds: Alex groaning into her open mouth. The naked desire of the moan sent a jolt through CJ's core.

She got them both onto the top of the bed, side by side, then she pushed her hips forward into Alex. They rocked together in their own rhythm, the heat like a flash fire between them.

"It's only you," Alex whispered.

CJ wanted to weep. "I know. I know. Touch me."

Alex got a hand between them, tugging the zipper down on CJ's jeans. Then she was cupping CJ through silk panties. With her other hand Alex slipped under CJ's shirt, tugging at one taut nipple.

CJ caught her breath, then pushed into Alex's caress as she continued to knead and grip Alex's breasts with her hands. Alex pursued CJ with her mouth. Tongues met, slashing and rolling, hot and wet.

CJ couldn't bring herself to climb onto Alex, nor to pull Alex onto her. She wanted this, the frenzied caressing while being caressed, inflaming and satisfying desire at the same time.

CJ dragged her hand away from Alex's breast, worked down inside her jeans. Alex was ready for her, soaked, hot and swollen. Caught in her desire, Alex stopped moving her hands on CJ.

CJ whispered urgently, "No. Touch me."

Alex opened her eyes a moment. CJ saw a flutter of surprise in the dark blue-gray, then Alex shifted her hand down CJ's hip, pulling the silk away.

CJ shifted her hips to urge Alex inside, and Alex filled CJ with her hand, moving easily against the slick heat. CJ got her fingers on Alex's swollen center, and heard Alex gasp as she began to rub her. CJ caught one more flash of surprise, then Alex closed her eyes against the intensity of the sensation, still working her own hand rhythmically in and out.

CJ listened to the ragged breathing, sensed every movement, while losing herself in the exquisite joy that was Alex moving inside her. She closed her eyes, focused and so aroused she could hardly remember to exhale. The sense of Alex next to her, building to her climax, was overwhelming as CJ felt herself drawing closer to her own orgasm.

"Yes, yes!" CJ moaned.

She felt Alex's body begin to stiffen. CJ pushed inside at the last second, filling Alex at the moment of maximum pleasure. She was rewarded with the contraction of muscles around her fingers, as if Alex were completely enfolded around her hand.

And in that moment, CJ surged into her own climax, thrusting her hips feverishly against Alex.

As CJ arched backward, she could feel nothing in the universe except Alex's hand, still inside her as she came. She cried out, incoherently.

When she returned to herself, she was lying across the bed, Alex holding her, wrapped around her. "Oh, darlin'," was all CJ could murmur.

Alex whispered, "I didn't think…have you ever…"

"No." CJ realized she was crying a little. "Not like that."

"Christ, sweetheart," Alex said, her voice rough from the tears she had shed. "I'm so sorry. I hurt you so much."

"Don't. Don't," CJ begged her. "Just hold onto me, for God's sake."

***

Sometime later they threw the rest of their clothes onto the floor and got under the sheets. They lay together, without talking, for a long time.

Eventually, Alex murmured, "Will you be all right?"

CJ moved against Alex's body and said, "Yes."

"CJ," Alex stroked her fingers through red hair, "I have to ask you something."

After a moment, CJ said, "Okay."

"You thought, the night of the shooting…you thought I'd been unfaithful to you."

"Yes." It still hurt her to think about it.

"And when we got home, when we made love…you thought I had cheated on you."

"Yes," CJ said again, softly.

Alex seemed unable to comprehend it. "Why?" she demanded incredulously. "How could you do that? I know how you feel about it. You couldn't be with me if you thought I'd cheated."

CJ didn't say anything, her head against Alex's shoulder, her fingers tracing lightly against Alex's ribs.

"I tried not to," she finally admitted. "I hated you, Alex. I hated what you'd done to me, to us. But I was wrong, I'm the one who's sorry."

Alex said, "You had plenty of reason to think it, I understand that. What I don't understand is how you could make love with me when you hated me for what you thought I'd done."

Could she admit it, confess her greatest weakness? There was nothing left to hide from Alex. She would say the truth, even if it left her completely exposed, naked, vulnerable.

"It didn't matter, what I'd thought you'd done," CJ answered. "Even after that, I still loved you, Alex. I was going to have to try to forgive you. I was going to forgive you, somehow. Because…" She took a deep breath, then released it slowly.

Alex touched CJ's hair again, running the silky strands through her fingers.

"Because I still needed you," CJ got the words out. "I think you can do almost anything, and I'll still love you. I hated you, and I still loved you. I can't leave you, Alex. It's too late. I don't think I can live without you."

It broke her heart, and mended it in the same moment.

Alex pressed her lips onto CJ's forehead and said against her skin, "I swear to you. I won't cheat, and I won't leave. I swear to God, CJ. I swear to you. I will never let go."

EPILOGUE: FEBRUARY

"I bought you a Valentine's Day present," Elizabeth said shyly, sitting in Chris Andersen's living room. They sat on the sofa in the semidarkness, watching the lights of the cars going up Hampden Avenue. Chris had her arm around Elizabeth's shoulders, feeling the warmth of her against her side.

"I told you not to," Chris said severely, tempering her tone with a gentle kiss to Elizabeth's temple. "You need every dollar for school."

Elizabeth smiled. "It wasn't expensive. And the best part is, you get to unwrap it."

Chris looked puzzled. They'd agreed last week to save the Valentine's Day celebration for the next weekend, but Elizabeth had shown up unexpectedly an hour before. Elizabeth had never come to her apartment after class. They'd dated mostly on weekend nights, working around Chris's job as well as Elizabeth's need to study.

Dated. Chris still couldn't believe she was "dating" anyone. Dinner, movies, walks in the park, for God's sake. It was like some stupid lesbian romantic comedy, except there wasn't any action hotter than holding hands and the one goodnight kiss she was allowed per date.

But it wasn't frustrating, to Chris's amazement. She didn't want to rush Elizabeth into bed, didn't want to rush her into anything. To her deep astonishment, Chris had finally recognized what was going on, and she was still walking around in a daze.

She'd fallen in love with gentle brown eyes, a shy smile, a woman who thought, for whatever reason, that Chris Andersen was wonderful.

Elizabeth had shown up at her door empty-handed. Was the gift in her purse? Coat pocket?

"You didn't have to," Chris said, "but it's really sweet that you did."

"I hope you like it. I think you will." Elizabeth stood and offered Chris her hand. "Come with me."

Chris stood, more confused than ever. "Is it outside? I can get our coats…"

Elizabeth leaned in and kissed her softly. "No," she said quietly. "We're staying here. All night."

Suddenly Chris was having trouble breathing. "Beth, are you saying that you're ready for this?" She fought disbelief.

Elizabeth said solemnly, "I love you, Chris. You've been wonderful, waiting for me, making sure it was right. I know this will mean something special to you as well as me." Elizabeth kissed her again, and whispered, "Where's your bedroom?"

But once they got there, Chris couldn't get her hands to work. Her fingers kept slipping off the buttons of Elizabeth's blouse. Elizabeth smiled and said, "Here, I'll help you."

She carefully unbuttoned her blouse, and Chris pushed it off her shoulders. She was wearing a lacy black bra and Chris inhaled sharply at the first sight of her.

"It's your present," Elizabeth said, a little shyly. "Do you like it?"

Chris brushed her fingers against the satin and saw that her hands were trembling a little.

Her voice shaking, Chris said, "I've never actually done this before."

"What? Had a girl in your bedroom?" Elizabeth gently teased her.

Chris laughed shakily. "That, either. You know there have been other women. I've, um, dated a lot, but I never brought anyone here."

"Oh, sweetheart." Elizabeth kissed her again, softly, barely brushing her lips against Chris's mouth.

"What is it you've never done?" Elizabeth asked her, after a moment.

"I've never had sex with someone I…with someone I care about," Chris admitted. "I've never actually really cared about anybody."

Elizabeth wrapped her arms around Chris's neck. Chris could see tears pooling behind Elizabeth's eyes, happy tears, she hoped.

"I love you, too, Chris. We're going to make love, you and me, together."

Chris leaned into her, kissing her mouth, then her cheek. "Are we?" she whispered into her ear. She heard her own voice shaking.

"Yes," Elizabeth answered softly. "You know I've never been with anybody before, but I'm not afraid. I want this, with you."

Chris carefully finished undressing her, stroking the soft skin and murmuring, "You're beautiful, so beautiful."

Then Elizabeth said, "May I?" and pulled at Chris's sweater.

Chris froze for a moment.

"Please?" Elizabeth whispered.

Chris surrendered. She wanted things she'd never desired before, to feel herself exposed, open to another woman. She wanted to feel Elizabeth naked, skin against skin, everywhere.

She wanted Elizabeth to undress her, something Chris had never let anyone else do. Elizabeth sighed happily over the curves of her breasts, the long runner's legs, the flat stomach.

Chris was trembling by the time they made it into her bed. It had been so long, she was overwhelmed with need that was sparking between her legs like fire. But it was more than that, somehow. The power of her emotions shocked her.

Sex was...well, just sex. Sex felt good, and then it was over. This was something different.

Chris covered Elizabeth with her body, and kissed her as she'd dreamed of doing, hard and deep and as long as she could before finally reaching for air.

"Oh, Chris," Elizabeth gasped.

"Baby, I need you so much," Chris whispered into her ear.

Elizabeth wrapped her arms around Chris and said, "Please, oh, please."

Chris went as slowly as she could. Elizabeth denied Chris nothing, letting her touch her everywhere, touch every part of her.

When Chris took her breasts into her hands, Elizabeth gasped again and pushed against her. When Chris put her mouth against one hard nipple, Elizabeth moaned and said only, "Yes. Yes. Yes."

Chris was as gentle as she could manage to be under the pressure of the passion building inside her. She pressed the palm of her hand against Elizabeth's center, felt her stiffen under her.

Elizabeth came easily against her hand, groaning noises that might have been words, but all Chris could hear was the beating of her own heart in her ears. Chris had never felt so satisfied in her life, holding Elizabeth as she climaxed.

When she finally felt Elizabeth relax, she kissed her, then said, "You are wonderful. And I want to make you happy."

Chris shifted herself downward, settling between Elizabeth's legs. Chris kissed her thighs, then gently parted her swollen, wet lips before sliding her mouth onto Elizabeth.

Above her, Elizabeth inhaled sharply, then said, "Oh, Chris! Please, yes, oh…"

She climaxed again within moments, surging off the bed in a spasm of pleasure more overwhelming than any Chris had ever seen.

She held her as the orgasm subsided, then returned to Elizabeth's shoulder, stroking her gently down the valley between her breasts. "Are you okay?" she whispered.

Elizabeth opened her eyes. "I didn't know," she managed. "I didn't know how it would be."

"It was good?" Chris asked, kissing her neck.

"Oh, Chris, yes! Yes. Only…"

Chris propped herself up on one elbow. "What? What do you need?"

Elizabeth was having trouble finding words, but finally said, "You didn't…didn't go inside."

Chris smiled a little. "Not every woman likes that. Since you'd never had sex, I didn't want to hurt you."

The dark eyes went wide. "You won't hurt me," she murmured. "Please. I want to feel you."

Chris smiled and kissed her. "Anything you want, baby," she said. "Anything."

Much later, Chris lay quietly in her bed, her arms still securing a sleeping Elizabeth next to her. Her body was completely satisfied, but more than that, her mind was calm, her heart full, content. It occurred to her that she should call Alex Ryan tomorrow and thank her for her advice.

**

CJ complained mildly, "You know, most women get roses, candy, a candlelit dinner on Valentine's Day."

Alex paused with the spoon of chocolate chip cookie dough ice dream halfway to CJ's mouth. "We do have the candles," she pointed out. "And you got a Doris Day movie on television, and your favorite flavor."

"True," CJ admitted. "You are my favorite flavor."

"I meant the ice cream."

"I know what you meant. Am I getting that bite, or are you taking it?"

Alex surrendered the ice cream and watched CJ lick the spoon. "Gee, Red, could you try a little harder? You're not quite sexy enough."

CJ gave her the slow smile that turned Alex to mush. "I've already seduced you," CJ pointed out. "We're in bed together. You're naked. I'm…" she lifted the sheet to verify it, "yes, I'm naked, too. What else would you like?"

Alex gave her a full smile. "I can't think of anything in the universe I need, actually."

CJ looked at her. "Are you sure? We've never actually finished the 'do you want a child' discussion."

Alex scooped out the last of the ice cream and set the carton on the bedside table. She said, "Honestly, sweetheart, I never seriously thought about having a child of my own. I think…I think I could be happy if I never did, but I want you to be happy more than anything. And I could be very happy raising a child with you, CJ."

She looked so solemn, blue-gray eyes light in the dim light from the candles. CJ brought her hand to her face and caressed her cheek softly.

"I just want this to be a conscious choice, not one forced on us by passage of time."

Alex said, "We still have some time. Well, you do. I can see forty very clearly in my rearview mirror. You're still a kid."

CJ laughed. "How lucky I am to have fallen for an older woman. I actually think thirty-five is about as old for a first pregnancy as most doctors recommend, so we're about at the limit."

Still looking at her solemnly, Alex asked, "Do you really want to get pregnant?"

"Honestly?" CJ asked, matching her serious mood.

"Yes, always," Alex answered.

"I really never longed to have a child of my own. There are things I would love about raising a child with you, but we'd be giving up things, too. Time together. One of us would have to cut back drastically at work, I think, and that would be me, I imagine."

"This does not seem like a fair distribution of responsibility. You have to be the one to get pregnant, and you think you should change jobs. Why?"

CJ smiled, just a little. "Because you, my darling, are going to be a chief of police someday. If not in Colfax, then somewhere. And I don't think you can take eighteen years or so out of your career at this point to raise a child. Besides, it doesn't matter whether I work or not. It's not like being a cop is my reason for living."

"And what would that reason for living be?" Alex asked, relaxing a little.

"Oh, I think you know."

Alex smiled and said, "I have another Valentine's present for you."

"I love presents." CJ sat up happily. "What is it?"

"I've been giving this a lot of thought," Alex said gravely. "And there's something I think I should tell you."

CJ cocked one eyebrow and waited.

"I think," Alex stopped, then continued, "no, I'm really sure."

"Really sure of what?"

"I'm really sure I'm a lesbian."

CJ regarded her with mock gravity of her own. "That's good to know. So long as we're clear that you're limited in actual field testing to one subject. And that would be me."

Alex leaned across and kissed her. "I'm very clear on that."

"Glad to hear it. And your last bite of ice cream is melting."

"Uh-oh," Alex said quietly. She put the spoon over CJ's chest and let the drips escape.

"Hey!" CJ exclaimed. "That's cold!"

"Let me see if I can help," Alex offered.

She leaned down and lapped up the drops of sweet cream. "Is that better?" Alex asked. "Are you warmer now?"

"Warmer?" CJ's voice was a purr. "Oh, yes."

Alex continued her efforts. After a minute or two, CJ murmured, "I think you missed a couple of spots."

"Since I'm a lesbian," Alex said, smiling, "I'll see what I can do about that."

≈